# CRIES OF A DYING WORLD

## A NOVEL

## G. MICHAEL HOPF

DOOMSDAY
PRESS

*For my girls*

# PROLOGUE

## PRESENT DAY

TRAVELING at 30,333 miles per hour and spanning over eleven kilometers in diameter, Asteroid Colossus made impact three hundred and thirteen miles northeast off the coast of the Hawaiian Islands.

The Earth shook. The seas heaved, and the planet groaned as massive chunks of itself were hurled into the lower atmosphere only to rain back down, causing further destruction. The torrid heat from Colossus' impact encircled the globe at a horrifying and inescapable speed of over nine thousand miles per hour. The inferno scorched and sterilized the planet, leaving nothing in its wake.

The impact crater covered an area over one hundred and ten miles in diameter. What lay in the miles-deep crater was nothing more than molten rock similar to the primordial soup that had been the planet six billion years before.

If one were to look back on Earth, they wouldn't recognize her. Gone were the vibrant colors of a once living planet. The deep blues and greens had been replaced by a searing red and charred black.

Hours after Colossus' arrival, over seven billion people were dead. Those who had found shelter deep in the bowels of Earth would eventually look upon those who died as the lucky ones, but theirs is another story entirely.

# ONE

TWELVE DAYS BEFORE IMPACT

EIGHT MILES WEST OF OCOTILLO, CALIFORNIA

HER EYES WERE a radiating emerald warmed with inner sea grass. He often got lost in them. And when she'd look upon him, it would pierce his soul with cries of love and desire. Her whisper, soft and quiet enough to make him pay attention, worked, it always worked. Her touch, gentle and loving. Her lips and kisses felt like home. Her aroma, sweet and alluring like rose petals. Her body curved right where it needed, and from her beautiful face to the bottom of her feet, she was perfect, but she always lovingly reminded him that no one was perfect, and that she was simply perfectly imperfect. While he'd relent on those details, these he'd never surrender: she was an angel, his queen, his soulmate, and the love of his life.

*"Ethan...I love you."*

Those were her final words to him as her radiant eyes closed for the last time. It took them an hour and three men to remove him from the mangled debris of shattered glass, twisted steel, transmission fluid and blood: both his and hers. When she let out her last breath, she not only left this world, but the unborn child she was carrying went with her.

The truck had come out of nowhere, or that was what he remembered. It was the police report, though, that told a different story. His blood alcohol was just over the legal limit, but he had felt fine, and they were only a mile from home. She had normally driven since becoming pregnant, but that night she was tired. What had started with a jovial birthday party for a friend turned into tragedy, and he was to blame.

Out of body. Surreal. There was no other way to describe how he felt as he watched them put her body in a bag while he sat in the back of a police car, his hands cuffed behind his back. Repeatedly he pressed his eyes closed and prayed that he'd open them, and all would be back as it was. The two of them holding hands and laughing. Chatting about the future, baby names and the neutral color they should paint the nursery. Yet, no matter how many times he had played this game of make-believe, using his imagination with hopes of changing the past, it never worked. He'd always open them to the reality that eleven months before, he had killed his wife and unborn child.

———

UNABLE TO SLEEP EVEN though he needed to, Ethan lowered his window and looked out over the moonlit desert landscape. Coyotes howled in the distance; their cries always sounded eerie to him. Whenever he heard a coyote howl, he thought of the prey they were pursuing. The animal's heart thumping as it raced to escape the jaws of death. For billions of people around the world, they too were praying and hoping to find salvation or an escape from what was coming. Maybe it was best to not know. Be like the coyote. It wasn't living in fear right now. It was hungry and doing what coyotes do: hunt and kill. Theirs was a simple existence, blissfully ignorant that an asteroid larger than the one that had killed the dinosaurs was hurtling towards them. He sometimes wished he too was ignorant of Earth's fate, but that wasn't to be. Nope, he had the privilege, or that was what his older brother, Eric, had told him. He had a spot, two actually, in a bunker that had been built so some would survive the apocalypse, this extinction-level event that was being caused by a piece of rock called Colossus.

*Who comes up with these names?*, he thought. Sounded like the name a screenwriter would come up with, or maybe it was just some twisted astrophysicist's joke; nevertheless, that was the name of this monster left over from the dawn of the solar system, which was on a collision course with Earth.

It had been two days since the new president, not sworn in a day at the time, had gone on national television to inform Americans and the world of their fate. A fate the previous administration had known about for five years, but now admitted had been covered up to prevent societal collapse years before. The irony is the powers that be weren't really concerned about the chaos of this knowledge on the average person, they just wanted the time to build their bunkers, and they had gotten the time. Five years to plan, build, and coordinate in relative peace and prosperity while everyone else went about their lives thinking they'd have a future. However, the new president had thrown a curveball. Those who believed they had a spot in the bunker, dubbed Ark, up until days ago soon discovered that spot wasn't secure. With a new president comes new rules, new policies, and new political friends to help.

This was why Ethan was on the side of Interstate 8 outside of Ocotillo, California, with a destination of Tempe, Arizona. Eric worked for the new president and had secured two seats, one for Ethan and one for Ethan's estranged son, Chance. The plane was leaving in ten days from Hill Air Force Base in Utah. All Ethan needed to do was get there and do so in the bitter cold month of January. It seemed easy enough, but when you threw in the fact that millions of people were coming to grips with their fate, with some acting out violently, this road trip probably wasn't going to go as planned.

Living was one of the last things Ethan had been doing or even wanted to since the accident. However, if he could save Chance, he owed him that. He had called Chance minutes after Eric made his offer, and to his surprise Chance had answered on the first try. Upon giving him the news, Chance agreed to go and to set aside past grievances, but before they could work out the details, the phone went dead. He hadn't been able to reach Chance since except for an occasional text which told him Chance was okay and eagerly awaiting his arrival.

A cool breeze brushed across Ethan's face, bringing with it the unique odor of creosote. In his lap his Sig P239 semiautomatic 9 mm pistol sat; he stared at it and even picked it up to feel the grip. He'd had the Sig for years, having bought it when he lived in Florida, and like him, it had found a home in San Diego when he moved. He and his Sig now had an unhealthy relationship, one of master and servant; and for now, he was still the master although there had been times over the past eleven months he'd almost surrendered his role. Life without Jen had been just bearable enough up until a couple of days ago; then the call came at the right time. He had a purpose now, something to do and someone to help. So for right now, the Sig would remain the servant. He opened the center console and set the Sig inside.

The coyotes howled again, but now their song began to lull him to sleep. Like he had done since losing her, he thumbed his phone to his voicemail, found the message he wanted, and hit play.

*"Hi, sweetie, I know I didn't get to say it, as I was in a hurry, but I love you so much. You're my life, my sun and stars. Have a great day."*

He hit play again; her words soaked into his soul. Over and over, he repeated the message until he fell asleep.

# TWO

## EIGHT MILES WEST OF OCOTILLO, CALIFORNIA

THE HORN of a car jolted Ethan awake. He sat up and quickly scanned his surroundings looking for the source, but saw nothing. He adjusted in the seat to allow his stiff legs to stretch before finally getting out to shake off the stiffness.

The chill of the evening still hung as a wind swept over, giving him a shiver, but the deep orange in the eastern sky portended the sun was about to crest the horizon and bring with it the warmth of the day. As he did his morning routine, he looked south across the rolling tan and brown hills. In the distance a small single-level house stood. The stucco siding showed years of weather, with the Spanish tile roof suffering the worst, as sections were missing. As seemed typical of solitary houses in the middle of the desert, their yards always had rusted old cars, a stack of tires, and tattered furniture. This house checked all those boxes but had one curious item Ethan found amusing. Lining the front of the house were pink flamingos, seven to be exact. *Why pink flamingos?* He chuckled to himself.

The whoosh of a vehicle traveling at a high rate of speed sounded behind him. He craned his head back to see a truck heading west. He wondered what their story was. Where were they headed? As he watched it speed up the hill, he said, "Del Mar, yep, they're going to Del Mar... Beach." Were they really going there, or was he just picking the destination he had chosen for himself before the call from Eric? Upon hearing about Colossus, he had picked Del Mar Beach as his final resting spot, it was a nice beach, not the most beautiful in the world by any stretch, but it brought back many memories of him and Jen.

He finished and made his way back to his truck. Hunger pangs came, along with his need for coffee or more importantly... caffeine. He opened the center console and paused for a moment when he saw his semi-automatic pistol sitting there. He pulled it out, gave it another weary look, then set it on the dash before diving back into the console to remove the bag of jerky along with a container of instant coffee. He opened a thermos, dumped a heaping amount of coffee into it, added water, closed it up and shook. It wasn't his French press from home with his dark roast coffee, but it was needed to stave off the headaches of withdrawal. The end of the world had some benefits, like free gas, which he found often, but the lack of good coffee brought to the forefront the good life many had taken for granted.

A car horn blared to the north of him. He shot a look, but a small hill obstructed any view further. Was this the same horn which woke him?

He took a bite of the savory jerky, his mouth watering as he chewed. His eyes found the pistol again; he stared at it.

The horn again blared, this time sounding for ten to fifteen seconds. His attention torn from the pistol and curious, he again looked across the highway half expecting to see a car barreling over the hill towards him. His senses kicked in; they were something he relied upon his entire life and usually were correct. Something was wrong, and he didn't want to stay around to find out. He tossed the bag of jerky on the passenger seat, closed his door, and started his vehicle, a white Chevrolet Suburban. The radio kicked on, the volume higher than he remembered, startling him. He quickly turned it down, shaking his head in disbelief that he had spooked himself; he also got a chuckle from the song playing. *'It's The End of The World As We Know It'*, by R.E.M.; clearly the DJ had a sense of humor.

He changed the channel and stopped when he heard a news report:

*"Based upon the data we have, Colossus will not strike us directly, but at an angle; the energy of the impact will be mostly directed out and up with about one to three percent going down into the ground. But it'll be enough to ring the*

*planet like a bell. We expect seismic waves will radiate across and through the Earth. As those waves move across the planet, the plates will be affected, and earthquakes of a magnitude higher than ten will occur. To give an example, Colossus will strike northeast of the Hawaiian Islands; the seismic waves will reach the western coast of the United States within fifteen minutes. Along with the quakes, fiery debris will also be raining down, causing forests to burn. Meanwhile the ejecta cloud from the blast will be traveling out in all directions from the impact site at a speed of sixteen thousand kilometers per hour. The ejecta cloud is superheated air; it will destroy all structures and bake the ground with unrelenting heat. And to make matters worse, millions of volts of static electricity will charge the cloud, making a vast electrical storm. This cloud will reach halfway around the world within an hour, and temperatures on the ground in Eastern Europe will reach three hundred degrees Fahrenheit. Within two hours, the cloud will encompass the planet and bury it in a superheated darkness.*

*"A global tsunami will also be produced. A wall of water a half mile high, traveling at speeds of over five hundred miles per hour, will wipe out the coastlines..."*

Hearing enough, he turned off the radio.

Picking up the pistol, he placed it in his lap, then put the vehicle in gear. As he smashed his foot against the accelerator, a gunshot cracked in the distance. It came from the same direction as the car horn. Not needing to look, he kept his attention on the road ahead and pressed the accelerator down further. He glanced in his side mirror and could see around the hill behind him. There he saw a trailer home and two cars. He wasn't sure what was happening, nor did he care. It was times like these, high stress and uncertainty, that produced situations he was all too familiar with, situations that still gave him nightmares. Not giving it another thought, he barreled down the road towards the rising sun.

# THREE

## FLAGSTAFF, ARIZONA

TRUST WASN'T JUST a word to Melody, she embodied and expected it from all she called friend or lover, and it had become something she was finding less and less of with her fiancé, Jared. She couldn't understand why they had been fighting more and more since the announcement of Colossus' arrival, but today's fight was the worst it had ever been resulting with him leaving. He'd said he was going out to get some air, but he'd been gone for over four hours. Acting as if she had a compulsive disorder, she looked at her phone several times per minute, somehow expecting to see a text message without a notification sounding. With each gaze, her heart sank, and the walls of her single-bedroom apartment became smaller. Sleep had already been a problem for her lately, from her getting up a couple of times per night to get sick, to Jared being distant, and their neighbors partying to all hours of the night.

She stopped at a framed photo of her and Jared. She stared at it and grew sad. The photo was from a trip to Las Vegas, they had gone to elope, but Jared had changed his mind, stating he wanted to marry her in a more dignified manner. That was three months ago, and two months after, she had gotten the news her cancer had returned. Maybe that was a sign. Maybe he had no intention of ever marrying her, and did it even matter now? Soon they'd all be dead anyway. Although the idea of being someone's wife before she died sounded romantic and checked off an item on her bucket list.

Unnerved by her negative inner thoughts, she moved on from the photo and continued her pacing. From the living room to the kitchen and on to the bedroom, she went. Where was he? Why wasn't he answering her texts? She looked at her phone, no replies. Calling was useless, as the circuits were busy, but texts were still going through, or maybe they weren't. Was that the issue?, she asked herself. She looked and saw the text notification read, DELIVERED.

She stopped herself in the narrow hall when she came upon a mirror. Dark circles under her sad blue eyes told a story of fatigue, worry and disease. *Why? Why is this happening to me?* She was only thirty-two. She'd already knocked on death's door three years before and overcame it, but cancer was a fucker, a tough opponent, and had come back with a vengeance. Now it didn't matter if she found a cure this very minute because in eleven days, she'd be dead, and this time from an asteroid. This was why she never gambled; her luck sucked.

A selfie he had taken of them a few weeks ago came to mind, it had been a sweet photo, and she recalled how happy it made her feel. She opened her phone and went to the Photos but couldn't find it. Maybe she hadn't saved it. Recalling he had texted it to her, she opened his texts, of course no reply from him, and hit the arrow next to his name. Another screen popped up and with it a map of his location.

She had completely forgotten she had the ability to track him. She had never had cause for concern, but now she did, and as if God was looking out for her, she now knew where he was. Pressing on the map, it opened a larger map. She zoomed in and saw he was a few blocks away and at a house.

She grabbed her keys and raced out the door.

# FOUR

## GILA BEND, ARIZONA

OVER THE YEARS, he had made numerous trips to Phoenix from San Diego, and the one place he always stopped to rest and refuel was Gila Bend and today would be like those times. He looked at the fuel gauge sitting just above a quarter tank. He needed gas; now he just hoped he could get it.

The town appeared normal; nothing looked out of place, giving him a sense that he'd be safe. Then again, it was the end of the world, and anything could happen. A couple of cars passed him, heading west; again he wondered where they might be going.

A Chevron sign ahead gave him his destination. As he closed in on it, he saw a large green glowing sign that read OPEN. He sighed in relief, turned right, and pulled up to an open pump. Two other vehicles were getting gas, and the occupants of the cars were out, with one group drinking alcohol, while the other group stood outside their large Suburban, armed with rifles as if expecting a skirmish to break out at any time. He laughed to himself. Two groups of people, two different reactions. One hyper-vigilant, the other not giving two shits, as they would say.

Just to make sure he wasn't walking into something dangerous, he did take a moment to look around. While he fell into the not-giving-two-shits camp, he was on a mission to get Chance to Utah, and he couldn't do that if he were dead. Feeling confident it was safe, he exited the vehicle, but not one to take things for granted, he slid his pistol in his waistband.

With his credit card in hand, he went to insert it in the pump but was prevented by a handwritten sign taped on the card reader, *FREE GAS, GOD BLESS.*

"Isn't that nice," he said with a smile. He took the pump and started filling while maintaining his situational awareness.

The hypervigilant group finished, loaded up, and drove off, followed by the beer-chugging group, leaving him by himself. Alone, he went to the cab, grabbed his mobile phone and tried to call Chance. Like before, the phone played the message: *"We're sorry. All circuits are busy now. Please try your call again later."* Frustrated, he tossed the phone back inside and went to finish fueling.

Topped off, he was curious if he could get water and some snacks. He locked his vehicle and made his way to the store. Stopping just before the entrance; he found another handwritten sign similar to the one on the pump. *EVERYTHING IS FREE, GOD BLESS.* Just below was a different message, *GET SAVED, IT'S NOT TOO LATE.*

Again, the sign made him smile. Some people clearly got the message about the end of the world: you can't take money with you.

He entered the store to find some had taken advantage of the 'free' option, with empty shelves for some items, specifically the beer cooler. Ethan went further down the cooler aisle to find the water was still there. Grabbing a basket, he loaded up what he could carry, nothing more, and a few more bags of jerky. As he headed for the door, two men entered. These were hard men by their looks, one had a thick scar on his cheek, and the other had what looked like fresh blood on his white T-shirt. Both men gave Ethan a stare that told him they were trouble. Not one to shy away, but also not wanting to engage, Ethan made eye contact, then looked away. He maneuvered around some loose items on the floor, around the men, and exited the store. With a slight turn of his head, Ethan kept the front door of the store in his peripheral vision.

Parked opposite him at a pump was a black Kia Soul, not the kind of vehicle he'd expect these two rough men to drive.

Making it to his vehicle, he unlocked it, tossed the entire basket inside, turned, and saw the men coming towards him. He pulled the pistol from his waist and raised it. "I'd stop right there."

Both men did as Ethan suggested, their arms up.

"Fellas, c'mon, really?"

"We need your rig," the man with the scar blurted out.

"For what? The world is being destroyed in about ten days. What are you gonna do, go four wheeling!" Ethan mocked.

Movement to Ethan's left caught his attention. He looked quickly and saw two more men; one had a rifle. "Shit." It had been years since Ethan had even held a pistol much less used one in any capacity, so he was a bit rusty. He was outnumbered and outgunned, as the man had an AR-platform rifle. Getting into a gunfight at a gas station was about the dumbest thing anybody could do, yet here he was. The men in front of him were twenty plus feet away, while the other two were three times that distance, but there was the rifle to consider.

His vision began to narrow while tension began to build. This was about to go down, and he hated it. He put all his attention on the closest threat, began to squeeze, but before he could pull the trigger on the man with the scar, a volley of gunfire came down on the men, striking them both.

Ethan took cover around the far side of his vehicle.

The footfalls of the other men approached, stopping next to the other two, followed by more gunfire.

With a white-knuckled grip, Ethan readied himself to fight. He peered above the hood of his vehicle to find the men digging through the pockets of the now dead men.

One of them caught him looking and called out, "We're not going to hurt you, bro; these guys stole my mom's car; we were just getting it back."

"Okay," Ethan answered. He didn't know what to believe, so he decided to stay put.

He followed the men's footfalls to the Kia, heard them get in, start it, and drive off. Feeling safe, he lifted his head and looked to find he was alone. Making his way around the front of his vehicle, his gaze fixed on the dead men. "Stupid is as stupid does."

Not wanting to wait around for another dangerous encounter, he headed out, thankful to be alive. He made one last look in his rearview mirror at the men who just moments before had been alive and threatening his life. *How stupid, but does it matter? They were dead men walking anyway.*

# FIVE

## ENOCH, UTAH

RUST, dust, and decay – that was what one would see if they stepped foot into 3030 Minersville Highway, Enoch, Utah, today. Built in 1897, the house was two stories with a walk-up attic, three bedrooms, two and a half bathrooms, a living and family room and kitchen. The exterior of the house had all the features one would expect of a Victorian home, with its stained glass, peaked Gothic roofs and cupulas, tall windows, ornate eaves, and a wide porch. When it was first occupied, the owner had been a prominent businessman who had moved from New York City to find his fortune in silver; from him it went to another businessman and his family and so forth until Everett John Pritchard inherited it. Everett wasn't like the previous occupants; he wasn't a businessman; he didn't have a fortune or was in the process of creating one; no, Everett just happened to be the only surviving relative when this asset became available after the death of his aunt.

He had grown up in Enoch and couldn't wait to leave to explore the world, then along came Susan Glassman. She was the checkout clerk at the pharmacy, and upon setting eyes on her, it was love at first sight. She had moved to Enoch just months before; a traveler of sorts, Susan was a runaway who needed some quick money, so she took a job upon seeing the sign in the window. The two were inseparable, and Everett found himself falling for her hard even though his friends warned him that Susan, or Susie, as Everett sweetly called her, was bad news. Everett wouldn't hear any of it and dove in. It wasn't long before she introduced him to the life of drugs and alcohol she had lived since she was fourteen, after her parents died in a car accident. From the tragic death, she bounced from foster home to foster home, eventually leaving one night when she was seventeen. The two had fun and partied, and months later she came to him pregnant.

Susie didn't want to have a baby at nineteen, but she too had fallen madly in love. They married and had the baby, a lovely girl, whom they named Savannah. Two and a half years later she gave birth again, a boy they named EJ for Everett Junior. She played house at 3030 Minersville Highway and enjoyed her life, even giving up drinking and drugs, but for Everett, he wanted something else. He'd sit on the porch and watch the cars and trucks go north and south and wanted nothing more than to be in one of them on his way out of town.

His drinking and drug use became legend in town,

with his time at home becoming less and less until one day he never came back.

Susie would sit on the porch waiting, but days turned into weeks, then months, and now years. As she mentally deteriorated, so did the house. She went back to the bottle to soothe her pain, but that was never enough, and before long she took her anger and sorrow of abandonment out on her children in the most brutal of ways.

The lives of her children became one of terror and torment until she got clean three years past. For Savannah, now twelve, and EJ, who had just turned nine, those three years of sobriety brought with them peace and harmony; it was as if the demon that had possessed their mother was gone, like a veil had been lifted. The memories of their tortuous early years began to fade until news of Colossus came.

———

"WHERE'S MAMA?" EJ asked; his long curly brown locks partially covered his tender nine-year-old face. He was small for his age, which led him to either be picked on at school or found to be adorable by adults. It was a curse, he said, as he'd heard his father had been tall and strapping. If one could be all consumed by something, his desire to grow big and tall was ever on his mind.

"Store," Savannah replied. She rocked back in the chair, her gaze just tall enough to see over the weathered railing of the porch towards Minersville Highway. She nervously fiddled with the gaping hole in the knee of her jeans. A chilled breeze washed over her and sent loose blonde hairs from her ponytail onto her face. She tucked the hairs behind her ears, her blue eyes still fixed upon the road.

The house fronted the road, which was busy for a town of a little over five thousand people. All her life she had been scolded not to play too close to the road and had received numerous beatings when Susie thought she hadn't listened.

Taking a seat on a rusty bucket next to Savannah, EJ picked up an old broom handle and began to push around the dried leaves from the old oak tree, which had stood in the front yard for over a hundred years.

The yard hadn't been cut before winter had set in, leaving the now dead grass tall and appearing more like weeds. A birdbath sat opposite the oak tree; the years of neglect showed, as the white marble was stained, and the bowl itself filled with murky water.

The mailman pulled up, opened the mailbox, the black paint cracked and flaking, and deposited mail.

Savannah thought it odd and gave him a puzzled look.

With a simple wave, the mailman acknowledged Savannah and EJ's presence before driving on.

"Why is he delivering mail?" EJ asked.

"I have no idea."

"He's stupid, then," EJ sneered.

"He must have his reasons." What they could be, she had no idea and didn't care, as she had bigger things to think about, like when Susie was coming home, and which Susie would they encounter?

"Will it hurt?" EJ asked.

"Will what hurt?"

"Dying."

Savannah took her attention off the road and fixed it on EJ. "Are you thinking about that?"

"You aren't?"

She didn't answer; she stared at him with amazement. For someone so young, he was a deep thinker with a profound mind. Maybe it was his childhood, she thought. *We are products of our nurturing, or lack thereof for us,* she chuckled in her mind. Many people had often commented about how mature she was for only being twelve. She hadn't paid much attention to those comments until a year ago. Her mother's sponsor, Chad, from AA, repeatedly said that of her. He'd comment about how she kept eye contact with everyone, especially adults, when she talked. She didn't deliberately tell herself to do such a thing; she had always done it. Speaking of her mother's sponsor, Chad, he'd called to check in, but after too many calls, Susie had disconnected the phone from the wall.

"Will there be a big explosion? Will it break into pieces and fall apart?"

Jarred from her thoughts, she shook her head and asked, "Huh?"

"The Earth, will it break into pieces?"

"I don't know."

"Will we hear it?"

Savannah cocked her head and asked, "Is this what you spend your time thinking about?"

"That and other stuff."

"Like what?"

"Do you believe in heaven?"

"Yeah, sure."

"Will...?" EJ scrunched his face. He put his lower lip in his mouth and sucked.

Seeing this, Savannah knew he was stressed. "What is it?"

He stopped playing with the dead leaves and looked at her. "If there is a heaven, and we all go there, will Mama be there?"

"Probably...I mean, yeah, she will." Savannah sat back and sighed, unsatisfied with her answer.

"But isn't heaven for good people?"

Savannah opened her mouth to reply but cut herself off.

"I don't think she'll be there. Nope. And I don't want her there," EJ stated firmly.

Savannah felt a wave of emotion rush over her. She hated her life and had dreamt about doing so many wonderful things; now none of it mattered. She didn't know much about religion or God, as she'd never been inside a church, not once. She had wondered if there was a God, and if there was, how could he make people suffer, especially children like them? What sort of God allowed this?

"I'm gonna go see what came; maybe it's something special," EJ chirped. He hopped off the bucket and ran down the red-brick sidewalk to the mailbox. He opened it and peered right in, as he and the mailbox were the same height. He reached in and came out with a stack of what looked like junk mail mostly. Cradling it in his arms, he carried it back, dropping a couple of flyers along the way. "I'll put it on the table for Mama."

Savannah shrugged her shoulders.

The sound of a rumbling engine came from down the road. It was familiar, one Savannah knew all too well. "Mama's coming!"

EJ appeared in the open doorway. "Should we hide?"

"I don't know but be prepared to."

Susie turned into the drive but pulled further in to allow a truck to park behind her.

Seeing this, Savannah knew what it meant. "Head upstairs."

"Is she mad?" EJ asked.

"Just head upstairs!" Savannah snapped and gave him a hard look.

Always obedient, EJ turned on a dime and raced down the hall and up the stairs.

Staying behind to get a good gauge of her mother's condition, Savannah waited.

The door of the Toyota Corolla creaked when she opened it. She put one leg out, then another and paused before standing. She looked towards the front porch and saw Savannah watching. "Hey, baby!" She hollered with her happy drunk tone. It was the way she spoke when she was flirting with men and wanted them to believe she was a good mother.

A man exited the truck and stumbled a few feet before getting his legs under him. "This where you live, huh? I always wondered who lived in this old house."

"Little ole me." Susie laughed, pointing a finger at herself. She took a half step back and almost fell back into her car. Giving the man a look, she asked, "Did you bring some beer?"

"You know it!" he exclaimed. He went back to the cab of his truck and removed a wet paper sack. He held it high. "Let's party like it's the end of the fucking world!" He caught sight of Savannah and laughed. "Oops, sorry."

"Pay no mind, she's heard worse," Susie smirked.

The contents of the bag broke through and onto the ground. A couple of cans burst open, spraying him with lukewarm beer. "Damn it!"

"Alcohol abuse!" She cackled. "Best shotgun those babies."

Savannah had seen enough. She knew exactly what tonight was going to be like. She got up, went inside the house, and climbed the twenty-six stairs to the walk-up attic, where she found EJ playing with some toys.

"Who's that with Mama?"

"A friend."

"Wanna play a game?" EJ asked with pleading eyes.

"Sure, let's play a game." She grabbed an old radio, turned it on, and cranked up the volume, as she always did when her mother came home with a *friend*.

*"There are reports circulating that Colossus will miss us. Folks, while I have prayed for that to be true, those reports are just plain fake news. Colossus will arrive with all its fury on February 2. So get your aff—"*

Savannah changed the frequency until she found a song she loved by the Beastie Boys titled, *"Sabotage"*, and turned it up loud. She had become a fan of harder music, like rock and heavy metal.

She faced EJ to see him holding up a deck of UNO and a regular set of cards. "You choose."

"Let's play war," Savannah said and sat down cross-legged.

EJ shuffled the cards as best he could with his small hands. "Savannah?"

"Yeah."

"Is Mama gonna hurt us tonight?"

"Can we not talk about it and just play cards?"

"I got a bad bruise from yesterday." He set the cards down and lifted his shirt to show the deep blue and black softball-sized bruise on his right side.

"I'm sorry, but mine is worse," she countered. She pulled up her sleeve to show a bruise and deep red scratch marks.

The two shared a glance only they could. Theirs was a shared experience.

"Why does she hurt us?"

"Mama is hurting herself. She's sad and doesn't know what to do with all that sadness."

"But we didn't hurt her."

"I know, but sometimes hurt people, hurt people."

"So daddy hurt her, so she hurts us?"

"Yeah, it's like that. Seems silly, but that's what adults do."

"Silly like the mailman delivering mail?"

"Yeah, like the mailman delivering mail."

EJ started to deal the deck.

"I'll do my best to protect you next time," Savannah said.

"You promise?"

There it was, that word Savannah hated. Promise? How could she do such a thing? She had heard that word from their dad and Susie all her life, and all they ever did was fail to live up to it. For her, she never wanted to utter that word unless she meant it.

EJ began to cry.

"What's wrong?"

"I don't want her to hurt me again."

Savannah's heart ached. She reached out, took EJ's hand, and said, "I'll protect you, and I promise she won't hurt you again, ever."

EJ leapt over to Savannah and into her arms.

As they embraced, Savannah pondered just how she was going to keep her promise.

# SIX

## FLAGSTAFF, ARIZONA

A SERIES of gunshots in the distance startled Melody and the large gathering of people she was passing on the street. She lowered her head and looked around for someone with a gun but saw no one. The group scattered, some running in front of her car to get away.

She weaved around two abandoned cars, a more common occurrence as people ran out of gas due to fuel shortages. Glancing at her phone to help navigate, she saw she was drawing close. She made a right turn, and there, three houses down, sat Jared's truck. Her heart sank, and a lump grew in her throat. She questioned what she was doing for a moment but came to the conclusion she needed to know whom he was with.

She parked a house down so as not to draw attention if Jared or whomever he was with looked out the window.

She was hoping to catch him by surprise. As she opened her door, a couple of teens on bicycles sped by. She yelped and took a pause to catch her breath. "Stupid kids," she growled under her breath. Out of the car, she again hesitated, her eyes fixed on the house.

She took a couple of steps and stopped. What would she say? What if he was with another woman, then what? She ran scenarios of encounters, and each one had her standing tall in righteousness, telling him how much of a loser he was. But deep down she couldn't escape the fact that she'd be devastated. *Could this really be happening?* Of course, when she got real, the signs were there. He was always on his phone, always posting to Instagram pics of him from the gym, this was no doubt to seek attention, or was it just narcissism? Probably both. She had vowed not to date another narcissist, yet here she was with one, and now he was probably hooking up with some woman from the gym or whom he'd met on social media. After her last disastrous relationship, she'd vowed to never date a controlling man, but she did; was it their confidence she found intoxicating or something else? Either way, it was her fault, as she'd never really done the real work on herself, and she'd met Jared online. A fact she hated to remind herself of was he had been dating someone at that time. This was karma for sure, she thought.

She took a few more steps and again paused. With a clenched jaw, she muttered, "Just do it, Mel." Fueled to just rip off the Band-Aid, she shoved her phone in her pocket and marched up to the front door. With a fist, she banged loudly, then listened.

Seconds went by and no response.

She banged more.

Curtains at the window next to the door moved.

"Jared, open this door."

"Go away, Mel," Jared shouted behind the closed door.

"I won't leave, not until you tell me what's going on."

Unintelligible chatter sounded behind the door.

"I hear you talking; open up!" she barked.

"No, I'll tell her!" a woman shouted before the door flew open.

Two feet separated Melody and this strange woman. Tabitha was her name.

With her arms firmly planted on her hips, a smirk of disgust written on her face, Melody sized her up. She was about her height, maybe an inch shorter, large breasts, long brown hair pulled back in a ponytail, and a sleeve tattoo on her left arm. Behind her, Jared cowered, his eyes unable to keep contact with hers when she looked.

"What do you want?" Tabitha asked.

"I'm here to see my fiancé."

"He doesn't want to see you."

Melody looked at Jared, who sheepishly looked down, and asked, "Is that true?"

Jared remained quiet. His silence drew condemnation from Tabitha. She cocked her head towards him and exclaimed, "Tell her!"

"Yeah, tell me!"

"You see..." Jared stuttered, then went quiet. He looked down at his feet and mumbled something unintelligible under his breath. For a man who stood over six feet with an athletic build, his stature was now diminished by his lack of confidence.

Tabitha fully turned around and faced him defiantly. "Tell her!"

"I am, I will...um, listen, Mel..."

Melody folded her arms and stood waiting.

"Maybe you should come in, and we can talk," Jared said. He looked to Tabitha for approval.

"This is bullshit!" Tabitha barked, then stormed off into the house.

"Please come in," Jared said, stepping out of the way.

Melody's chest felt like an elephant was sitting on it, and a slight sweat had built on her brow. She crossed the threshold and waited just inside.

"Can I get you something to drink?" Jared asked. He headed for the kitchen, which sat to the left. On the right was a small living room, with a couch against the window overlooking the street.

"No, what I need is an explanation," Melody replied, following him into the kitchen.

"I need one...a drink, that is," Jared nervously said. He opened the refrigerator and pulled out a beer. "I'm still shocked the power is still on. I'm ready for it to go off any minute now. I mean, who's running anything anymore? Who's doing –"

"Are you fucking her?" Melody blurted out.

Jared coughed and stood speechless.

"You are, aren't you? Last time I checked, you were my fiancé."

"Listen, it's complicated."

"Complicated? Either you are or you aren't."

"You see, I was going through a tough time with you being sick..."

"Wait, you're using me as an excuse? You're putting the fact you're cheating on me with this whore on the fact I have cancer?"

"No, it's not that, it's, you see, remember when I needed some space a couple of months ago?"

"Yeah I remember, you were going to dig deep, blah, blah, blah. I didn't know that meant going deep with another woman!"

"Stop, Mel! It's not that..."

"Then what the fuck is it, Jared!" Melody screamed at the top of her lungs.

"I love her!" he replied, his tone showing a lack of conviction.

"You love her?" Melody's voice cracked, and tears came to her eyes. She took a deep breath, hoping it would clear the heavy and painful sensation in her chest. "I...I can't believe this."

"I'm sorry," Jared said softly.

His apology hit her ears like a loud bang and chased away what feelings of sorrow she had. In the emotional vacuum, anger raced in. "You love this whore, this home-wrecking bitch!"

Jared's eyes widened.

"How dare you call me a whore!" Tabitha screeched.

Melody looked over her shoulder to find Tabitha coming at her, fist clenched tight. She stepped out of the way and, using Tabitha's forward momentum, shoved her.

Tabitha spilled to the floor, her chin hitting hard on the laminate flooring.

"Damn it!" Jared howled.

"You fucking bitch!" Tabitha snarled. She got to her feet quickly, touched her chin, and found blood. Her eyes widened and bulged with anger broiling behind them. She saw a paring knife on the counter, snatched it, and launched herself at Melody.

Reacting with speed, Melody pivoted out of her way, but her maneuver placed her in the ninety-degree angle of the counter with nowhere to go.

Jared hollered in protest but stayed clear of the altercation.

Fueled by rage, Tabitha again pressed the attack, this time managing to clear the distance. The only thing that stopped Tabitha from plunging the knife into Melody was the fact she'd blocked her arm.

With her right hand, Melody searched the counter for her own weapon to use. She'd have to find something quick, as her strength was waning.

"Stop it!" Jared wailed from across the kitchen.

The knife inched closer to Melody's face. Her eyes fixed on the blade as her right hand kept searching.

Animalistic grunts came from Tabitha. The downward pressure was working, as she could feel Melody slowly relenting.

She found something. She knew what it was by the feel, grasped it firmly, and swung hard. The marble rolling pin struck Tabitha against the side of her head near her temple. Melody swung again, once more hitting the same spot.

Tabitha dropped the knife and let out a groan.

Running on survival instinct, Melody hit Tabitha one

last time. This blow produced an audible crack from Tabitha's head.

Tabitha's knees buckled, and she toppled to the floor.

In shock, Jared stared for a moment. "You killed her!" He went to Tabitha's side and could easily see she was dead. Blood began to spread underneath her body. "You killed her!"

"I didn't have a choice."

"You fucking killed her!" Jared groaned, taking Tabitha into his arms.

Sweat poured off Melody and dripped onto the floor. Her body trembled and became weak. She dropped the rolling pin. It hit the floor with a heavy thud.

His attention on Tabitha broken by the rolling pin, he shifted his glare to Melody. His expression had changed from anguish to rage. He furrowed his brow and sprang from the floor. His hands found Melody's throat, and squeezed. The two toppled to the floor, with Jared on top of her. He tightened his grip on her neck.

Melody scratched and clawed, but she was already too weak. Like before, she searched for something within arm's reach and found the paring knife just in time, as she could feel herself slipping away. She took a firm hold of the handle and came up hard. The blade easily slid into Jared's neck. She removed it and once more stabbed him.

Jared let go and recoiled. He placed his hands on his neck and gave her a shocked look. Thick blood oozed between his fingers and streamed down his chest and onto the floor. He coughed, and more blood flowed. He fell off her, landing on the floor faceup. He squirmed for a few moments, then fell still, his eyes open with a death stare to the ceiling.

It took all she had to lift her head. She saw Jared a few feet away, and just beyond him was Tabitha, both positively dead and by her hand. A heaviness overtook her, and with it came an unconscious darkness.

# SEVEN

## TEMPE, ARIZONA

THE DRIVE into Phoenix seemed like a scene out of an apocalyptic movie with thick black billowing plumes of smoke dotting the skyline, abandoned vehicles and debris strewn about the freeway. With each mile he got closer to the inner city, the number of abandoned vehicles grew. He piloted around those and the random person or group of people walking until he reached the exit ramp. By his recollection, he was about five minutes away from Chance's apartment; he just prayed he was there.

He found his phone, thumbed to Chance's number, and called. Like the other times, the same message broadcast. He wondered if this was the case everywhere, or was it just in this region?

As he approached, a nervous energy began to build. It had been years since he'd seen Chance, and their last conversation before the call the other day had been bad.

Words like *hate* were used, not by him, but by Chance. He didn't want to believe Chance hated him; then again, every time he had tried to reach out, Chance never answered or ever called him back.

He made the last right turn, and there it was, Cactus Rose Apartments. The complex was a series of four, two-story buildings. In the center was a common area with barbeques, a pool, and a hot tub. One with such knowledge could tell the buildings had been constructed in the 1990s based upon the architectural design. The heavy Spanish influence, which included the use of random colorful tiles, stucco siding, arched entryways, heavy wrought iron, and a clay tile roof, was in style then versus the more contemporary style of the present day. It was a safe complex and convenient for those who attended Arizona State.

Chance was in his third year of what would have been many more, as he'd just changed his major to engineering and away from kinesiology. It was a decision Ethan was happy with, especially since he paid the tuition. He, like most, enjoyed going to the gym, but personal trainers don't really make money, and to get a degree where his choices for jobs were relatively low paying didn't seem like a sound investment when compared to engineering.

He pulled up next to the main entrance and parked. He had a clear view of the common area and saw dozens of people. It looked like a party, with pool toys and water splashing.

"Well, no time like the present," he said out loud. He took one large breath, exhaled, and exited the vehicle. He paused when he felt the weight of his pistol in his waistband. He removed it, his eyes giving it the familiar stare. He went to place it in the console, then stopped; he shoved it back in his waistband and pulled down his shirt to cover it.

Hoots, laughter, and the sounds of merriment rang from the pool and common area. Scantily clad women and men played like children, with a couple openly having sex. Near the barbeques, which were smoking with the savory smell of meat cooking, was a keg. Several people were gathered around it, filling their cups. Outside of the sex, nothing made this scene too out of the ordinary for an apartment complex that primarily housed college students.

Like a car wreck, Ethan couldn't help but look. He didn't judge, the world for them was coming to an end soon, and this was how they were choosing to spend the last days. He did question why some hadn't gone home to family. *What was their story?*

He made a beeline for Chance's apartment, number 24, top floor, back corner unit in building 4. He scaled the stairs, stepping out of the way as a man and woman in their mid-twenties raced down, drunken smiles on their faces.

Ethan cleared the stairs. His thoughts shifted from the rowdy party to seeing Chance. He played out their encounter in his mind and only chose to see it work out with love and harmony, and maybe one contentious conversation that would quickly turn positive.

At the door he raised his hand to knock, but before he could, the door opened. Chance stood, his lean face now covered in weeks' growth. "Hi, Dad."

"Chance," Ethan replied. He couldn't help but stare into his familiar eyes. He was a Kinkaid without a doubt. Like Ethan, he was tall, a little shy of six foot one inch, with broad shoulders, muscular build and lean face. His dark hair was thick, but a widow's peak was already present.

Chance embraced Ethan tightly, pulling him close.

Taken aback by the display of affection, it took Ethan a moment before he put his arms around Chance.

"I'm so glad you're here, I was getting worried, the phones have been down, and you didn't reply to my texts."

Ethan pulled back from the embrace and asked, "You texted me?"

"Yeah, constantly."

Ethan furrowed his brow as he searched his memory, had he even checked text messages since the day before? He wasn't one for technology; he stayed clear of social media and the phone in general most of the time, and after Jen died, he all but gave it up. Embarrassed and needing to know that moment, he pulled out his phone, flipped past his home screen, and searched for the text app. Upon discovering it, he saw Chance had sent six texts. He groaned and said, "I'm such a tech idiot. I didn't..."

"It doesn't matter; you're here now. Come in." Chance warmly opened the door fully.

"I don't understand why I didn't get these."

Chance snatched his phone and, like a professional from tech support, scrolled through, clicking and swiping. "You had your texts set to no notification."

"I did?"

"Yep." He handed the phone back to Ethan. "Notifications back on, and I put the text app back on your home screen. It was literally nowhere to be found."

Ethan wasn't shocked. After Jen died, he hated the attention from everyone, so he turned off notifications. He looked at the phone and saw he had over one hundred unread texts which went back almost a year.

Two drunken twenty-somethings sprinted past, one almost clipping Ethan.

"Let's get you inside before you end up covered in beer or worse," Chance said, motioning with his hand for Ethan to enter.

Ethan crossed the threshold and immediately felt the coziness of the apartment. He recalled Cactus Rose Apartments had a reputation for being clean and safe, but one negative was the size. Chance's one bedroom was just above one thousand square feet, barely large enough to even have a bedroom.

The short hallway was dark and narrow; the white walls were bare except for a single print of a sunflower in a vase. Ethan found it odd that Chance would have it up, as he was a rock and rap-band-poster type of person. Walking past the kitchen, he spotted something else out of sorts: the apartment was clean. Chance had always been untidy; the fact there wasn't a dirty dish said something was off.

They entered the small twelve-by-sixteen-foot living room, to the left was a small dinette table, and to the right a plush couch sat against the wall facing a seventy-five-inch television.

Again, Ethan took in just how neat and clean it was.

On the small glass coffee table was a stack of magazines; he looked closer and saw *Women's Health* and a Bible. Now it all made sense.

"Ahh, Dad, I, um, I..." Chance stuttered, a nervous band of sweat on his brow.

The bedroom door opened, and out stepped a woman.

Ethan looked at her, and when he saw her belly, his chest tightened.

The woman walked up to Ethan with a confidence not usually seen in someone her age. She embraced Ethan warmly and said, "Hi, I'm Annette. It's so nice to finally meet you." She pulled back, took his hand, and continued, "I've heard so much about you. And I can see where Chance gets his looks."

With a crooked smile, Ethan replied, "Hi, nice to meet you too." He shot Chance a look and said, "I'm sure you've heard a lot."

A nervous smile stretched across Chance's face; he said, "It's not been all bad, I swear."

"So, congratulations are in order, I see," Ethan said, his face showing the shock as he turned his gaze back to Annette.

"Yeah, we're very excited," she said, rubbing her belly. "It's gonna be a boy."

"Oh, wow, this is very exciting," Ethan said. He struggled to keep his tone from showing his deep concern for the situation.

Chance could see the stress on Ethan's face. "Can I get you a beer?"

"Sure."

Annette waddled over to the couch and slowly maneuvered herself to the cushion. Settling in, she let out a sigh. "Could be any day now."

With eyes as wide as saucers, Ethan spun around and went to the kitchen.

"We have a problem."

Holding two bottles of beer and a flavored club soda in his hand, Chance grinned. "I know what you're going to say, but I thought if we just showed up, they're not going to say no to a pregnant woman."

"That very well may be the case, but we have a long drive, and she's about to pop."

Looking over Ethan's shoulder, Chance urged, "Please keep your voice down, Dad. She's already upset about everything."

"Son, seven billion people are upset right now."

"Call Uncle Eric; he'll make it happen."

"Call? Did you just say call?"

"Then text him."

"You haven't changed, have you?" Ethan scolded.

"What does that mean?"

"We have a chance to survive this, and just to complicate the situation, you knock up some girl. What if I don't reach your uncle, or he says they can't give us an extra spot for your pregnant girlfriend?"

Chance shoved the beer into Ethan's chest. "I see *you* haven't changed, still an asshole. If you can't help us, then leave." He pushed past him but stopped short of leaving. He turned back around and snapped. "And she's not my girlfriend, she's my wife." Chance exited the kitchen.

With a heavy sigh, Ethan took a swig of the cold beer; the strong hoppy flavor tasted good and reminded him of better times. He set the beer on the counter, pulled his phone out, and scrolled through until he found Eric's number. He pressed call and waited. Nothing but the same message of 'circuits busy'. "Ugh." He went to the text messages and saw the four from Eric.

Call me, ASAP, bro.

Need to talk, answer your phone.

Glad to have reached you. Have this with you when you arrive, the QR code is important, it's your ticket to ride. Get to Hill Air Force Base in Utah, just north of Salt Lake City by February 1st, plane is scheduled for wheels up at 1pm. Don't be late. Love you, brother.

Can't wait to see you soon.

"Here goes nothing," Ethan groaned as he typed out the message.

Hey brother, ran into an issue with Chance, need two extra spots.

He pressed send and waited. A notification appeared below, DELIVERED. He waited a moment longer to see the dots of someone replying, but nothing. Making sure he'd know if a text came, he took his phone off silent mode. He took another swig of beer, let out an audible sigh, and joined Chance and Annette in the living room.

---

THE THREE TALKED until the late afternoon turned to evening. The raucous sounds of merriment penetrated the walls, reminding them another world existed outside the pleasantries of family getting to know one another.

The aroma of macaroni filled the air as Chance could be heard in the kitchen.

"I can see he's still gourmet," Ethan quipped.

"Actually, he's become quite a good cook," Annette said, her lips raised in a pleasant smile. "One thing I truly love about Chance is he's intellectually curious and always willing to learn. He shows an earnest desire for knowledge."

Ethan dug through his memories briefly to confirm Annette's assessment, only to come up short. Not wanting to seem like he didn't know his son as well as she did, he nodded. "Yep, he's always been that way."

"I'm so eager to learn more about Chance, about his childhood years and such. He doesn't tell me too much. I hope you don't mind if I ask questions about him from time to time."

"Sure," Ethan said. He found himself relaxed in Annette's presence. She was young, but there was a maturity about her, a confidence and authenticity that gave him a sense of peace.

"Who's hungry?" Chance came into the living room carrying a tray. On it were three heaping and steaming bowls. He set the tray on the coffee table, handed a bowl to Annette and one to Ethan. He raced out and quickly returned with fresh drinks, another beer for him and Ethan and another flavored soda water for Annette.

"Shall we pray?" Annette asked.

Ethan quickly shot a glance to Chance, his brow raised.

Ignoring his father, Chance nodded and said, "Yes, good idea. But do you mind doing it? You're much better than I am."

Annette smiled sweetly and reached her right hand out to Ethan and her left to Chance.

Chance took her hand without hesitation, while Ethan felt a bit awkward at first but relented.

"Heavenly Father, thank you for all the blessings we have and for the continued blessings you bestow. Today we rejoice, as Chance's father is here. Lord, we are grateful that you have given Chance his father back and that our son will have a grandfather. Lord, thank you for this food and the hands that made it. I send this prayer to you through your son, Jesus, amen."

Happily, Chance opened his eyes, smiled, and said, "Amen."

Annette tenderly squeezed Ethan's hand and gave him an adoring smile.

Taking his hand back, Ethan returned the smile and, so he didn't feel like the odd person out, said, "Amen." He picked up the bowl, and before he took a spoonful, looked at Chance. "Some things never change."

Chance looked and saw Ethan motioning with his head to the bowl. "What who doesn't love mac-n-cheese?"

"Well, you always have." Ethan laughed. "We could be having steak and lobster, and Chance would ask for macaroni and cheese without fail. I think he lived off it from three to twelve."

"And beyond, it got me through my first two years of college."

"And then he met me. I opened up his culinary palate."

"Admit it though, you love this stuff. This golden bowl of cheesy pasta goodness."

"Gold?" Annette laughed. "More like orange."

"I see golden goodness," Chance said, shoveling a spoonful into his mouth.

Ethan watched the two banter and laugh. Each time Chance would look at Annette, a glimmer would sparkle in his eyes, and she seemed to find him the funniest person alive, something Ethan would adamantly disagree with. Theirs was a love, a love he found familiar. A heaviness began to weigh on his chest, and his thoughts turned to Jen. He slowed his eating and played with his food.

"Are you okay?" Annette asked, noticing Ethan's expression and composure had changed.

He lifted his gaze to meet hers. "I'm just happy to be here, and it's so nice to see Chance truly happy."

A large smile graced Annette's face. She reached her hand out and took Chance's. "We are truly happy."

An audible ping sounded from Ethan's pocket,

drawing everyone's curious eyes. Ethan set his bowl down and reached into his pocket.

"Who is it?" Chance asked.

"I'm thinking it's your uncle Eric," Ethan replied. A rush of anxious energy surged through him. The screen illuminated to show it was from Eric. He unlocked his phone and read the message.

> Hey brother, I can't secure you any more spots. Sorry. If more become available, I'll let you know. Now get to the base as soon as you can, some details have changed, can't send it via text. Be safe, shit's really hitting the fan.

Sitting pensively, both Annette and Chance awaited the update.

Ethan did his best poker face. He knew if he answered honestly he risked losing Chance. He had days to figure this out, and if he didn't, then he'd just not go. Death was something he was already prepared for anyway. But what would happen if she had a baby, would they count the child as a spot?

"Well?" Chance asked.

"Uncle Eric can make it happen; you, my dear, have a seat."

"I knew it. I knew Uncle Eric would make it happen!" Chance cheered. He jumped to his feet and pumped his fist.

Tears streamed down Annette's flush face. "God is good. I knew he'd come through for us. He always does."

"I knew it. I told you, Dad, I told you!" Chance cheered.

"You were right." Ethan smiled.

"We need to celebrate," Chance exclaimed and made his way to the kitchen.

"Hey, champ, let's not do too much celebration tonight; we need to get on the road in the early morning."

Chance returned with a bottle of whiskey and two glasses. He sat down, opened the bottle, and just as he poured, the power turned off.

A combination of groans and cheers echoed from the common area.

"I was wondering when it was going to finally shut down." Chance chuckled. He felt for the end table; his fingers fumbled to open the drawer. Once open, he searched, his hand gliding over numerous objects until he touched what he wanted, a small battery-powered lantern no bigger than a baseball. He took it out, pulled, making it telescope a couple of inches, and turn on. The bright LED illuminated the space and cast long shadows on the wall behind them.

"We got this and some other items after last summer's brownouts," Chance said, a prideful smile on his face.

The lack of power seemed to amplify the chatter and overall activity outside, specifically at the common area and pool.

"Here," Chance said, handing a half-full glass of whiskey to Ethan.

"Thanks, but like I said, let's take it easy; we have an early morning and a long drive ahead of us."

"Here's to God delivering, as he always does, and to Uncle Eric," Chance said, his glass lifted.

They all touched glasses, Annette still drinking her soda water, and took a drink. She sighed heavily, leaned back, and groaned, her hand rubbing her stomach. "He's moving tonight."

"Maybe you should get some sleep," Chance said, a concerned look on his face.

"I think you're right." She struggled to sit up, only to struggle more to get to her feet. "Good night."

In unison, Ethan and Chance said, "Good night."

"You should go in with her," Ethan said, swirling the whiskey in his glass. He liked the taste but just wasn't in the mood to drink.

"I thought we could talk," Chance said, taking a seat on the couch, the glass of whiskey in his hand. He tossed it back and poured another.

"How come you never told me you were married and had a kid on the way?"

Chance shifted his weight on the couch, his gaze on the glass in his hand. A smile broke out on his face.

With a furrowed brow, Ethan asked, "What is it?"

"Is it really a mystery?"

"To me it is, yeah. My only son getting married and having a kid on the way. Most people kind of expect a call, maybe a text."

"If it were a text, you wouldn't have gotten it," Chance quipped. He took a big swig, almost emptying the glass. "And, Dad, I saw the dating app on your phone. Never thought you were one for those sorts of things."

"Dating app?" Ethan asked, unaware of what Chance

was talking about. He pulled his phone out and scrolled. "Where?"

"It's there. Match.com."

Thinking he found it, he held his phone out. "Is this it?"

"Yep."

"Oh, a friend downloaded that and said I needed to move on. Ugh, who tells someone to move on after their spouse dies? I never even went on the stupid thing."

"One day you'll want to."

"I don't think the app will work."

"No, find love again."

"Maybe."

"God didn't create us to be alone. We're made for companionship. People who say they're happy to be alone are lying. No one is happy to be alone; in fact too many people talk about happiness, finding it, you know. What they don't know is happiness can only be found inside yourself and through God."

"Look who's the philosopher."

Chance smiled.

"How did you meet?"

"Here, yep, she used to live a few doors down."

"Let me guess, as soon as you saw her, you just knew."

"Yep."

"That's how it was for me and Jen. The first time I saw her, I just knew, it was as if I had found a missing part of me."

Chance nodded.

"She was backing out of a parking space and almost hit me as I was walking. She got out, and we started chatting, the chatting turned to laughter, and her eyes, those eyes, man, I was hooked."

"We're both romantics, then."

"But you're the philosopher king."

"I keep trying to be a better man each day."

"I'm assuming this is Annette's influence because this isn't the rap-music foulmouthed kid I raised."

Chance chuckled and took a swig of whiskey.

"What's so funny?"

"Raised?"

"You're still upset because I wouldn't lend you that money?"

"Let's drop this. I shouldn't have said that."

Ethan couldn't; that chuckle annoyed him. "Or does this go back to the time when you were thirteen and wanted me to disrespect your mother."

"Let's not talk about her."

"I'm not talking about her, just mentioning you gave me a six-month silent treatment after that."

"I miss her," Chance said; his tone turned somber.

Ethan thought about his next words and decided to lower the temperature of the conversation. "She was a good person."

"She was a great mother," Chance said. He finished his glass, set it down, and reached for the bottle.

"Son, ease up; we've got a big day ahead of us."

Ignoring Ethan, Chance opened the bottle and poured. He gave Ethan a wink and took a big gulp.

Ethan curled the corners of his mouth and shook his head gently.

"Does the dad in you not approve?" Chance mocked.

"No, I don't. I don't need you hungover."

A loud bang at the front door startled them and provided a perfectly timed break from their deteriorating conversation.

"Who can that be?" Ethan asked. He set his glass down and stood.

"Probably just a neighbor asking for something." Chance took a step; his foot caught the corner of the coffee table, causing him to stumble a few feet. Whiskey spilled from the glass onto him and the floor. "Ugh."

"Let me go get it."

"No, I got it. Sit down, drink." Chance disappeared into the darkness of the hall.

Ethan got up and followed, his hand placed on the backstrap of his pistol, which was still tucked into his waistband.

Chance opened the door to find a woman, a flashlight in her hand. "Hi." He recognized her as the young woman, about early twenties, who lived in an apartment two doors down.

"You have any beer?" she asked, swaying from side to side.

"All out, sorry."

She looked at his hand and saw the glass. "What's that?"

"Oh, um, this is whiskey."

"Can I have some?"

"Um, I don't think that's a good idea."

She took a step forward, bumping into Chance.

"You're drunk."

"So what?"

"Maybe you should go to bed."

"What are you, my mother? Like, who cares? We're all gonna die soon anyway," she blared, her words slurred together. She took another step forward to walk inside.

"Ahh, I don't think I invited you in."

She reached down and rubbed her hand on his crotch. "I'll take care of you if you take care of me."

Her breath smelled of stale beer and vomit. Chance pulled away and said, "I'm married, and my wife is in the other room."

"We can have a threesome." She winked and bit her lip, her hip cocked out in a seductive pose.

Chance put his free hand on her shoulder and gently pushed her away. "I can't help you here. I'm sorry." He stepped back and closed the door.

"Fuck you!" she screamed. "You probably have a small dick anyway!"

Watching from the shadows, Ethan smiled. He was impressed with Chance's discipline. Many men were weak and would have succumbed to the temptation.

Chance locked the door. He took a deep breath in, emptied the contents of the glass, and headed back towards the living room.

"Bravo," Ethan said.

"What the?" Chance's eyes widened. "Were you spying on me?"

"Not spying, just watching your back. We had no idea who that was, and if it was someone with no good intentions, I wanted to be ready."

"Did you hear her?"

"Yeah, bravo. You turned away sex. Most people would have been unable to do that."

"I'm married now, and that's a sin. Poor woman has only days left, and she freely sins. What she should be doing is seeking God and forgiveness."

"Give her a break."

"A break?"

"She's lost and alone. And it's obvious she's depressed about the fact she'll be dead in a little over a week. Plus, you don't know if she'll find God just before."

"That's true."

"Maybe we should be less judgmental these days. I'm not saying we walk around foolishly, but maybe a bit more humility and grace towards people. Pretty much everyone you see will be dead soon, and they're coming to grips with that realization, either one drink, sexual partner or prayer at a time."

"Look who became a scholar and sage."

"None of that. I've just had my share of loss."

A pregnant pause held them both to silence.

"I'm sorry I didn't make Jen's memorial service."

"You were missed, and I won't lie, it upset me, but I'm over it now. You had your reasons."

"Can I tell you why?"

"Please."

"I was paying you back for not coming to Mom's."

"I told you why I couldn't make hers, there was no time to make it back, and you all had to have it specifically three days after her death. I really wanted to be there."

"I'm like you, I'm over it, but I was upset at the time." He paused. "And I was just mad at you and her. She didn't do anything to me; she was just with you. I acted like a child, immature, and I'm sorry."

Ethan smiled; a warm feeling spread over him. One he hadn't felt in some time in relation to Chance. "I have much to apologize for too. I haven't been the best father."

"Well, that's true," Chance quipped, the alcohol fueling his attitude.

"Ouch."

"Shall we have another?" Chance asked, holding his empty glass up. He headed towards the couch.

"How about we call it a night."

"Oh, come on."

"No, I want to get up early and start heading north."

"Fine." Chance moped. He set his glass down, shot Ethan a glance, and strutted towards him.

Standing like a statue, Ethan could feel the energy coming off Chance as he headed at him.

Chance embraced Ethan, warmly wrapping his arms around him, and squeezed. "It's good to see you, Dad."

"It's good to be seen," Ethan said, his arms firmly around Chance. "You've gotten muscular."

"Been working out for a while now. I do one hundred push-ups a day and other calisthenics on top of my gym routine."

"One hundred per day, hmm, I bet your old man could still beat you in a push-up challenge."

Pulling back, Chance grinned. "I'll take that bet. Tomorrow morning, first thing. Best get some rest...old man."

The two parted ways.

"There's a blanket and pillow in the hall closet. Good

night, Dad," Chance said just before disappearing into the bedroom.

Alone, Ethan took in the day. It had been a full one at best. He got the blanket and pillow and stretched out on the couch. He turned off the lantern and stared into the darkness.

Outside, the laughter and partying continued, with the occasional beam from a flashlight cutting through the black in the room from the window.

As it did each night, Ethan's thoughts drifted to Jen. Like a movie he'd seen a hundred times, he played the moments he enjoyed the most before revisiting the night she died, with the thoughts ending with her words, *"Ethan...I love you."*

He picked his phone off the coffee table, found the voicemail, and hit play. He adjusted the volume so as not to disturb Chance and Annette. Over and over, he played the voicemail. Tears formed and streamed down the sides of his face.

Waking like she did numerous times each night to go to the bathroom, Annette heard someone talking in the living room; she opened the bedroom door just a bit but stopped short of going out when she heard the message end and start over again. She knew who it was and what Ethan was doing. She closed the door quietly, leaving Ethan to his memories.

# EIGHT

## FLAGSTAFF, ARIZONA

CONFUSION. Melody opened her eyes and stared at the unfamiliar ceiling above. The cold hard floor beneath her wasn't her bed nor her couch.

Pain. An ache in her right arm and that ever-present sensation of nausea were there. She rolled her head to the left and looked at the cherry-stained cabinets, then to the right and saw the bodies. Jolted by the sight, she pushed herself up, her elbows supporting her weight. She was a nurse, had been for a little over a year, but had never seen so much blood as what was covering the floor. She fully sat up, her back against the far cabinets of the kitchen, staring at the bodies of Jared and Tabitha; she was in disbelief. Tabitha's head showed the damage done by the rolling pin, and Jared's neck had two small but perfectly positioned holes that led to his jugular. Jared's eyes were open, staring blankly at the orange-peel-textured ceiling above. His dark brown eyes had turned gray, an odd thing to see. *How did it come to this?* She only meant to come over and get the answers she rightfully deserved. The scene itself was a shock, but so was the fact he had cheated on her, and she never knew about it. She never saw this coming, but there were the signs she had thought about earlier. This was on her, she told herself, not that she deserved to have her fiancé cheat, but because her weakness of mind had prevented her from seeing what was clearly in front of her.

A wave of nausea overcame her. She leaned over and began to vomit. *Was this a reaction to what just happened, or was it the medicine she'd taken before coming over?* After emptying the contents of her stomach, she got to her feet. Light-headed, she gripped the counter and held fast until the feeling subsided enough for her to traverse from the kitchen to the living room couch. A crushing fatigue began to build, which she blamed on everything that had occurred coupled with her disease. Needing to get off her feet, she fell into the couch; the cool leather felt good against her hot skin. She went to adjust herself to get more comfortable, but her hand slipped on something wet. She looked and noticed her hand was covered in blood. Taking a moment, she then saw it went down her arm, with blood splatters on her shirt and jeans. Disturbed, she ripped off her shirt and jeans and headed down the hall, looking for a bathroom. Entering the master bedroom, she paused when she came upon a framed photo of Jared and Tabitha. Anger welled up in her. She took the picture and threw it with all her might against the far wall. Shards of glass showered the floor like hail peppering a lawn.

"Lying bastard!" she screamed.

Marching into the bathroom, she stopped upon seeing her reflection in the mirror. Splatters of blood were spread across her face and in her thick brown hair. Filled with a range of emotions from disgust to utter despair, she began to sob. Warm tears streamed down her cheeks, turning red as they went through the dried blood. Not able to look at herself any longer, she spun away, turned on the shower, and got naked.

The hot water felt good; she stood without washing for an unknown amount of time, her thoughts jumbled. *What should I do? Where will I go?* She thought of going back home to her mother in New Jersey, but the reality was she hated her mother. She had no other relative nor close friends around her since Jared had moved her to Flagstaff the year before. This was what made his betrayal the more painful. She had given him all of her, and this was how he treated her. She was alone and sick, and now the world was coming to an end.

She hated having to do it, but she needed clothes, and Tabitha's would do since she was about her size. Dressed and back in the living room, she stood for a moment staring at them. On the kitchen bar, she saw his phone. An idea came to her. She had nowhere to go, and no idea of what to do with herself, but maybe she could find some answers to why he'd left her, why he was with this woman. She snatched his phone from the counter and made her way back to the couch and sat. Tucking her wet hair behind her ears, she browsed through his text messages.

As she read his messages to Tabitha, she felt sick, and her chest hurt. What infuriated her more than him telling her how much he loved her was the cat emojis he used when talking about her vagina.

"You're a piece of shit," she snarled at Jared's body.

While it was painful to go through each text between Jared and Tabitha, she did get the answers she was looking for and that her illness had played a role in him seeking someone outside their relationship. Did it make what Jared did right? No, but now she knew his excuse, and it was a piss-poor one. He had turned her battle with cancer into a narcissistic pity party so that he could get sympathy. He'd leveraged her pain, her sickness for his own carnal pleasure and then had the nerve to tell her he was on a spiritual journey. What a joke and, it turned out, a lie!

Her sadness turned to anger. She wanted to throw the phone across the room, but her curiosity got the better of her. She needed to know what else he had going on. *Was Tabitha just one of many? Who else was he lying to?* She went to the next text from a number she didn't recognize. Confused by what she was reading, she reread it several times.

HILL AF BASE...DEPARTURE 1300 HRS...FEBRUARY 1...SHOW GUARD QR CODE...ACCESS FOR TWO.

*What did this mean? Were they going somewhere?* Then she recalled seeing a piece of luggage on the bed in the master. There was no other information in the text telling her what it meant. *Where were they going? A flight to where?* Then it dawned on her. She cocked her head in his direction and barked, "You were going to the Ark? You were going to leave me here to die?" She recoiled her arm and was about to throw the phone at his body when she remembered the QR code. *Can I use it?* Well, there was only one way of finding out. She got to her feet with purpose and headed for the door.

# NINE

## ENOCH, UTAH

THE SNORES COMING from Susie's bedroom were loud enough for Savannah to sneak down the creaking stairs and into the kitchen. She found some food for her and EJ and raced back up. Just before she cleared the last step, Susie cried out.

"Who is that?"

Savannah froze. Her gaze locked with EJ's, who sat wide-eyed inside the attic, his hand over his mouth to prevent even his breath from making a noise.

"EJ?" Susie called out from her bedroom.

Hearing his name, EJ shook his head with a panicked look now washing across his face.

The two had slept in the attic. Something they had done before, and since it wasn't a rare occurrence, Savannah kept blankets and pillows there.

"Savannah?" Susie called out.

71

EJ removed his hand and mouthed, "Don't say a word."

Savannah didn't want to reply. She pressed her eyes closed, gulped, and prayed she would fall back to sleep.

Unintelligible voices came from Susie's bedroom, followed by heavy footfalls, then the sound of someone urinating in the master bathroom. The heavy footfalls continued to the master bedroom door.

"See you later?" the man asked.

"Maybe," Susie replied, her voice craggy.

The man exited and closed the door behind him. He pulled a T-shirt over his head and slipped into a flannel.

Savannah craned her head back and looked down at him. He was younger, or at least appeared so, than her mother. He had thick curly brown hair, which hung just below the top of his ears. His face was covered with thick stubble, and his overall appearance was that of someone who paid little attention to grooming. He wasn't an unattractive man even with his large nose, which protruded out and hooked down. He was lean and not because he worked out; he just happened to be one of those lucky people who could live however they wanted and not gain a pound. Savannah just stared at him. Not for any other reason than to remember this man who had just slept with her mother. She found them both repulsive and wished he would just leave.

The man looked up the stairs and saw Savannah. He shot her a wink, then put his finger to his lips, signaling for her to remain quiet. He gave her a slight grin, turned, and left the house.

Savannah pondered why he'd motioned for her to be

quiet. Did he also know her mother was cruel? Was her tone calling out to her enough for him to pick that up? Or was he just being playful, knowing that kids will be kids.

The deep guttural roar of the truck starting filled the air and tore her away from her thoughts.

"Psst, I'm hungry," EJ whispered.

Savannah took a soft step and froze when Susie boomed in her typical demanding voice, "Savannah, get your ass down to the kitchen and make me breakfast!"

Savannah didn't move. She looked at EJ, who shook his head with disappointment.

The bedroom door opened and Susie emerged wearing a soiled and ill-fitting nightgown; around her was a halo of smoke. She walked to the base of the stairs and looked up. "There you are. Are you deaf or just being a little shit and ignoring me?" She took a long drag from her cigarette and exhaled. A phlegmy cough followed. "Well?"

"Yes, Mama," Savannah said. She turned and slowly descended until she was in front of her, her arms filled with the bread and jars of peanut butter and jelly.

Susie looked at the food, shook her head, and said, "Tell your brother to come down and help."

"Yes, Mama," she said timidly. "Eggs and bacon?"

"Sure, sounds good." She took a long hard drag on the cigarette, her eyes taking Savannah in. She reached out and touched Savannah's long blonde hair. "Did you see him?"

"Who?"

"Don't play stupid with me."

"The man?"

"He's a looker, isn't he?"

Savannah looked down. She hated these sorts of questions.

Susie moved her hand down towards Savannah's chest. "You're not maturing like I did. Good thing. Men like Dave take notice when you're more...developed. You can't trust men like him." She inhaled a drag; the tip glowed, illuminating her weathered face. As she exhaled, she continued, "You can't trust men, period."

"Then why did...why was he here if you don't trust him?"

Susie smiled. She lifted her hand and caressed Savannah's cheek. "You're still so innocent."

Savannah tensed her body in anticipation of what usually came next, her eyes still focused down. She looked at Susie's bruised and scrawny legs. They were like sticks with shriveled meat attached, no real muscular definition.

"It's sad, you know," Susie said, her hand now brushing through Savannah's hair.

"What's sad?"

"You'll never know what it's like."

Savannah's stomach tightened, and every muscle in her body became rigid. Her mind was screaming to run, yet she stood frozen and accepting of what she was sure to come.

"And you're such a pretty little thing. I am sorry, I truly am, that you won't get to know the pleasures of life. Ugh! This fucking asteroid, it took it all away. It's taking everything away."

"I should get breakfast going," Savannah said.

"You go ahead."

Savannah quickly pivoted, like a soldier turns when given an order.

"And, Savy," Susie said.

Savannah took a few steps before acknowledging her. "Yes, Mama."

"Next time I call for you, answer me."

"Yes, Mama," she said and hurried into the kitchen, breathing a sigh of relief she hadn't been hit.

Susie shuffled back into her bedroom and closed the door.

Fearing she might pass out, Savannah sat at the dinette table and took in a couple of deep breaths.

EJ appeared in the doorway of the kitchen. "Where's Mama?"

Savannah jumped. "Darn it, EJ, you scared me."

He walked up to her and again asked, "Where's Mama?"

"She went back to bed. Now help me make her breakfast."

"What are we making?"

"I hate her," Savannah growled.

EJ stood, an expression of shock on his face. "You'd best be quiet. If she heard you say that, she'd beat you bad."

"Just shut up and go set the table," Savannah snapped back. She tossed the items she had in her arms onto the counter and began prepping to cook.

EJ didn't say a word. He stood next to the small dinette table in front of the window that overlooked the backyard. The table was like everything else in the house, weathered and in disrepair. He fiddled with his fingers, his nails long with grime underneath. His face was smudged with dirt, as he hadn't had a bath nor washed in some days.

Savannah placed a frying pan on the stove top and went to the refrigerator. She stopped and shot EJ a look. "Go wash your hands and face first."

EJ did as he was told, not a word uttered.

"Ugh," Savannah groaned when she saw there were only a few eggs left. She took what they had left and walked back to the stove top. "Are you setting the table yet?" She looked back, and EJ was already doing it. "I'm sorry if I'm grumpy. Mama was..."

"I know."

"I'm sorry."

"It's okay. Can I go to the bathroom first? I need to pee."

"Just get the table set, then go."

He shuffled to a set of cabinets next to Savannah, pulled over a stool, climbed up, and opened the dingy white door of the upper cabinet. Inside were plates; he took them down one at a time. Each movement appeared choreographed to ensure he didn't drop one.

Savannah poured a bit of vegetable oil into the frying pan. While she waited for the pan to heat, she watched EJ take the plates down. Her heart ached for him. Every person is born different, some softer and with tender hearts like EJ. While she had been able to suffer through Susie's abuse, EJ was struggling; his mental well-being was in peril.

Hacking coughs from down the hall tore Savannah from her thoughts. She looked and saw the oil was beginning to burn and smoke. "Ugh!" she barked. She quickly turned off the heat and picked up the pan and went to place it on a cool cook top. In her haste she hit the egg carton, sending it to the floor and breaking all the eggs but one.

Startled by the eggs falling, EJ dropped a plate. It fell, smacked the counter, breaking into four large pieces, and then onto the floor, where it shattered into dozens.

Both stood motionless, looking at each other, waiting for the wrath to come.

"What was that!" Susie hollered from the bedroom. She burst out and marched heavy footed down the hall and into the kitchen. Standing with fire in her eyes, she glared at them both.

"I'll clean it up," Savannah said, already on her knees, doing her best to recover what eggs she could.

EJ stood shaking on the stool and began to sob.

Susie stared at the eggs, then the plate. "Are you both useless?"

EJ's shaking became worse as a puddle began to form on the stool and floor below.

"We'll get it cleaned up fast, promise. EJ, get down and clean the plate up." Not hearing any movement except his sobbing, she looked over her shoulder and saw the growing puddle. "No."

"I...I...I'm sorry," he sobbed.

Susie exploded with rage. She raced over to EJ, snatched him from the stool, and started to whip him with her open hand.

EJ screamed in pain and terror.

Angered, Savannah shot up and went towards Susie. "Stop! Leave him alone!"

Shocked by Savannah's response, Susie stopped hitting EJ.

Savannah took EJ's hand and pulled him close. "Leave him alone. Just stop it!"

Susie recovered from her shock and took a step towards Savannah, who stood in front of EJ. "If you touch him again, I'll…"

"You'll what?" Susie asked. She stopped feet from Savannah; her defiance paused her advance.

"We're your kids, your babies. Why are you hurting us?"

She recoiled from the question.

The two were in a stalemate. Savannah stood tall while Susie contemplated what to do next as her mind processed.

"We love you, Mama. Please stop hurting us," EJ whimpered.

"I'm teaching you all a lesson," she fired back. "Life is hard, so you must be prepared."

"What life? It all ends in a week!" Savannah reminded her.

Susie's nostrils flared, and her eyes narrowed. With an open hand she smacked Savannah across the face and stormed out of the kitchen.

Both the children stood quivering.

"Thank you," EJ softly said. He wrapped his arms around Savannah and squeezed.

It took more than a moment for Savannah to recover. She took in a few deep breaths and said, "Go change your clothes."

"But the…" he said and pointed at the floor.

"I'll take care of it. Go, get on a clean pair of pants, and you didn't wash your face like I asked. Go get cleaned up, then come back."

EJ ran out of the kitchen and down the hall towards his bedroom.

The eggs were now past recovery. She surveyed all that needed to be cleaned and began with mopping up after EJ. With that done, she opened the cabinet beneath the sink to get paper towels and a cleaning spray. As she dug, she spotted an old box of rat poison. She stared at it; her mind went to dark thoughts.

EJ reappeared. "Clean!" He had changed all his clothes, and the shirt he wore was one she had given him last Christmas. "Look, it's the shirt you gave me."

She gave him a sweet look but was immediately reminded of the incident that had just occurred when Susie called out from the bedroom, "Where's my breakfast?"

An anger rose in her; she looked at EJ and said, "Get the oatmeal out; we'll have that instead."

# TEN

## TEMPE, ARIZONA

A SCREAM REVERBERATED through the apartment complex.

Ethan stopped and turned around. He had been on his way to his vehicle with a box of supplies for the road trip ahead, but by the sound and tone of the scream, he knew something was wrong.

A second even more intense scream sounded.

This was enough for Ethan to set the box down and race back towards the complex.

People stirred, with some exiting their apartments. Weary heads lifted from lounge chairs at the pool, their final resting place after a night of drinking and debauchery, to look around.

Ethan reached the common area and called out, "Where's that coming from?"

A man, early twenties and with a dazed and confused

look on his face, pointed towards the second floor of Chance's building.

A third scream came.

Ethan sprinted up the stairs. When he crested, he saw Chance coming from his apartment, a concerned look upon his face. For a moment, Ethan thought something was wrong with Annette; then Chance took a turn and entered another apartment. Ethan followed.

The floorplan of the apartment was like Chance's.

Cries and unintelligible chatter came from the bedroom.

A group of six people were huddled in the living room. Ethan pushed through them and into the bedroom, where he was welcomed by a pungent mildew odor. Chance and several others stood at the foot of the bed; all had their eyes fixed on the body of a naked woman. Several bottles of prescription drugs lay on the bed and nightstand along with loose tablets, beer cans and an empty bottle of vodka. Trash and strewn clothing littered the floor. The woman's eyes were open, and dried vomit stuck to her cheek.

Stepping next to Chance, Ethan asked, "Do you know her?"

"It's the girl from last night."

Ethan hadn't gotten a good look at her, so he would never have made the connection.

"Did you know her from before last night?"

"Yeah, I'd see her now and then, but can't say I knew her. Annette had some conversations while getting the mail or coming and going," he replied. After a moment's pause, he continued, "I feel bad now."

"There's nothing to feel bad about. This was going to happen whether you let her in or not."

"But still."

Ethan put his hand on Chance's shoulder and squeezed. "Come on, there's nothing you can do."

"Yeah, you're right."

They turned, and there, standing in the doorway, tears in her eyes, was Annette. Her gaze fixed on the woman. She rushed past them and to the side of the bed. Sitting down, she took the woman's hand and held it.

Murmured chatter broke out in the room.

Chance and Ethan looked on.

Annette bowed her head; tears streamed down her face.

The chatter continued.

"Show some respect; she's praying for her," Chance scolded the others.

"It's fine," Annette said just above a whisper, her eyes still fixed on the woman. She moved the woman's hair from her face and closed her eyes. "Help me wrap her body."

Chance sprang into action. He untucked the sheet and helped Annette drape and fold it over until the woman was swaddled completely. "Now what?"

"We should bury her," Annette said, now standing next to Chance. "Poor thing, she was a lost soul. I prayed that she found peace."

All Ethan heard was the word *bury*. "We don't have time to do that, and who has a shovel, anyway? I say we seal the room and call this a mausoleum."

Giving Ethan a tender look, Annette nodded. "Very well."

"But I, um, I do respect you for wanting to do that for her," Ethan said, feeling he needed to acknowledge her thoughtfulness.

Annette, with Chance's hand in hers, faced Ethan. "I've got my bag in the apartment. We should go."

"Agreed," Ethan said happily. He turned and exited.

"You're a good woman," Chance whispered into Annette's ear.

"I only did what was right."

Chance escorted her out of the apartment. "Stay here."

"What are you doing?"

"Finishing what needs to be done." He went back in the woman's apartment and made everyone leave. He locked the door by pressing the button, and closed it behind him.

With a sweet and subtle smile on her face, Annette said, "Look who's doing the right thing."

He gave her a peck on the cheek. "I had a good teacher."

# ELEVEN

## ENOCH, UTAH

STEAM BILLOWED FROM THE BOWL. A half-melted dab of butter, along with a healthy sprinkling of brown sugar, coated the top of the oatmeal.

EJ stared at his bowl, his eyes wide with excitement at the prospect of shoveling the first spoonful into his mouth. Without lifting his head, he asked, "Can I have just a little?"

"Wait for Mama."

The two had been sitting for over five minutes and still no sign or sound of Susie.

Impatient, Savannah called out, "Mama, breakfast!"

A loud creak came from the hallway. Footfalls and then a loud thud.

EJ jumped from his chair and was about to go see what had happened, but Savannah waved and gave him a nod, indicating he needed to stay put.

Susie let out a groan along with a few curse words. She got to her feet and puttered into the kitchen. Seeing the children sitting patiently waiting, she cooed, "Ahh, were you waiting for me?"

"Yes, we were, Mama," EJ replied, a smile gracing his face.

She sauntered over and looked at the food in the bowls. Her brow furrowed, her eyes narrowed, and the muscles in her jaw tensed. "What's this?"

"Um, the eggs, I broke them, and there wasn't enough," Savannah replied nervously.

"I wanted eggs."

"You like oatmeal," Savannah reminded her.

"Yeah, Mama, you love it," EJ said, hoping his jovial tone would turn her around.

"I wanted eggs and bacon."

"Try it, Mama. It's good," Savannah said.

A long uncomfortable pause had the children nervous. She stood, a blank stare on her face now as she gazed at the steaming oatmeal.

"Mama?" EJ asked.

Silence.

A strong wind whipped, causing the large tree's branches to slap the house, startling the children.

Savannah held her spoon tight in her grip, but now wished it were a knife.

The anger melted away from Susie's face. She sat down and chuckled. "Wow. What a night."

Not knowing what to say, both children shot each other an awkward glance. It was as if Susie had rebooted her brain.

"Best eat while it's hot, Mama," Savannah urged.

With a broad smile, Susie turned her head in Savannah's direction and said, "Thank you for making oatmeal."

"You're welcome."

"You used to love oatmeal as a toddler. I'd make it, and you'd eat it up. Ah, you were such a sweet baby." A smile on her face. She tilted her head towards EJ and said, "Go ahead, eat; don't wait for me."

EJ didn't need to be asked twice. He dove in and pulled out a heaping spoonful and shoved it in his mouth.

Savannah couldn't eat. Her stomach was in knots.

"Did I ever tell you about the time when you were eating oatmeal, you were two, maybe three, and you took the entire bowl and placed it on your head, upside down. I almost lost it, but your daddy, he, um, he thought it was the funniest thing he'd ever seen, and you know what he did?"

EJ, spoon down, listened intently.

Savannah's stomach twisted, and a cold sweat broke out on her brow. *Shut up and eat the oatmeal!* she screamed in her mind.

"He picked up his bowl and did the exact same thing. I wanted to kill him and you because of the mess, but he laughed, and you laughed. I stopped and just watched. I was mesmerized. You two had such a connection. He really loved you."

*Yeah, so much he left me with a crazy person. Now eat the oatmeal!*

Now look at you, you'll be..." She paused and took a gulp of air. "You would have turned thirteen, but this fucking asteroid!" She slammed her fist onto the table.

EJ jumped.

"Mama, the oatmeal is going to get cold. Please eat it," Savannah urged.

Ignoring Savannah, Susie sat back in her seat, her gaze up as she reminisced again. "Your daddy was so handsome. I can still see him walking into the pharmacy that day."

"That was so good," EJ said, licking his lips. The bowl in front of him was empty.

"Did you like that, baby?" Susie asked.

Anger welled in Savannah. Susie's sweet act was just that, she could turn on a dime, and it could happen at any moment. *Now eat the oatmeal!*

As if she could read her thoughts, Susie picked up her spoon and was about to dive into the oatmeal when she paused. "He's a real nice guy. I might see if he'd like to come over again tonight." She sank the spoon into the bowl.

Savannah's eyes widened.

"Does this mean you're leaving us home alone again?" EJ asked.

Susie, now with a spoonful herself, brought it to her mouth, but stopped when EJ blurted out his question. She lowered it, gave him a scolding look, and asked, "Are you my parent now? Huh? Do I need your approval to go out?"

EJ recoiled, and his body stiffened. "Ah, no, Mama."

"Are you questioning me?"

"No, Mama, not at all."

Savannah couldn't even hear the back-and-forth. Her attention was on the hovering spoon. *Eat it!*

"I'm sorry, Mama," EJ said. Tears welled in his eyes.

"Oh no, don't cry," Susie said, her voice softened.

"I just miss you, that's all," EJ explained.

Susie once more lowered the spoon, but this time put it back into the bowl. She reached out and took EJ's hand. "I'm sorry, Boo. Would you like me to stay home?"

Wiping his nose and the few tears that had broken free, EJ nodded.

Savannah couldn't stop staring at the bowl of oatmeal in front of her mother. Her stomach tightened more than it ever had in her life. This was a monumental event that was about to occur. She would be murdering her mother. She began to question herself and the decision; guilt and fear of getting caught raced through her darkened thoughts. *What if the poison isn't enough to kill her?* She hadn't done this sort of thing before. *What if she doesn't die? Would she make EJ suffer the most for it?*

Susie lowered her head and sniffed. "This smells so good." She picked her spoon up, then paused. "You know, I think I'll grab a bite out, see if Brad wants to come over. Here, you have it." She slid the oatmeal in front of EJ.

Savannah panicked. With catlike reflexes, she lunged across the table and pushed the bowl off the table. The bowl smashed on the floor, sending oatmeal everywhere.

"What in the hell?" Susie wailed.

"I, ah, I think I saw a bug in it!" Savannah cried out.

"No, you didn't, you wanted it for yourself, and look at you, you haven't even eaten yours yet." Susie stood and took a step towards Savannah.

"No, Mama, leave her alone!" EJ screamed.

Susie halted. She craned her head back and sneered. "Are you telling me what to do...again?"

EJ froze.

For whatever reason, EJ was mostly her primary target when she became enraged. Savannah concluded it must be because he was male and looked like their dad.

Susie turned and advanced on EJ.

"No, Mama, please!" EJ wailed.

Savannah stood, she wasn't sure what she should do, but knew she had to do something.

Susie came around the table, but EJ didn't stay still this time. He jumped up and raced to the opposite side of the table.

"You come here, boy!" she growled. With her bad knee, she couldn't move as quickly as EJ, but she'd try. She pushed the table out of her way and marched towards him.

EJ froze again.

"Over here," Savannah called.

EJ looked and saw Savannah standing tall, her hand out, beckoning for him to come. He did just that. He sprinted and got behind her.

Susie stopped and nodded. "So you two gonna team up?"

"Stay away," Savannah warned.

"You too? Telling me what I can and can't do in my own house."

"Just leave, go, come back when you're not going to hurt us!" Savannah commanded; her voice boomed with authority.

"You bitch and your smart mouth!" Susie snapped. She took two steps but paused when Savannah brandished a knife.

"Mama, just go...now!"

"You gonna stab me? Your own mother? You'd do that?"

EJ sobbed, his hands clinging to Savannah's shirt with his face buried in her back.

"Just go."

Susie lunged.

Savannah raised the knife and stood defiantly, her pose clearly showing Susie she wasn't going to back down.

Stopping inches from the tip of the blade, Susie sneered. She licked her dried and cracked lips and gave Savannah a foul look. "I'll leave, but when I come home, you'd best be gone. You hear me, gone!" She stomped from the kitchen and into her bedroom.

Standing firm and not moving an inch, the two children waited.

Moments later, Susie burst from her room, wearing jeans and a sweater. In her hands she had a pair of Uggs. "You hear me, bitch, you'd best be gone."

Savannah didn't reply; she kept the knife out in front of her.

Susie threw open the front door and walked out without closing it.

When the tinny sound of her car hit their ears, Savannah lowered the knife. She walked to the front door and watched as Susie backed out and drove in the direction of the bar.

"Are you gonna leave?" EJ asked. "Please don't go, please."

She lowered herself to look into his eyes. "There's

nowhere to go, we'll stay here, and if she comes at us, I'll use this." Savannah still held the knife.

Looking at the sharp edge of the blade, EJ cringed. "I'm scared."

She wrapped her arms around him and squeezed. "I'll keep you safe. She's not going to hurt you, I promise."

This time her promise was uttered without hesitation or question. She felt empowered. For the first time in her life, Susie had backed down. She knew they'd have to be vigilant, but if they played it safe, they could ride out their last days in the attic and in peace.

# TWELVE

## FLAGSTAFF, ARIZONA

BEING ORGANIZED WAS a trait Melody took pride in. Even in her childhood she'd had a clean room; it was a feat her mother complimented, something rare for her to do. But today there wouldn't be the normal inventory list of socks and underwear to ensure it was the same. No, today she tossed every pair she had into her luggage. This would be her last trip, and she wasn't sure if she'd ever be able to get new ones ever again. She did the same with T-shirts but kept her jeans to a minimum of seven. Unsure of where she was going, she did toss in a few sweaters and set aside a thicker down jacket with a knit hat. When it came to her toiletries, she again ensured she took every toothbrush and tube of toothpaste, and included every feminine hygiene product she had.

As she went back and forth from her dresser and closet to her luggage, she listened to music to get her mind off Jared and Tabitha and what had happened, but found it difficult. Her thoughts then drifted to what was happening in the world. She hadn't paid any attention to the news since she'd heard about Colossus, and for good reason. What was the point? However, she was now traveling a long way, and if the news could give her a glimpse of the road ahead, she needed to know.

When she turned on the television, the movie *Groundhog Day* was playing. She watched for a few moments and was drawn back to a happier time. The movie held nostalgia for her and no doubt many others who were watching it at this very moment. A smile stretched across her face as she watched Bill Murray going through one of his days. If only life were similar, if only she could go to sleep and wake to a new day, a day where she didn't kill Tabitha and Jared. She regretted the altercation and knew she was still in a state of shock. One day she'd have to face the horrible truth she'd killed two people, but now was not that time.

She flipped through the channels, looking for a news broadcast. She first went to a major cable news channel, but soon decided to see if the local channels were still broadcasting. What she needed was reliable local information. One by one she turned on the local channels to discover they were also showing movies. She understood; who would still be working? She felt foolish for thinking so and went back to one of the major cable news channels.

She chuckled out loud when she looked at the upper-right-hand corner of the screen. Written in a scary-looking font, with a clock showing the days, hours, minutes and seconds underneath, were the words *COUNTDOWN TO ARMAGEDDON*. They were treating it like they had treated every major news story, no matter how gruesome or serious, with a cartoonish approach to boost ratings. She didn't need to go to any other large news channel because they all were the same. The chyron at the bottom of the screen was an endless parade of reports about mass migrations, government activity, news on the Ark, and pulled local reports from around the world concerning violence and civil unrest.

*"...coverage of Colossus. As you know, we have a dedicated team who will remain with you until the end. We're here to give you what information we feel is pertinent and will help you either cope or survive. My co-host, Angela Rodriquez, has gathered reports on people finding what could be adequate shelter in caves around Lake of the Ozarks. Angela, what have you found out?"*

*"Thanks, Brett. Lake of the Ozarks is..."*

Melody switched the channel, and like she had assumed correctly, there was a graphic; this one showed a fireball with another clock ticking down to the impact with just the name Colossus in a large bold font. Again, she chuckled. The chyron underneath was essentially identical to the other channel, but they were reporting on the impact of a smaller chunk of Colossus in Brazil.

*"What has been described as a companion to Colossus has impacted sixty-seven miles west of Sao Paulo, Brazil. The*

*initial reports are tragic, with an estimated death toll that will reach the tens of thousands..."*

Frustrated, she turned off the television and turned her attention back to packing.

"Tragic?" she blared. "Those people merely died early; everyone is going to die, Jackie, or whatever your stupid name was, including yourself." Newspeople were like old dogs; there wasn't teaching them a new trick; they looked and acted the same. She now felt stupid for even spending the couple of minutes watching.

"Where was I?" She scanned the luggage and various clothing items still perfectly stacked and folded on her bed next to it.

Yells came from the walkway outside her front door.

Curious, she went to the front door and peeked through a small window to find her neighbors – DeShaun and his girlfriend, Ester – near the top of the stairs. In her left arm she had their son, DeShaun Jr., and in her right she was pulling a roller suitcase.

"No, baby, don't go, please! I'm sorry; it meant nothing," DeShaun pleaded, his hands clasped together as if praying.

To Melody he looked pathetic. It had nothing to do with what he was wearing, although his baggy oversized athletic shorts and tank top didn't help. His energy just felt like a man who had been caught cheating.

"You want that bitch, you can have her," Ester screamed.

"No, baby, I want you!"

A third person emerged from behind DeShaun, a

woman, and she didn't look happy either. With her hands firmly planted on her hips, she scowled at DeShaun and Ester.

"Just go, woman, leave him," Melody said, her mind reliving the events of yesterday.

"You can't want me if you had her; it don't work like that, DeShaun!" Ester howled.

A voice boomed in the distance, "Shut up!"

"No, you shut up, bitch!" Ester barked back. She scowled at DeShaun and said, "Me and DeShaun Junior are going to stay with my mama."

"Come back inside," the woman urged DeShaun, her hands desperately trying to interlock with his.

He shrugged her off and advanced towards Ester. "Please, baby, please."

"You made your choice; enjoy your last days with your whore!" Ester marched down the stairs and out of sight. "And don't think about coming to Mama's; she'll put a cap in your ass!"

"Let her go," the woman pleaded.

DeShaun took a step forward, then back. His mind was filled with confusion and fear.

The woman stepped up to him, her breasts barely contained by her low-cut top. She pressed them against him in a seductive manner. "Come on, baby. We can go to my place if you want. Fuck her."

A look of desperation teetering on the verge of derangement spread across his face. "No!" He pushed the woman off and sprinted down the stairs, with the woman going after him.

Garbled screaming echoed from the parking lot below.

Melody could no longer see what was happening. Her curiosity was there, but she'd seen enough. She had to finish getting packed and start her journey to Utah. She felt a kinship with Ester. She, like her, was another woman scorned by a man, by the one who said they loved them. *What horrible timing*, she thought. *How many others were dealing with this now?* Just when you needed someone, they go and mess it up. *What is wrong with people?* she asked herself. If she survived this, would she ever meet someone she could trust? Were humans just built to lie and leave? Her life experience confirmed this, from her father dying when she was young, to her mother abandoning her briefly when she was a teen, to Jared's cheating and leaving.

She found herself back in the bedroom and hovering over the luggage. Aware her thoughts were her enemy, she dismissed them with intention and put her mind back to the task of getting packed and heading north. Needing something to distract her, she opened her phone, flipped to Spotify, and hit her favorite playlist.

The sweet melodic sounds of Taylor Swift's song "Maroon" came on. "Nope, can't listen to that." She scrolled to the Cure and hit play on "Fascination Street". She loved the Cure; no one sounded like them. She connected her phone to the Bluetooth speakers, turned up the volume, and got lost in the music.

# THIRTEEN

## SIX MILES SOUTH OF FLAGSTAFF, ARIZONA

TALL PINES on the west side of the highway cast long shadows across the snow, which lay piled up on the shoulder of the interstate. Three inches of fresh snow had fallen since the plow had last come; tire and tread marks of cars had compacted it, leaving some of it hard and slick.

Ethan drove carefully, his hands fixed to the steering wheel. The drive north to Flagstaff had taken almost seven hours, almost three times as long as it should. The number of abandoned cars and the conditions of the road made for slow driving. Calculating how long it had taken them just to get where they were, Ethan began to consider the total drive to Hill Air Force Base could take them a day and a half or even two.

The drive had started with conversation, but after two hours, Chance and Annette had crawled into the back and fallen asleep, a luxury Ethan would have to wait for until later.

A large, spray-painted sign on the side of the road read *FREE GAS NEXT STOP*.

"Do we need gas?" Chance asked, his voice groggy.

"Welcome to this side of consciousness," Ethan quipped. He gave Chance a look through the rearview mirror.

"I guess I was more tired than I thought. Want me to take over?"

"You know, that's a good idea," Ethan said. He turned the wheel and began to ascend the off-ramp in the direction of the *free gas*. "And yes, we need gas, but I'm hoping there's some here. I tried a few exits back; pumps down or out of fuel."

"Do you always drive without listening to music, oh, wait, you're old, talk radio?" Chance hung his arms over the front passenger seat and rested his chin on the headrest.

"If you find news, it's depressing, and I swear every DJ has taken it upon themselves to just loop that REM song or the other one that was popular a few years back."

"Song about the apocalypse?"

"'Radioactive'," Annette answered from the far back.

"Rise and shine," Ethan said with a smirk.

She lifted her head, looked around, and with a voice that sounded like a chirp, said, "Ooh, snow."

"Yeah, good ole snow, beautiful to look at, a bitch... oops, sorry, a pain to drive in," Ethan said. He came to a stop sign at the end of the ramp, looked right, nothing but an abandoned car and snow, then left down a snow-covered overpass. He made the left turn and headed towards the Shell station.

"Where are we?" Annette asked.

"Just outside of Flagstaff," Ethan replied. He came to another stop sign, looked in either direction, and crossed over the street and into the gas station. "Power's still on up here." He looked around, making sure he wasn't pulling into another dangerous situation like Gila Bend.

"How nice they're giving the gas away," Annette said as she ran a brush through her hair.

"Can't take it with you," Ethan said.

Three teenage boys on bikes sped just in front of the truck. Ethan slammed on the brakes and hollered. The last teen raised his hand and pointed a middle finger at Ethan.

"Idiots, I almost hit them."

"Something tells me they don't care." Chance laughed.

The station was empty. Lights were on in the convenience store, but no sign of anyone.

"Looks quiet," Chance said, his eyes looking all around.

"Good," Ethan said, putting the truck into park in front of a pump. He hadn't detailed his incident in Gila Bend and decided he wasn't going to.

"I'll fill it up," Chance said, getting out and working the pump. When the gas flowed, he called out, "It's working!"

Needing to not only stretch his legs, but wanting to provide watch, Ethan exited the truck, his Sig in his waistband.

Annette joined him, her arms folded tight in front of her to shield herself from the chilled air.

"Don't you have a coat?" Ethan asked.

"Yeah, I'm just too lazy to get it out." Her long blonde hair blew as a wind whipped past them. She shivered for a bit, took a glance of the store, and said, "I need to find a bathroom. The little guy doesn't give me much room to work with anymore."

"I'll come with you, um, not to the bathroom, of course."

"I know what you meant, but you don't have to accompany me," she said.

"I insist, and I want to see if there's anything good in there for the rest of the road trip."

"Oh yeah, some good road-trip junk food. What's your favorite?" she asked, a devilish smile on her face.

"I'm more of a salty versus sweet kind of guy, but..."

"Oh, let me guess."

The two walked across the snow-dusted parking lot.

"You look like a traditional guy. I'm going to say regular Lays potato chips, the ones in the yellow bag," she said with confidence.

"Yeah, they're good, but I wouldn't buy them. If they're in a lunch pack, I'll eat them, but wouldn't go out of my way for them."

"Let's see, those cheddar sour cream Ruffles?"

"Same."

"Doritos?"

"Close, Funyuns."

"Funyuns, yum, that's kind of what kids eat."

"I am a big kid at heart." He laughed.

They walked into the store.

Her eyes darted around, looking for the bathroom, but stopped when she heard the television.

Like her, his attention was drawn to the television on in the corner.

*"The president and his administration have not denied reports of a massive bunker facility in Antarctica, but they are also not confirming. While the president has been relatively forthright since announcing to the country and the world of Colossus, he has remained suspiciously silent on this development," Aaron Simon, the commentator, said.*

*"And there are now reports of people massing near military bases with hopes of getting on a transport to what's being called Ark. What do you make of this, Aaron?" the female commentator asked.*

*"I understand the previous administration was doing what government does best, looks out for itself, but what I'd like to know is how did those people going to the Ark get picked? Was this solely based on merit like what some sources have said, or is this just the same game of politics and favors we've seen in Washington forever?"*

*"Well, did you get picked?"*

*Aaron laughed. "No, I did not. Something tells me reporters are the last people they want."*

*The woman commentator laughed. "Let us now turn to Puja in Northern Nevada, where hundreds of thousands of people of gathered to celebrate the last Burning Man. Puja, what's it like out there?"*

"What's Burning Man?" Annette asked.

"It's an event in the middle of the desert where millennials gather to smoke pot and hook up."

"Oh dear."

"Not your scene," Ethan quipped.

With their attention off the television, they found the store had been ransacked, but there was enough spare bags of chips and other assorted snacks to make it worth their while.

"I think it's sad," Annette said, her arms filled with packs of Twizzlers and Sour Patch Kids.

"What's that?"

"That those people are still working. I mean, what's the point? Don't they have family to go back to?"

"Speaking of family, what about you?" He walked and scanned the aisles and floors for anything good.

"A mom and dad...married thirty-two years."

"Wow, impressive. Any brothers and sisters?"

"Just two older brothers. I'm the baby."

"I'm the youngest too."

The two met at the corner of the aisle; she looked up at him and said, "I never got a real opportunity, but I'm sorry about Jen."

He looked down for a moment, then back at her. "Thank you."

"We can only trust God that there was a reason."

"Well, if you find out, let me know," he snarked.

She reached out and touched his arm. "We must not lean on our own understanding."

"Please don't take this the wrong way, but I'm not a religious person. Heck, I don't think I can believe in God right now. First, he took my wife and unborn child, and now the world is about to end and with it seven billion plus people."

"I understand, I do."

He looked deep into her eyes and could feel she was being honest. What he wasn't sure of was how she could have faith in a God that was about to destroy the world.

———

A TIRE IRON can be used for many things besides tightening and untightening lug nuts, some good, some not; but Melody needed it to do just that. Her only problem was she had a flat to remove, but not the spare. She stared into the trunk, the tire iron in her hand, shocked and annoyed she didn't have what she needed. *How could this be?* she thought.

Her annoyance turned to anger, and she threw the tire iron into the trunk and slammed it shut. "This can't be my life right now, ugh!" She walked from the rear of the car and slipped on a patch of ice. Quickly she reached out and steadied herself by holding onto the car. She let out a hearty laugh, as she thought falling on ice and possibly hurting herself would have been par for the course.

Her initial instinct was to call someone, but who would come? She didn't know anyone, and it wasn't like she could call 911 or AAA. This was it; she had a flat tire with no spare and now had to find one.

A wave of emotion overcame her. She put her weight against the hood of her car and began to cry. It wasn't as if she wouldn't be able to find a spare tire, but how long would it take? How far would she have to go looking for one? She felt lost and utterly alone.

*Why is this happening to me?* she thought. Her life over the past few years had been one disaster after another.

Four years ago, she'd tried to commit suicide; her friend saved her, only to have that friend die shortly after. Their death gave her new meaning in life. She got healthy, both physically and mentally, finished her degree, and got the career she'd always wanted in nursing. Then boom, cancer diagnosis. She fought it, only for it to just come back. Thinking she'd fight it but with the help of her fiancé, she found that all to be a lie, and to add insult to injury, an asteroid was coming to destroy all life. She would be hard-pressed now to find someone who didn't feel like she did, hopeless and defeated.

She looked up at the gray illuminated sky. A glow from town cast above the trees to the north, and to the south lay open road. She needed to be headed north and now.

A car coming northbound sounded in the distance. She had an idea. Maybe someone could be a Good Samaritan. Maybe they could take her to find a tire. It was worth a try.

She waved her arms and prayed they'd stop.

The car made the turn and was headed her way; its headlights hit her. A feeling of hope welled up, but was dashed as the car sped by without even slowing. Aggravated, she raised her hand and gave them the middle finger. "Thanks!"

She leaned against the car and pondered her next

move. She couldn't rely on someone stopping, and if they did, could she trust them, and would they spend an enormous amount of time looking for a tire? Time was critical to her. The drive to Hill Air Force Base was one you could do in less than a day during normal times, but these weren't normal times. She opened her door, popped the trunk, and took out the tire iron. If she was going hunting for tires, she'd need that, and if someone came hunting for her, she'd need it; nothing like a tool that had diverse purposes.

———

THE DOOR CHIME caused Annette and Ethan to look towards the door.

"You find anything good?" Chance asked. He shook his body and yelped. "It's chilly out there." Like the two before him, his attention soon gravitated towards the television. He looked at the chyron, raised his brow, and asked, "Ahh, Dad?"

"Yeah."

"Where was it you said we were headed?"

"Hill Air Force Base."

"Well, it appears everyone else will be too. Look."

Ethan craned his head back and looked at the television to read:

*"HILL AIR FORCE BASE IN SALT LAKE CITY, UTAH, DESIGNATED AS AN EVAC LOCATION FOR ARK."*

"That could cause us some issues," Chance said.

"I'm hoping they'll figure it out, but we should expect it could take us a while to gain access."

"Look at the number of people there!" Chance pointed at the screen, which showed the main gate was crawling with a massive swarm of people, many screaming. The guards at the gate stood their ground, stress and focus etched on their faces.

"The sooner we get there, the better. Let's finish our little shopping spree and get back on the road. I think we'll need a couple more stops."

"Make that four or five...maybe six," Annette said and pointed at her stomach.

"Then even more reason to get on the road with haste," Ethan said.

Chance nodded and made his way to the bathroom.

Right after Chance disappeared into the bathroom, Annette let out a grunt. "Whew, that was a big kick."

"You okay?"

"Ahh, yeah...oh wow, another one," she said, dropping a few items. She backed up and sat down on a stack of boxes filled with windshield wiper fluid.

With concern written on his face, Ethan approached. "You're not looking good."

"I think I'm having Braxton-Hicks."

"Having what?"

"Brax...wow!" She dropped the remaining items in her hands. She leaned back against the large glass window and braced herself. Her body tensed, and she gritted her teeth. "Ugh, that was powerful."

"Are you going into labor?"

Sweat glistened on her brow. "No, I think these are Braxton-Hicks.... false contractions."

"That doesn't look false."

"Oh, they're real contractions, just not the ones where the baby is coming. I'll be fine; give me a moment."

Chance exited the bathroom, saw Annette was in distress, and raced to her side. He took her hand, kissed it, and asked, "Is the baby coming?"

"No, I don't think so."

"You're having..."

"Braxton-Hicks," Ethan chimed in, proud to have learned a new term.

Annette's body went rigid as she again braced for the intense contraction.

The two men could only watch and show support. This was the bane for many men. Having to watch a loved one, your spouse, go through pain, but be unable to help or do anything. Ethan recalled the many years ago during Chance's birth and how useless he'd felt.

The pain subsided. Annette relaxed. She reached out and took Chance's hand. "That was intense." A joyful smile graced her face.

Chance wiped the sweat from her brow and face and gave her a peck on her forehead. "How about we get you back in the vehicle. You can rest there."

She nodded.

Ethan didn't hesitate. He headed for the door.

"Hey, don't forget the Twizzlers," Annette called out.

Looking back, Ethan stopped. "You really want them?"

"I grabbed them for a reason."

"Let me get a basket. We can haul everything out in

that," Ethan said and went to the front door where he'd seen them.

Annette got to her feet, her left hand still firmly holding on to a rack to ensure she stood stably.

"And you're sure they're just Braxton-Hicks contractions?" Chance asked.

"I'm positive."

Ethan loaded up all the items she had been holding, including his, and went for the door.

She took a step and stopped. Her body tensed. "I'm having another."

Both men again waited and watched, Chance next to her, his hand touching her back, and Ethan near the front door.

She grunted through the pain, which felt like a severe cramp or tightening in her lower abdomen, followed by a wave of pain. She felt a wet sensation in her panties, then down her leg. "Oh no."

Eyes wide with concern, Chance asked, "What is it?"

"Babe."

"Is that what I think it is?" Ethan asked.

Chance held on to her tight.

She looked at Chance with fear in her eyes. "I don't think these are Braxton-Hicks."

"No?" Chance asked.

She looked at the growing pool of amniotic fluid on the floor and replied, "Sweetie, I think the baby is coming."

———

THE CHILLED breeze from earlier had turned into a frigid gale, and with it came flurries of snow. Already fatigued, Melody was finding the hike taxing on her system. She thought about turning around and going back to her car, but she had walked over a mile, and by the glow ahead of her, she was close to something.

"You can do this," she said to herself.

She crested a small rise and discovered the glow came from a Shell gas station. She saw an SUV parked at the pumps, and with no one else even driving by, she committed herself to asking if they could help her.

The wind blew the fresh snow across the road, with little whirlwinds kicking up here and there.

Unable to hold the ice-cold tire iron, she tucked it underneath her armpit and shoved her numb hands into her pockets. She had set out with only a coat and knit cap, no gloves or scarf, and now she was regretting her poor decision.

She saw movement inside the convenience store, two men from what she could make out, one kept appearing and disappearing, like he was kneeling and standing, while the other moved around inside and had even come out to the truck, only to return with a blanket.

She didn't know what to expect, and even contemplated not stopping, but something told her these people weren't going to harm her; plus, she needed to warm up.

———

SHOCK. Chance thought he was prepared for the day when Annette would give birth, but his reaction so far showed a man who wasn't quite ready. He watched as Ethan did his best to prepare Annette for delivering a baby. He wanted to do more, but he knew nothing about childbirth except for what he'd seen on television or in movies. Even the birthing classes he and Annette had attended didn't prepare him.

Annette cried out as another contraction surged, sending pain throughout her body. She was covered in sweat, and her skin radiated heat. In the moments between contractions, her mind would play out fearful scenes. She knew neither one of the men knew what they were doing, and even with her deep faith, she was having a difficult time controlling the darker thoughts.

"I'm going to remove your jeans," Ethan said.

Annette nodded. Gone was any sense of modesty.

"I, um, Dad, I can do that," Chance said. He got to his knees and unfastened her jeans.

Ethan had no problem having this responsibility taken from him. He stood and thought about what else he should be doing. Thinking they needed fresh water, he found several gallons of distilled water on the bottom shelf in the center aisle and returned.

Chance removed her jeans and tossed them aside. His hands shook, and he was doing his best to remain calm. She needed him, and he couldn't be an emotional mess.

Another contraction came, and Annette let out a guttural grunt.

"We should be timing these, right?" Chance asked Ethan.

"Ah, yeah, good idea."

Deep-rooted fear began to set in for Chance. He didn't

know a thing about delivering a baby and could tell Ethan didn't either. His fear was rooted in the fact Annette's life and that of their baby was on the line. Of course, women had given birth often in the past without doctors, but the incidence of dying during childbirth was also much higher then. He gave Ethan a look of concern and asked, "Do you remember anything from when I was born?"

"Um, no, not really. I, um, I helped her with a breathing technique. You should be doing that, and I'll time the contractions."

Annette howled in pain as a contraction took hold. She tensed her body and gritted her teeth. She squeezed Chance's hand so hard he too let out a howl of pain. "Dear God...please Lord..." she grunted. She looked deep into Chance's eyes and said, "I'm scared."

"I'm here, baby. We will do this together."

"I'm really scared."

"God is with us."

"I know...I...ugh!" She squeezed his hand and clenched her jaw as pain surged through her body. Her face was flush, and sweat poured off her face.

Ethan watched as if he were a voyeur.

"Maybe we should go find a doctor," Chance said.

The idea sounded tempting to Ethan, but he didn't like the idea of leaving them here.

"Dad!"

"How about we take her to a hospital?"

"Are they even open anymore?"

"I don't know. How the hell would I know!" Ethan snapped.

"Find out!" Chance fired back. "Go!"

Ethan turned to leave but stopped when he saw a woman standing just inside the door. It was Melody, and she stood, tire iron in her hand and a look of surprise at the situation unfolding.

"Hi," she said, her hand clenching the tire iron more firmly.

Ethan opened his mouth to speak but found himself unable to utter a word.

She looked over Ethan's shoulder to Annette on the floor, her legs spread, and a look of desperation and fear written all on her face. "Do you need help?"

"YES!" Annette howled.

"Are you a doctor?" Ethan snarked.

"No, but I'm a registered nurse."

# FOURTEEN

ENOCH, UTAH

FOR SAVANNAH, the strong, unpleasant, acrid smell of mothballs meant she was hiding in the closet of the walk-up attic. It was her and EJ's go-to sanctum. Just a whiff of the distinct odor and she'd be transported to other times where fear and pain ruled.

EJ's whimpering jolted Savannah out of her thoughts and to the present situation.

"Be quiet," Savannah whispered.

"She'll find us anyway."

"She hates coming up here," Savannah replied confidently. "Plus, her leg has been bothering her more lately."

"I hear her," EJ whimpered.

Savannah listened intently. "I don't hear anything."

"She's out there. I hear her."

After Susie had left that morning, they hadn't seen her since, leaving them to just play games and enjoy themselves. The day had turned to night, and even though Savannah had tried to remain awake for Susie's arrival home, she and EJ had fallen asleep. This sleep had been disturbed by Susie's screams from below.

"We stay here. She won't come up, especially after what happened yesterday. We will be fine, trust me."

"But what if she does?"

"Can you just be quiet?"

"I'm scared."

"EJ, please. I love you, but please stop."

The door swung open, splashing light from the attic's three sixty-watt bulbs into the closet. Towering over them, Susie barked, her words slurred from another solid day of drinking. "I've been looking for you two brats!"

EJ wailed in fear while Savannah cowered, her earlier confidence vanquished. "No, Mama, don't hurt us."

"What have you been doing all day, huh?"

EJ clung to Savannah, his head buried in her shoulder.

"Just leave us be!" Savannah screamed at her, a mix of fear and anger in her tone.

"You didn't clean up the kitchen."

"I'll clean it," Savannah said.

Susie stumbled backwards a few steps, then lurched forward. Savannah called this her drunken pose. She reached into the closet, her skinny fingers attempting to grasp EJ.

"Leave him be!" Savannah cried out, batting away her hand.

Turning her ire to Savannah, Susie took a hold of her long blonde hair and pulled hard.

The pain shot through Savannah's scalp. Using both hands, she grabbed Susie's arm and tried to pry her loose, but she wasn't strong enough.

Susie braced her left hand against the doorjamb and pulled using all her strength.

Savannah inched out of the closet with each tug until she was fully out. She looked up to see Susie had blood on her face, and her lip was cut. The odor of alcohol and fresh dirt hung in the air.

Susie knew she had the advantage and, with fury and rage running through her veins, raised her left hand, clenched it, and came down hard like a hammer against Savannah's face.

Savannah grunted in pain.

Susie repeatedly punched Savannah.

EJ sprang from the closet. "Stop it!" He saw Savannah wasn't responding to the punches any longer and feared she could be dead. He grasped Susie's right arm and pulled to no effect. He clamped down with his teeth; this time it produced the desired result.

Susie's grasp on Savannah released; her limp body fell over, with her face hitting the hardwood floor with a thud. Susie turned her ire towards EJ, who fled down the stairs, screaming hysterically.

"You come back here!" Susie wailed. She hobbled to the open doorway and began to descend, taking each step slowly.

EJ stopped at the ground floor; he looked in either direction and wondered where he should hide, but knew there wasn't a place out of reach of his mother. He looked straight ahead and saw the front door and ran towards it.

"You get your ass back here now!" Susie shrieked. She carefully placed her foot onto the ground floor and stared ahead at the open front door. "You get back here!"

Savannah opened her eyes, her face ached, and a coppery taste hit her lips and tongue. She reached up, touched, and pulled her hand back to find blood-covered fingers. She groaned as she rose to a seated position. Susie's screams sounded distant in her ears, followed by EJ's. Slowly and with effort, she got to her feet; her head swooned. She knew EJ needed help and made her way down the stairs, the back-and-forth screams leading her to the front door. On the porch stood Susie, and in the yard, EJ.

"You killed her!" EJ wailed.

"No, I didn't. She's just playing possum is all. Now get back here!"

"I won't, no!"

"If I gotta come get you, it'll be worse," Susie barked. She stepped down the porch stairs and headed for him.

EJ froze. Where else could he go? His head swiveled, looking for an escape route. The sound of traffic from the highway gave him an idea. He spun around and headed for the road.

"No, EJ, don't," Savannah said quietly under her breath in disbelief as to what she was witnessing. She stepped onto the porch, her vision blurred, and her head still swooned.

EJ ran onto the highway and waved his arms in the direction of an oncoming truck. "Help!"

"EJ, no!" Savannah screamed. She leapt from the

CRIES OF A DYING WORLD

porch, hit the ground, and tumbled when her knees gave out.

Susie stood motionless, her eyes fixed on EJ standing in the highway, the truck barreling towards him, its headlights shining on EJ.

"Help!" EJ screamed. His arms waved frantically.

The truck kept its speed, which was easily over the legal limit of fifty-five miles per hour.

"EJ!" Savannah yelled. She got to her feet and raced towards him.

He heard her, lowered his arms, and looked at her with a smile.

Savannah tripped on a loose brick and fell hard, her knee taking most of the impact. "EJ, get out of the road!" She got up and started towards him.

EJ turned, his face glowing with excitement at seeing her. "Savannah, you're –"

The truck struck EJ, his body rolled underneath, and the rear tire crushed him.

Savannah wailed in sorrow. She ran onto the road, dropped to her knees, and reached for his battered, small lifeless body.

The damage was fatal. EJ was dead.

"Is he...?" Susie asked feet behind Savannah.

Savannah had no words for Susie. She picked up his body, cradled him in her arms, and brought him back to the house.

Susie followed. Tears flowed, and nonsensical drunken comments left her mouth.

Savannah, in shock and operating on instinct, took his body to his bedroom and laid him in the bed. She positioned him as best she could to make it appear he was sleeping, but it was impossible. His body was shattered.

"I told him to come back, I told him, and I've told you to stay out of that damn highway," Susie muttered. She lit a cigarette, took a long drag, and nodded as if agreeing with herself. "Yep. I told him many times, stay out of the road."

Tears flowed like a raging river down Savannah's face. She sat on the bed, held EJ's hand, and sobbed.

The single lamp on EJ's nightstand cast long shadows and showcased the collection of snow globes he'd collected over the years.

"Now look, see what happens when you don't listen to your mama."

"Shut up!" Savannah barked.

Susie took a nervous drag of her cigarette. "Ahh, what did you say to me?"

Not looking at her, Savannah kept her gaze fixed upon EJ. "I said shut up."

"I know you're upset, but I was his mama. You can't understand the pain I'm feeling," Susie fired back. She picked at her fingers and kept her focus on anything but EJ.

"You might have given birth to him, but you weren't a mother."

"I wasn't his mother? Ha!"

Savannah set EJ's hand down calmly, stood and faced Susie. The front of her clothes was drenched in blood, and her face was streaked with blood, sweat and tears.

"You'd best change that tune, girl."

"Or what?" Savannah asked.

"I'll whip ya!"

"Try it!"

Susie took another long drag and exhaled the smoke in Savannah's direction.

Savannah kept her eyes locked on Susie, who couldn't keep eye contact with Savannah for more than a few moments.

Susie felt the shift in dominance, much like what had occurred yesterday. She wanted to leave but convinced herself Savannah was merely a child, and this was her moment to reclaim her position. She needed Savannah to fear her again. She lifted her gaze, locked eye contact with Savannah, and flicked her cigarette at her.

Savannah stepped out of the way.

Susie came at Savannah. She cleared the few feet quickly and took hold of Savannah by the throat, but Savannah wasn't just prepared for this assault mentally and emotionally, she had already planned what she'd do, and executed it. She grabbed one of the snow globes and swung hard. Savannah's swing provided the force needed when the globe struck Susie in the temple.

Susie groaned. She stumbled backwards and fell against the chest of drawers.

Fueled with hatred born from years of abuse, Savannah pressed the attack. She stood above her, looked down, and came down hard. The globe shattered when it contacted the top of Susie's head. Blood poured from the deep gash, but it wasn't the death blow Savannah was looking for, and Susie wasn't going quietly. She pushed Savannah away and crawled towards the door.

Savannah jumped on her back and, with her fists,

began to punch. She spotted her next weapon, an old metal Tonka dump truck that had been their dad's. She picked it up over her head and slammed it into the back of Susie's head repeatedly until Susie stopped moving.

A pool of blood spread out from Susie's head.

Savannah's breath was labored. She stood but was overcome by vertigo. She stepped out of the room, hit the wall, and slid down. She went unconscious before she hit the floor.

# FIFTEEN

## SIX MILES SOUTH OF FLAGSTAFF, ARIZONA

MOMENTS BEFORE, cries of pain had filled the air of the Kwik Stop; now the sounds of a suckling newborn and the whispers of love and adoration from Chance could be heard.

Melody's evening had started with a flat tire and ended with her delivering a baby. She felt pride, and who wouldn't? Having the skills and knowledge to bring a new life safely into the world was something to be proud of.

"Thank you," Ethan said to Melody, who was feet away from him, drying her hands. She gazed happily, a smile on her face, at Annette and the baby. Since she had stepped foot into the Kwik Stop, he hadn't been able to take his eyes off her. It was so shocking to him that he purposely forced himself to look away numerous times. She was beautiful by societal standards, with her long dark hair, light eyes, and lean figure; but there was something more about her that he couldn't quite peg; it was a feeling, a familiar feeling he got from her. Something radiated from her presence that drew him in, and it was strong enough to make him feel uncomfortable.

"It's literally my job, or was. I'm glad I could help," she said, tossing the towel aside.

"You came at the perfect time."

"Timing is everything, isn't it."

"I'm Ethan." He held out his hand.

"I'm Melody."

"I don't know how to thank you," Ethan said.

Melody chuckled. "I do."

Ethan laughed. "Do tell."

"I need a tire, specifically a tire for a Nissan Sentra."

"A tire for a Nissan Sentra?" Ethan asked, a puzzled look on his face. "So, you are missing a tire?"

"I have a flat tire about a mile from here, and my dipshit fiancé, sorry, former fiancé must have taken the spare out of the back."

"Depending on how far you're going to drive, you could just toss on one of those tiny spares, you know the ones."

"I don't have either, but I really need a real tire," she said flatly.

Ethan wanted to help, but he felt pressed for time. The need to get from A to B when traveling was something he'd always had his entire life. He was the guy who hated the journey. He never understood how people could just be so laissez-faire and take their sweet-ass time. And with the current circumstances, his desire to be moving towards his destination was even stronger. As he processed just how he'd go about finding a tire quickly, he stood without saying a word, his expression blank.

Seeing the expression on his face and filled with a high level of defeat from the past few days, she said, "Listen, forget about it."

"Wait, hold on."

"Help her!" Annette called out.

"I am," Ethan replied.

"No, forget about it. I'll find one and get out of this Godforsaken town." She threw open the door and exited.

"Ethan!" Annette barked. "Help her!"

"I never said I wouldn't. I don't know why she up and left."

"Stop her; tell her we will help."

He opened the door; a brisk frigid wind swept in. "Melody, come back. I'll help you."

Melody heard him but kept walking.

"We're so grateful for all you did. Please let us help you."

Melody stopped and, without looking back, asked, "Are you sure?"

"Yes, now come in here. Help me get Annette and the baby in the truck, and we'll go scouting for a tire."

Melody turned around and again asked, "Are you sure?"

"Yes, I'm sure. But we're in a hurry."

"We both are," she replied.

# SIXTEEN

## ENOCH, UTAH

SAVANNAH OPENED HER EYES. She looked around to find she was in her bed, and the morning light was casting through the blinds. What made this unusual was she had no recollection of going there. She tossed the covers back and discovered she was in clean pajamas. The aroma of bacon hit her. Her body tensed. Who was here?

She swung her weary legs out of bed and gingerly placed her feet on the cold wood floor. She went to stand, but as soon as she put all her weight on both legs, they shook, and her head swooned. Out of the corner of her eyes, she saw a medicine bottle. Had someone given her something? A hum came from down the hall in the direction of the kitchen. Who was here? She began to fear she hadn't killed her mother. An odd thought to have, especially being fearful that you hadn't killed someone.

She looked for a weapon, something she could defend

herself with. A bat sat in the corner, but the six feet to it seemed like a mile. She took a step. Her legs wobbled, and her vision narrowed. She reached for the bed to support her, but she missed and fell. Her elbow connected with the floor first, followed by her shoulder. Pain shot through her arm. She rolled onto her back and grimaced. She opened her eyes and saw the bat. Unable to get to her feet, she rolled back over and began to crawl; one arm after another she pulled herself along the floor. Each arm length felt like it was taking her an eternity. She was there; the bat was just one more reach. She extended her arm.

The door opened, and in came a man and the sound of a radio. "Savvy, what are you doing?"

She looked up, but her vision was blurred. The tone of the voice was a man's, but she couldn't make out who. This gave her some ease, but not enough to stop her attempt to get the bat.

"What on earth are you doing, girl?" the man asked. He knelt, grabbed the bat, and handed it to her. "You want this?"

She took ahold of the bat, but now could barely lift it. Her strength was gone, lost along the six-foot stretch. She opened her mouth to talk but couldn't utter a word.

"Come, let's get you back in bed," the man said. He scooped her up, bat still in her grasp, and carried her over to the bed. Tenderly he set her down and covered her with the sheet and blanket. "You need to rest."

She blinked repeatedly. "Who...?"

"Those drugs have you loopy. I ought to know, they used to be one of my go-tos."

She swallowed hard and consciously tried to widen her eyes with hopes she'd see more clearly.

The man bent down, gave her a kiss on her forehead, and said, "Just rest, your daddy is home, and he's gonna take good care of you."

# SEVENTEEN

## SIX MILES SOUTH OF FLAGSTAFF, ARIZONA

WHEN HE LOOKED in the rearview mirror, Ethan smiled. It was then he was happy he'd gotten an SUV versus a pickup truck. He had always wanted a truck, but with Jen having a baby and her car being a sedan, the choice had made sense and now proved to be invaluable.

It had taken them some time to rearrange the seating and storage, but this would be the last time they'd need to do so for the journey north. Chance rode shotgun, with Melody in the middle row and Annette and the baby in the back cargo area, lying down.

The daylight would make looking for the tire much easier, and for Ethan, he also preferred being able to just see.

"Do you have a name picked out yet?" Melody asked. She had her arm over the seat and kept an eye on Annette and the baby.

"We've come up with some, but with all that's happened, we haven't decided on the final. I wasn't expecting him to be born yet. I'm early."

Melody touched the baby's small hand and softly said, "He's beautiful."

"Do you have any children?"

Melody didn't answer.

"I'm sorry, that was rude of me."

"Oh, no, not at all. It's not like I can't; it's just...it's just that I haven't yet."

Annette opened her mouth to say something positive but stopped herself.

Melody too kept quiet. She looked at the baby, and her heart ached.

"So where are you headed? To see family?" Annette asked.

"I'm going north."

"So are we," Annette chirped happily.

"Family?"

"Not exactly, but my family is on the way."

"On the way to?"

Annette ignored the question and put her attention on the baby. "He latched right away. I was worried about that."

Caressing the baby's arm, Melody replied, "That can be a concern."

"You said Nissan Sentra, right?" Chance asked, his head going from left to right, looking.

"Yes, a Nissan Sentra."

"That looks like a Nissan Sentra," Chance said, his finger pointed in the direction of a parked car.

"That's not it," Melody answered.

"It doesn't have to exactly be a Sentra, just a similar Nissan, I'm assuming."

"You said you were going north; maybe we could take you," Annette said.

"It's pretty far north," Melody said before putting her attention back to looking for a car. She didn't want to tell anyone where she was going out of fear they'd try to take the passes away from her.

"Are you going to Utah, by chance?" Annette asked.

"No."

"Oh."

"Are you?"

"Yes, my family lives in Spanish Fork."

"Where's Spanish Fork?"

"Just south of Provo. It's such a beautiful place. I call it God's country."

The baby yawned, his tiny mouth agape.

"He's so sweet," Annette said. She ogled him and tenderly caressing his rosy cheeks. "How is it possible to love someone so quickly? I mean, I just met this little guy, and I'm so in love with him."

"That's the motherly bond; all women have it."

Tears formed in Annette's eyes.

"You okay?"

"I'm just so happy. God is so good."

"It'll be nice for your family to meet him, considering everything."

"Yeah, it'll be nice." She kissed the baby's face and continued, "Just you wait until your nana sees you. She's going to eat you up. You'll love your nana, that's guaranteed."

"Who's Nana?"

"My mom, she likes to be called that. He'll be their second grandchild, but the only living one, as my brother's daughter died."

"How sad."

"It was horrible. It rocked my family."

Melody enjoyed the conversation, but also found it fleeting. All she could think was this poor woman and her child would be dead soon. The silver lining of it all was that she got to meet her baby before they all perished.

"Colorado?" Annette asked curiously.

"Huh?"

"Are you going to Colorado?"

"Ah, no."

"I know I sound like I'm prying, but I'm just curious is all. I'll stop."

"I'm going to Utah," Melody blurted out.

"You are? But you said you weren't."

"I did?" Melody asked. She grimaced and felt stupid for getting caught in a lie. "I'm sorry, I must have misunderstood you."

Annette gave her a sweet smile and said, "It's been a stressful time for all. So where in Utah?"

Not knowing any other city in Utah, she replied, "Um, Salt Lake City."

"I've got an idea," Annette said, her eyes wide with excitement. "You can come with us. We can take you to where you're going, drop you off."

"Oh, um, I don't think that's a good idea. I don't want to intrude on your road trip."

"You must. You shouldn't be driving all alone," Annette insisted.

Melody again grew quiet.

Seeing the shift in Melody, Annette changed the topic. "How long have you been a nurse?"

Melody was growing weary of the questions. She didn't want them to know where she was going, and the more Annette peppered her with questions, she feared she'd accidentally disclose her destination, and she'd already messed up.

Facing to the front, she ignored Annette's question and said, "Maybe a Nissan dealership. There's one in town."

"Where?" Ethan asked.

"It's just off..."

"She's going to Salt Lake. I think she should come with us," Annette blurted out.

Ethan shot Melody a glance in the rearview mirror.

She returned the look. "I told her that it wasn't a good idea."

"It's not safe out there, you know, for a woman to be driving by herself, and we're headed that way anyway. Plus, I could use the help, you know, her medical expertise," Annette said.

"Listen, I don't think it's a good idea. I don't want to intrude, and to be quite honest, I don't know you all that well. Heck, I don't know you at all," Melody said. She hated that Annette had mentioned where she was going.

"Where in Salt Lake?" Ethan asked. He was now curious if she was also headed to the base.

"Just Salt Lake," Melody answered.

"Oh, look, that's one, I know it!" Chance exclaimed. He bounced in his seat like a kid. "Yep, that's one right there."

Ethan turned the vehicle in the direction of the car in question.

"Why don't you want to come with us? I promise we're good people," Annette said, her voice booming from the back.

"You all seem nice, but I'd rather get a new tire and be on my way...by myself."

Ethan parked the vehicle and asked Melody, "Well?"

"Well what?"

"Is that like your car?" Ethan motioned with his head towards the direction of the car.

She looked at the car; it was a Sentra but a newer model. "Yep, that's a Sentra."

"Then it's time to get you a tire," Ethan said. He put the car in park, grabbed a knit cap from the center console, and exited the vehicle.

Chance rolled down the window and said, "I'll stay in here with Annette unless you need me."

"That's okay," Ethan replied.

Needing to get away from Annette and her many questions, Melody said, "I'll help."

"Nope, I got this. You can keep warm."

"No, I'm fine. I need to stretch my legs anyhow." With her tire iron in hand, she exited the vehicle.

"Which one do you want?" Ethan asked, his arms folded in front of him as the chilled air washed over them both.

"Doesn't matter," she said and handed him the tire iron.

He took it and started to loosen the left rear tire. "Once I get this, I'll need the jack from my vehicle."

"I can get it now," she said. Melody had her arms folded against her body to shield herself from the cold air that whipped around them.

"Not yet."

Curious about their destination as much as Annette was, Melody asked, "So where are you headed?"

"To see family."

"Annette's family, right?" Melody asked even though she already knew the answer.

Ethan grunted as he pulled up. The lug broke free and turned. "Yeah." Like her before, he had zero interest in telling anyone their real destination.

"Annette said Idaho?"

"Yep, Idaho."

With his lie confirmed, Melody suspected they weren't going to see her family but somewhere else they didn't want to disclose. She didn't have anything to really lose, well, maybe getting this tire, but she had to know. "Can I ask a personal question?"

Ethan stopped working on the tire for a moment, thought, and replied, "Shoot."

"Are you going to Hill Air Force Base?"

Ethan stopped and gave her a curious look.

"You are, you're going to that air force base, aren't you?" Melody chirped.

He stood up straight and asked, "How do you know about that base?"

Sensing they were going there, she decided then and there to confess. "Because that's where I'm going as well."

Ethan's eyes widened. "Really?"

"Yes. Can I ask you a question?"

"Shoot."

"You got a place in the Ark, don't you?"

Feigning ignorance, Ethan said, "Ark?"

"Cut the BS."

He stopped working on the tire and gave her a hard look.

"Do you?" she asked.

"You're asking me if we have a spot in some bunker and that we will survive the apocalypse?"

"Yes."

"And if I did, why would I tell you?"

"Because what if I told you I have a spot?"

"Do you?"

"Yes," she blurted out.

"You have a spot in the Ark?"

"Yes."

"Prove it," Ethan insisted. He stood tall and cut his eyes at her. He was cynical by nature and didn't want to admit to anything until he had proof.

Melody removed Jared's phone, unlocked it, and went to the text that had the QR code. She held it up for him to see. "I've got two spots."

"How did you get a spot?"

"No, now your turn," she said defiantly. She pocketed the phone and returned his hard stare. "You didn't answer my question."

"Yes, we have a spot."

"I knew it."

"When do you fly out?" he asked.

"February 1. You?"

"Same."

The two stared at each other, unsure of what to say next.

"Are you gonna finish with the tire?" she asked.

He looked over her shoulder and into the vehicle, where he saw Chance near the back, attending to Annette. "What you did for us, that was special."

"It's my job, literally."

"But you showed up at the right time."

"Does seem like it was fate."

"I'm not one to believe in fate, but luck, yeah, we got lucky," he said and again looked over her shoulder. She had come at the right time, and she brought with her a skill set and an extra spot, not enough for him, but if the baby needed one, there it was.

"Can I see your pass?" she asked.

"Why?"

"Because I trusted you enough to show you mine. Can I see yours?"

He removed the phone from his pocket and thumbed to the text from Eric. Finding it, he held it up.

"That's the one. Looks like we're gonna be neighbors."

He paused. He was tempted to ask for her second pass but relented because he didn't want to be in need.

The two again just stared at each other, the frigid air showing their breath.

"I've got a thought," she said.

"I do too."

"And?"

"Why don't you come with us; there is…"

"Safety in numbers," she said, finishing his thought.

"True."

"And I can trust you?"

"Melody, I'm not here to hurt you or anyone. I just want to get my son, his wife and my grandchild to the Ark."

"I believe you. I can see it in your eyes." She held out her hand.

He took it and shook. "I guess I can stop."

"Yeah, let's go get my stuff; it's not far away."

Ethan and Melody got back in the vehicle.

"Does the tire not work?" Chance asked.

"We don't need the tire anymore," Ethan said.

"Why?" Chance asked.

"On account Melody is coming with us."

# EIGHTEEN

## ENOCH, UTAH

SEEING THE OATMEAL TRIGGERED SAVANNAH. It was as if she were having a sick and warped dream. She looked into the steaming bowl to find the brown sugar Everett had generously poured on top swam in the puddle made from the melted tab of butter. The room was cold, not enough to see your breath, but a chill had taken over the entire house.

The radio played in the background.

"Don't you like oatmeal anymore?" Everett asked. He sat across from her at the dinette table, in the seat EJ had been in just days ago. "You really slept. I'm happy you got the extra couple of hours in."

Savannah looked up from the bowl and stared at her father's weathered face. He looked much older than the last time she'd seen him; in fact, the years had not been good to him. The skin on his face was heavily tanned, almost leathery, with deep wrinkles around his eyes and in the center of his brow. Darker brown splotches dotted the parts of his face she could see not covered by a thick beard. His hands also showed the harshness of the life he'd lived. They were big, his fingers long and thick but covered in small cuts and callouses. It was surreal seeing him there. He'd been gone for so long, years, and now here he was, but why?

"Go on, eat," Everett said. He nudged the bowl towards her and gave her a broad smile. His teeth were big and surprisingly white.

"I'm not hungry," she said timidly. She folded her arms and shivered. She wore a sweater, sweatpants and thick socks, but it wasn't enough. "Why is it so cold in here?"

"Power is off. Now please eat; the hot oatmeal will warm you up."

She stared at the bowl, and after her experience with oatmeal the other day, there wasn't a chance she'd take a bite. "I'm not hungry, and if the power is off, how is that radio playing?"

Excited, he jumped up and grabbed the radio from the counter. He brought it back and set it near her. "It's one of those wind-up radios. I got it on my way back. Isn't it cool?"

She shrugged her shoulders.

They stared at each other while the radio broadcast a news interview.

*"There was an attempt to deflect the asteroid three years ago, but the mission failed. NASA, along with the European Space Agency, developed the mission parameters from the*

*successful DART mission in 2022. But due to the size of 2028AK, the mission was a failure."*

"You have to be hungry. Now please," Everett said as he nudged her bowl.

She looked up at him and asked, "Why are you here?" Her tone was mixed with genuine curiosity and anger.

He leaned back in the chair. It squeaked as his weight shifted.

"After all this time, now you show up," she said. "And can you turn that off?"

He did as she asked and turned the radio off. He clasped his fingers together and leaned on the table. "I wanted to see you; that's why I'm here."

"Now?"

"Yes, now. The world is ending, and I didn't want it to end without seeing my kids."

She chuckled.

"What's so funny?"

"You're a little late."

He shook his head in a sign he was aggravated by her comment. "What happened? Did someone break in?"

She rolled her eyes.

"You're not going to help, are you?" He again shook his head and put his attention towards the side yard. "I buried them late last night after getting you cleaned up and tucked in bed."

Unaware, she looked out the window but couldn't see the graves.

"I was hoping we could say some prayers over them later."

"Prayers? You found God?"

"Not exactly, but I believe."

She chuckled again.

"What is so darn funny?"

"You've been gone for years. You left us with a person who was evil. You say you believe, but your belief wasn't more than your need to get drunk."

"Wow," he replied. He was shocked by her words.

"You don't like what I'm saying. You're shocked by it? What are you going to do, slap me like Mama did?"

"I'd never hurt you, never. And your mama, she never was abusive, ever that I recall. Had I known…"

"Too late for that."

He nodded. She was right. He had hurt her in a way that was about equal to Susie's abuse.

"I'm going to my room." She pushed away from the table and headed around it to avoid him.

He got up and went to her. He took her arm gently and said, "I'm sorry."

She shrugged him off, stared into his eyes, and replied, "There is nothing you can say, no apology you can give. Now leave me alone."

# NINETEEN

## PAGE, ARIZONA

THE GLEN CANYON DAM was eerily quiet. The hum of pumps and flowing water was gone. The only sounds now were the occasional vehicle that drove by.

Ethan relaxed against the hood of the SUV. His attention was fixed on the red and brown painted landscape beyond the dam to the northwest hills where the sun was about to descend.

As warned, they had stopped earlier than he would have liked, but it wasn't so Annette could relieve herself. No, this was so Melody could attend to some bleeding Annette was experiencing.

Chance walked up. "She's going to be fine. Melody said this is normal. She has torn down there, and she said bleeding after giving birth is normal. It's called lochia. She said it's how your body gets rid of the extra blood and tissue from the uterus. She said the bleeding is heaviest the first few days, so we shouldn't worry. She's going to stitch –"

Ethan raised his hand. "TMI."

Chance laughed. "Sorry."

"This is one of those times I'm happy to be a man."

Chance leaned against the hood and inhaled deeply. "It's beautiful here."

"It is. Even the dam. There's a beauty in some of the things man has built; dams are one of them. Incredible achievements."

"I'm sad too. All this beauty, all that has been built and created will soon be gone. Wiped clean."

"That's Mother Nature."

"Or God."

"Yes, God. Sorry, I should give him credit. I can't fault the guy, he did create all this, so he does have the right to destroy it all," Ethan mocked.

"You lost your faith," Chance said.

"Faith? Not sure I ever really had it."

"It was Jen's death. When she died, your faith died."

"Son, I never really had faith. At least not like many who are religious."

"But you used to take us to church."

"Only occasionally and mainly on holidays."

Chance laughed. "We were Chreasters."

"We were what?"

"Chreasters. Means we mainly went to church on Christmas and Easter."

Ethan laughed loudly. "Never heard of that. That's good."

A flask appeared in Chance's hand. He twisted the top off and took a swig. He offered it to Ethan.

"No, I'm good. And ease up, okay. We should be clearheaded."

"It's just a drink."

"You drink a lot for a Christian."

"The Bible doesn't say we can't drink, just that we shouldn't get drunk," Chance replied and took another swig. He twisted the cap back on and pocketed it. "What do you think the Ark will be like?"

"I'm imagining a big concrete jungle of passageways and large cold sterile rooms."

"How long do you think we'll be there?"

Ethan took his gaze off the horizon and put it on Chance. "I think we're going to die there."

"Die?"

"I mean we will live out the rest of our natural lives there."

"My boy will only know the Ark, kinda sad."

"Kinda amazing that he'll be able to live. I think you should be grateful."

A whimper came from inside the vehicle. Both men looked back.

Melody raised her hand and shouted, "She's fine. I just started suturing."

The men nodded and put their attention back on what was in front of them.

"I am grateful, I really am," Chance said.

"I've been thinking a lot since Jen died. A lot about how I wasn't the father you needed years back, and I know I messed up. I could have tried harder. I could have done more during those years. I know you were mad at me, but I allowed your anger to keep me away."

"Listen –"

"No, let me finish." Ethan cleared his throat and lowered his head in thought. "I'm sorry. I really am. I know it doesn't bring back those years you didn't have a father, but I am truly sorry."

Chance smiled and threw his arm over Ethan's shoulder. "Dad, I forgave you a while back."

"You did?"

"But I still thought we should have some space. I forgave you but never forgot. And no, you weren't the perfect parent. I know they say kids are resilient in divorce; it's a joke. We suffer. We suffer a lot more than you know."

"I'm so sorry."

"I also wasn't the perfect son. Annette has shown me a way of life that is beautiful. My walk, while, again, not perfect, is I hope headed in a better direction. While we missed time together during my teen years, you're here now, when it's a life-and-death situation, and I'm grateful beyond words."

Ethan's chest tightened. A warmth that emanated from his heart spread across his body. It was love, pure unconditional love. He lifted his gaze, eyes wet with tears, and said, "Thank you."

"You're my dad, you're the only one I got, and I'm happy we're here together and that I got to give you a grandson."

The rumble of a car engine sounded to the north. They looked and saw a blue Honda Civic; its exhaust system had been modified to make it sound throaty. The car stopped on the bridge behind a few others that were parked there. A man exited, turned, and reached inside, and when he came back out, he was holding a toddler.

"What do you think is going on there?" Chance asked.

"Not sure, ran out of gas maybe."

The man walked to a large hole cut into the chain-link safety barrier along the side of the bridge. He carefully stepped through it and stood on the edge, the toddler in his arms.

"Whoa! Is he going to jump?" Chance yelped.

Ethan didn't reply. He took off running. "Don't!"

The man looked at Ethan; tears streamed down his face. He looked back towards the dam and stepped off.

"No!" Ethan yelled.

The man with the child in his arms disappeared out of sight.

Ethan reached the hole in the barrier and looked over. The distance from the bridge to the water below was two hundred feet. They were gone. Only the ripples from where they had gone into the water were visible.

Chance ran over. "Are they?"

"Yeah."

"Oh my God."

"That...that right there is why you should be grateful. That man didn't have hope."

"What does gratitude have to do with that?"

"Grateful people don't kill themselves."

"Oh really?"

"Trust me on this," Ethan snapped back with an edge. The situation had triggered him. "Being grateful fills you with joy, and when you're filled with joy, there's no room for sorrow."

"You're talking in riddles."

"I'm talking from experience."

"And what does that mean?"

"Son, trust me, be grateful for all you have because one day it can be taken away. This life isn't certain; in fact, the only thing certain is the uncertainty of it."

"All I'm saying is he didn't have to kill himself, and more importantly, he didn't have to murder his child."

Ethan was done talking. His emotions were riding high, and all he wanted was to get away from the scene. He walked around Chance and back towards their vehicle. All he could see in his mind's eye was the man's expression. He'd seen that look before. That hopeless and lost look. It was him. It was what he had seen in the mirror every time he looked after Jen died. He understood the man's decision because, in some way, he was that man.

# TWENTY

## ENOCH, UTAH

SAVANNAH STOOD over the bloodstained floor and stared into EJ's bedroom. She replayed the events of that day, which culminated in her killing Susie, and the one thing that kept coming to mind was she didn't feel any remorse. It was odd, she thought, to not regret something so harsh. Was something wrong with her? Her answer was always the same: of course there was. How can one suffer such abuse and not be changed for the worse? She had lost out on being a child, on the innocence and love all children need. Susie's pain was so great, she'd generously shared it with her children. Maybe it was a good thing that soon she'd be dead. She wouldn't be passing on this legacy of anger and pain.

She turned and walked off when she heard Everett exit the master bedroom. She exited the house through the front door, stopped when the chilled air hit her, but decided she'd be fine without a coat and continued. She found herself in the side yard next to the graves. She sat in front of EJ's and looked at the cross Everett had made for him. In red paint he'd spelled out EJ's full name and even added his date of birth and death.

She picked up a clump of dirt and held it. As she rolled her thumb over it, she said, "I'm sorry. I hope you'll forgive me."

"I'm glad you're out here," Everett said. He had quietly walked up behind her.

Savannah didn't say a word.

He sat down to her left and in front of Susie's grave. "Should we pray?"

She rolled her eyes and laughed.

"C'mon, Savannah, I'm trying here."

She cut her eyes and snapped, "Trying! Now you try?" She suddenly caught the strong smell of alcohol. "Have you been drinking?"

"I only had one drink."

She looked into his eyes and could see his pupils were dilated; it was the same thousand-yard-high look Susie would have. Disgusted, she pushed away from him. "You're pathetic."

"I know I'm not perfect, but we only have a week left. Maybe we should make the most of it."

"Where were you? Huh? Where did you go that was so much better than being with us?"

"I thought about you and EJ every day," he replied, his head hung low.

She laughed.

"This isn't funny."

"No, it's not. All those years we were being beaten and abused. No, it wasn't funny."

"I'm so sorry; had I known…"

"Had you cared, you would have known. You never called, not a card, nothing."

"I fucked up, I know."

Savannah jumped to her feet.

"Please don't go."

"Then you go, get out of here, and leave me alone. When I die next week, I want to do so alone, not with you, not with a father who abandons his children to a monster."

"I didn't know she was like that. I never knew." He got to his feet and tried to reach for her.

"Don't you touch me. I want you to go, get out of here. Go back to wherever you thought was better than here!"

His eyes filled with tears. "Please, Savannah, let me explain. Give me a chance."

"EJ needed a chance. He died because of you. He was so terrified of Mama that he ran into the road and was hit by a truck."

"Is that what happened?"

"Yeah, he died trying to get away from her."

Hot tears streamed down his face. He wiped them on his sleeve.

"And Mama, she was mean. She was evil, and I…I killed her. She tried to hurt me, and I hit her over the head with one of EJ's snow globes, and when that wasn't enough, I took that old toy of yours and beat her until she died!" Savannah wailed, and tears burst from her eyes.

Everett reached for her, but she slapped his hands.

"Don't you touch me!" she screamed.

"Baby, please."

"I need you to go, leave! Get the hell out of here! I hate you!"

He wiped more tears onto his sleeve and stood, a broken man, his shoulders hunched over. "Give me a chance."

"No!"

He couldn't look her in the eyes. Instead, he kept his gaze towards the ground. "You killed your mama?"

"Yes, and she deserved it."

"And EJ, he, um, he got run over?" Everett's voiced cracked with sorrow at the thought of EJ's small body getting run over.

"Yes. He was so terrified of Mama he ran into the road to get help. You see, he thought I was dead, she had beaten me so bad." She pointed at her face and continued, "I passed out. He ran away, looking for help, for someone to save him. That's what daddies do, they protect their children. They save them from bad people. But EJ and me didn't have a daddy; that person left us a long time ago. To us he died."

"I'm right here."

"No, you're not him. You're not my daddy, you're just a drunk and deadbeat. A weak man who ran away to find whatever you defined as happiness. I'm twelve, but I know that happiness can only come from here. It's never found outside of us."

Everett sobbed. "Where am I to go?"

"I don't care."

"I have nowhere to go. Please." He reached for her, but she recoiled.

"Don't touch me."

"I'm sorry, please." He sobbed; tears and snot ran down his face.

The more he cried, the angrier she got. "Now get out of here, or I'll do to you what I did to Mama."

# TWENTY-ONE

## TWO MILES SOUTH OF ORDERVILLE, UTAH

THE HEADLIGHTS HIT a sign that read *HIGHWAY CLOSED AHEAD, TAKE DETOUR TO INTERSTATE 15.*

"Dad, wake up," Chance said. He reached over and shook Ethan.

Ethan popped up, eyes wide. "What?"

"Look."

Ethan rubbed his eyes and leaned closer to the windshield. "Highway closed. Shit!" He looked around for anything out of the ordinary, but it was dark out. "We have no choice; take the detour."

"I also need to take a piss, and I'm getting tired."

"Pull over, then," Ethan said.

Chance took the exit towards the detour and found a spot along the side of the road. He got out, stretched his legs, and went to find a spot to relieve himself.

Ethan sat half awake. His ears perked up when a news broadcast on the radio started.

*"My name is Dr. Janice Flores, I'm from NASA's Planetary Defense Coordination Office, and I've been given the privilege of updating the American people on the current status of 2028AK, commonly known as Asteroid Colossus. Based on satellite readings, we are still expecting an arrival on February 2 at approximately eighteen thirty hours eastern time. For those in need of support during these last days, FEMA and Department of Homeland Security facilities will remain open indefinitely. As it pertains to those evacuating to ARK, please get to those locations as soon as you can. We understand that many telecom towers are down, so you're not receiving up-to-date information. Again, if you are traveling to ARK, please arrive as soon as you can. We are seeing large numbers of nonauthorized people arriving, causing bottlenecks. To those traveling to predesignated evacuation centers without the proper documentation, please do not. You will not be allowed access. The more you interfere, the greater the chance we cannot get those people on a transport to ARK."*

"Wow," Ethan said under his breath. "What a cold-hearted bitch."

"Yeah, so another way to say it is, if you're one of the unlucky, just go somewhere and wait to die," Melody said, her arm dangling over the driver's seat.

Ethan hadn't seen her and was a bit startled. "Oh, good..." He looked at the clock. "Morning." He turned the radio down and gave her a smile.

"Where are we?" Melody asked, her voice groggy. She lifted her head and yawned.

"I don't know." He took out his phone and went to the map app but didn't have a signal. "Oh no."

"What?"

"No signal. Cold-hearted bitch was right; towers are going down."

"Mel," Annette moaned.

Melody spun around and leaned over the seat. What light the dashboard gave was just enough for her to see Annette's face, and her expression showed distress. "You okay?"

"I think something is wrong."

"Talk to me."

"I think I'm bleeding again."

Melody looked to Ethan and asked, "Do you have a flashlight?"

Ethan produced a flashlight and gave it to her.

Melody climbed into the back, careful where she stepped and placed her hands. She turned the light on and instantly discovered Annette was correct. Blood covered her clothes and the floor mats.

Annette saw the blood and cried out.

"You're going to be fine. Let me see what's going on." Melody removed Annette's pants and could see blood, lots of blood.

"Is everything okay?" Ethan asked.

"One sec," Melody replied. She put her attention back on Annette. "Sweetie, let me examine you real quick. Then we will get you cleaned up."

Annette nodded.

The front passenger door opened and startled Ethan. "Okay, Pops, your turn."

Ethan motioned for Chance to come with him. He exited and closed the door. "Hey, listen. I don't want you to get alarmed, but I don't think Annette is doing well."

"What?" Chance asked and turned to go open the rear passenger door.

Ethan took a hold of him. "No, stay here. Let Melody do what she's going to do before you go back and get Annette worried more than she already is."

"But she might need me."

"Annette may not need anything. I just got a sense from Melody that she's not doing good. What I think Annette needs is for you to stay strong. If something…"

"But –"

"Hold up. If something is wrong, she will need your strength. Do you hear me?"

Chance took a deep breath. "Yeah, I hear you."

"Now you can get back in, but don't be an alarmist. If we need to do something, we will, and we will do it calmly."

"Got it," Chance answered. He got in and looked back to see Melody holding the flashlight in her mouth as she worked on cleaning up the blood. "How's it going?"

Melody mumbled.

"Hi, baby, how are you?" Annette asked, her voice low and slow.

"I'm good. How's our little boy?"

"He's right here. How about you take him for a bit while Mel helps me out."

Not needing to be asked twice, Chance climbed into

the rear passenger seat and looked over to see blood, lots of it. It was on rags and Annette's thighs and clothes. He recoiled for a moment, then recalled Ethan's advice. He took a deep breath and calmed himself. He wasn't one to get queasy at the sight of blood, it was just her blood, and by the looks of it, a lot, and that made him uneasy and scared.

"It's fine, sweetie; just take him," Annette said. She held up the swaddled baby.

Chance took his son and held him close. "Can I help?"

"Just care for the baby. I've got this," Melody said; the flashlight in her mouth distorted some of her words.

Chance faced the front and held the baby close. He hummed and tried to get his mind off what he feared was happening.

Melody cleaned up the blood, placed a new pad in a fresh pair of pants, and put them on Annette. She caressed her face and said, "Hon, it'll be okay."

"Thank you," Annette said and placed her hand on Melody's arm tenderly.

Melody checked Annette's pulse and found it to be weak.

"Am I okay?" Annette asked.

"Yes, you're fine. I just need you to rest."

"I'm so tired."

"Just rest," Melody said. She opened the back of the vehicle and got out. She closed the door and immediately inhaled deeply, then let out a loud sigh.

Ethan came around the back. "Talk to me."

"You want the truth?"

"I wouldn't want you to give me anything else but that."

"It's normal to bleed after giving birth. I explained this to Chance, but I fear she's losing too much."

"And?"

"She could have a postpartum hemorrhage. Her pulse is low, and her complexion is waxy."

"And?"

"I've helped women give birth before, I've never had this occur on my watch, and to be honest, there's not too much I can do without some of the benefits of modern medicine."

"You're saying we need a doctor?"

"I'm saying we need a hospital."

# TWENTY-TWO

ENOCH, UTAH

A LOUD CRACK WOKE SAVANNAH. She opened her eyes but was engulfed in darkness. She listened intently. Silence. She didn't know what time it was but assumed it was early morning. She was exhausted; she hadn't fallen asleep right away upon going to bed. She had lain there listening to Everett cry, curse, and stomp around the house. By his tone, she could tell he was drunk or high.

Curious as to what the sound was, she tossed the sheet and blanket off to find her room was frigid. She slipped her feet into slippers and put on a thick robe. She shuffled to the door and placed her ear against it and listened. Silence.

The knob was cold to the touch. She turned and opened the door to find the hall dark, as expected. "Dad?"

Nothing.

She stepped into the hall and, using her left hand,

guided herself towards the kitchen. She noticed a dim light, which resembled the flicker of a candle, coming from the kitchen. She entered to see a vanilla-fragranced candle burning on the dinette table, and next to it was a sheet of paper and pen. She made her way there to find the paper was a handwritten note. She picked it up and read.

> Dear Savannah,
>
> I am so sorry for what happened to you and Everett Jr. It was never my intention to hurt you. Had I known your mother was like that, I would have stayed. But you must try to understand that I had to go. I needed to get away, away from her. Much like you, she abused me, but mine was emotional. I should have known, I should have, that she could resort to such acts. I wish I could take it all back, but I can't. I made my decision, and I take ownership of that decision. Please know that I did and still love you. You're my baby girl.
>
> Goodbye, your daddy

She set the letter down and saw a photo. She picked it up. It was an image of a younger-looking Everett holding a baby. She presumed it was her. She flipped it over and read the inscription. *"Baby Savannah."*

She tossed it down atop the letter and saw the sky was getting lighter. Dawn was coming and with it a new day. A feeling of relief washed over her. He was gone, and she didn't care. She walked to the window and looked out towards the graves to see he was lying on the ground. She leaned in because his body was in an awkward position. She stiffened. Her eyes caught sight of something lying next to him, but she couldn't make out what it was. Her stomach tightened. She raced out of the house.

As she approached him, a wave of nausea hit her. She could see the object on the ground was a pistol, and the dirt around him was soaked with blood. She stopped feet from him and stared. The nausea grew more intense until she couldn't hold it back; she leaned over and vomited. She emptied the contents of her stomach, wiped her mouth, and stumbled back towards the house. She thought about going back and burying him, but it all seemed overwhelming. She'd seen enough death that she just couldn't bring herself to even touch him.

She sat in the chair on the front porch, leaned back, and stared across the highway. She had asked him to go, and he'd followed her wishes. She didn't want him dead but also wasn't going to blame herself. No, she wouldn't feel shame or guilt; he'd made that decision, not her, she thought.

A car whizzed by.

"Now what?" she asked out loud. She was alone, all alone in a world that would soon end. It was moments like these that you wanted the opposite. A tinge of fear hit her as she thought about the pending impact of Colossus. Would she feel it? She recalled EJ asking her these questions. They were good questions. Would she see it, or would it happen in a flash?

An idea popped in her head. She went inside and into the kitchen. She dug through the pantry until she found what she was looking for, a bag of chocolate chips. She carried it back to the front porch and sat back down. She reached in the large bag, scooped a handful, and brought it to her mouth, where she poured a few in. "Hmm."

If she only had days to live, she was going to do and eat whatever she wanted. She was going to live it up as best she could. She looked at the car, and another idea came to mind.

# TWENTY-THREE

## TWO MILES SOUTH OF ORDERVILLE, UTAH

CHANCE PACED the length of the SUV, chewing his fingers nervously as he went. Dark thoughts and images raced through his mind.

"We will find someone to help," Ethan said. He could see the strain and stress on Chance's face and wished like hell he could take it all away.

"Where? Where do we find a doctor? Just go to a hospital? We're in the middle of nowhere!" Chance barked.

"There has to be a town close by. Back on the highway, the road closure, there was a town just north of there," Ethan said.

"Then let's go," Chance said. He turned to get in the vehicle, but Melody stopped him.

"I doubt that town has a hospital. We need a hospital;

we need a pharmacy; she'll need some drugs too," Melody insisted.

"We have to try!" Chance snapped as he took a step towards her aggressively.

Melody took a step back. She'd seen patients' relatives get heated before, and even though she was accustomed to it, she never enjoyed it and always felt repelled.

Seeing Melody react, Ethan inserted himself. "Chance, son, I need you to calm down. I understand the urgency of the matter. We will find the help we need."

"Don't tell me to calm down!" Chance growled.

"This right here isn't going to fly. Now, calm down," Ethan snapped back.

"Fuck you!" Chance yelled.

Ethan felt his pulse rise. He understood why Chance was upset, but never liked being told to go f-off.

"Stop it!" Melody exclaimed. She stepped in between them and gave them both a stern look. "Listen, Annette needs us all to remain calm so we can think. We will find a hospital or maybe a good urgent care clinic that can help. But we need a doctor who knows how to deal with this."

Chance and Ethan looked at her, then back at each other. Without uttering a word, Chance began to pace again while Ethan walked to the vehicle, opened the driver's door, and pulled out the map he'd gotten earlier along the trip. He unfolded it and started to look.

After letting out a long sigh, Melody approached Ethan. "Maybe we should drive into that town, see what we can find."

"I defer to you. I don't know how much time we have. If we have time to drive around looking, then fine, but if we need to drive directly to a city we know will have a hospital, then we should do that."

Melody bit her lip as she thought.

He intently watched her in deep thought, her lip between her teeth, and found it alluring. He pushed his impure thoughts quickly out of his mind.

"Mel," Annette said weakly from the back.

Melody and Ethan looked up.

With concern in her step, Melody raced back and opened the back. "Yes, sweetie."

"My uncle," Annette said, her voice barely above a whisper. Her face was ashen, and she didn't lift her head to speak or even look in Melody's direction.

"What's that?"

"My uncle..."

Chance appeared. "What is it, baby?"

"Uncle Barry..."

"What about him?" Chance asked.

"He's a...he's a doctor," she answered.

"How does that..."

Melody silenced Chance and asked Annette, "Does Uncle Barry live in Spanish Fork?"

Annette shook her head. She tried to open her eyes, but the crushing fatigue she felt made it impossible.

"Where is Uncle Barry?" Melody asked.

"Cedar City," she replied.

"Found it!" Ethan yelped. "And there's a hospital there!"

"Then let's go!" Chance exclaimed. He raced to the driver's door, but was stopped by Ethan.

"I've got the wheel; you stay with your wife. I'll get us there."

"Thanks, Dad."

Melody got in the front passenger seat while Chance crawled in next to Annette.

"Uncle Barry, here we come!" Ethan said loudly as he smashed down the accelerator.

# TWENTY-FOUR

## ENOCH, UTAH

NERVOUS ENERGY SURGED through Savannah when she put the key in the ignition. She'd never started a car, much less driven one, but she'd seen Susie do it enough to give her confidence. She turned the key and placed her foot on the accelerator. The car turned over with ease. A prideful smile stretched across her face. "Nice."

She peered out the grimy and bug-littered windshield and saw Everett's body, which lay exactly where he'd fallen. She'd not done a thing about it and didn't intend to.

She put her attention back to driving. Now she needed to back out of the driveway. She looked at the gear shift and tried to get it to move, but it wouldn't. She tried a couple more times, but it wouldn't budge. She sat back and tried to recall Susie driving. An idea came to mind; she placed her foot on the brake and engaged the shift. It moved. She put it in reverse and let her foot off the brake. The car moved slowly. She touched the accelerator, and the car lurched backwards. Scared, she slammed on the brakes.

"C'mon, Savannah," she grunted in frustration.

She let her foot off the brake. The car moved slowly in reverse again; this time she gingerly touched the accelerator. The car moved at a speed she felt comfortable with. A smile broke out on her face. She was driving. Filled with joy about what she'd accomplished, she didn't pay attention to any traffic that was coming on the highway.

A horn blared behind her.

She slammed on the brakes. Looked behind her to see a car swerve around her. Her heart raced.

"Stupid, stupid."

With wide fearful eyes, she looked around; no other cars were coming. She again let her foot off the brake and with focus steered the car onto the highway. She braked, put the car into Drive, and like reverse, touched the accelerator. The car moved. She applied more pressure, and the car moved faster.

Her heart thumped, and sweat appeared on her brow and forehead.

She pushed against the accelerator more and more until she was going twenty-five miles per hour, slower than the posted limit, but a comfortable speed for her.

Her hands gripped the steering wheel tightly, and her heart rate was through the roof. She was driving, and she'd never felt more liberated in her life.

With laser focus, she kept the car in between the lines and straight. Ahead, she spotted a familiar stop Susie would hit to get cigarettes and snacks. This would be her first stop on her adventure. She slowed the car and pulled over. Sitting out front on a bench was Tim Niles, the owner and a familiar and friendly face.

She hit the brake harder than she intended and whipped her head forward. "Oops." She let out a laugh.

Tim cocked his head and gave her an amused look.

She exited the car and waved. "Hi, Mr. Niles."

"Why, hello there, Ms. Savannah."

Tim Niles was an older man in his mid-seventies. He had thick silver hair with a beard that matched, and his portly belly gave him a Santa Claus appearance.

"Are you open?" Savannah asked.

Tim leaned forward once he could see her clearly and, with concern in his voice, asked, "My dear, what happened to your pretty little face?"

Savannah had forgotten about her deep purple and black bruises. "I, um, I fell down. Me and EJ were horsing around."

"Fell down, eh," he mused, doubt front and center in his tone.

"You open?"

"Sure, but not much in there, cleaned out pretty much," Tim replied. "But go help yourself."

Savannah smiled and entered the little store, which was nothing more than an old house converted to a market. Inside, she discovered Tim wasn't exaggerating; the shelves were bare. Nevertheless, she wandered the short aisles, looking for anything that fancied her. In the candy aisle, the only thing left was a handful of Almond Joys. She'd never had them and thought why not. She picked them up and continued to the chips, and there she only found pork rinds. Not a fan, she passed them by. She went through the store in record time and only ended up with the Almond Joys. She exited to find Tim where she'd left him. "How much?"

He lifted his bifocals and leaned in to see what she had. "Oh boy. Those are gonna cost ya."

She pulled out a wad of bills from her pocket.

"Let's call it free hundred."

"How much?"

"Free hundred." He smiled.

"I don't have a hundred."

He tenderly tapped her hand and said, "Sweetheart, they're yours, free; keep your money. What's it worth, anyway?"

"Thank you, Mr. Niles."

"Say, where's your mother? I haven't seen her in a couple of days."

"She's at home, watching EJ."

"Hmm. Well, let her know I'm out of smokes. Got cleaned out yesterday. But if she's looking for more, I'd suggest she go to Cedar City."

Savannah's eyes widened. "Cedar City, you say?"

"Yep. I heard some stores still have stuff down there."

"Thank you, Mr. Niles," Savannah said. She held up the candy and rushed to the car.

"Ms. Savannah, in normal times I'd ask why you're driving, but these ain't normal times."

Savannah gave him a smile.

"You be careful now."

"Goodbye, Mr. Niles," Savannah said and got in the

car. She knew she'd never see him again. How odd, she thought. As the hours and days drew closer to Colossus' arrival, she'd be experiencing many last things. She quickly put the morbid thought out of her mind and put it towards driving to Cedar City.

# TWENTY-FIVE

## CEDAR CITY, UTAH

THE CITY WAS QUIET. A few cars drove past, and some people were strolling along the sidewalks, acting as if it were any other day. What was surprising to Ethan was the violence he imagined would befall society in general wasn't materializing as widespread. Then again, Cedar City was a small city, or a big town, depending on how you wanted to classify it. Maybe the mayhem and societal breakdown was happening in the big cities, he thought; and for him, did it even matter? No, it didn't.

Melody navigated him as best she could to the hospital entrance, where he honestly thought they'd find no one.

"Take a right," Melody said, pointing to the street ahead.

"Okay."

"And there it is." Melody sighed. "How is she doing?"

"Her breathing is shallow," Chance replied.

"We're almost there," Ethan said. "She'll get the help she needs soon." He did his best to stay optimistic, but he just couldn't imagine people would still be working. He parked out front and promptly got out and ran inside. The automatic doors opened, which was a welcome sign. "I need help!" he cried out.

A woman wearing a nurse's uniform appeared from a hallway. "Where?"

"Out front," he replied and led the woman out to the vehicle.

Melody met the nurse. She introduced herself and explained what she felt was happening. The woman went back inside and came out with another nurse and a gurney. They got Annette on it and quickly rushed her inside, with Chance carrying the baby, and Melody in tow. Ethan followed but stopped short of going down the hall.

Ethan was exhausted and was going to take the moment alone to rest his body and mind. He found a seat in the lobby and sat down. His mind spun with all that had occurred over the past twelve hours, and he concluded that he couldn't trust his assumptions. He never imagined anyone would have been at the hospital, and lo and behold, there were people. He couldn't explain why, yet here they were, working to save lives.

His eyes grew heavy, and he was about to doze off when the automatic doors opened, and in came a man, frantic, hollering and screaming.

"Help, I need help. My wife, she's hurt badly!"

Ethan sat up and looked around. He expected to see the nurse appear, but she didn't.

"Help me!" the man wailed. He was covered in blood, and tears streamed down his panicked face. Seeing Ethan, he ran over to him. "I need help, please!"

"Sure," Ethan replied as he got to his feet.

"Where are the doctors and nurses?" the man asked.

"They're here, but let me help you."

The man rushed out.

Ethan followed.

Parked behind Ethan's vehicle was a white Audi Q7, the passenger-side door was smeared with blood, and a bloody handprint was on the window frame. The man ran over and threw open the door. "It'll be okay, baby, I swear."

Ethan came up behind him and paused when he saw the woman. Her body was battered; blood was everywhere. Her left arm had a compound fracture and was twisted at an awkward angle. On her other arm a large gash laid open the flesh so much it exposed the bone beneath. He recoiled when he saw she was pregnant and in the late stages. Visions of Jen flashed through his mind. He glanced up and saw her eyes were open, but she wasn't blinking. Then he noticed she wasn't moving at all. Her blank stare was that of someone dead. Ethan had seen that look before. He took a few steps back.

"Help me!" the man yelled at Ethan when he saw he had backed away.

"She's –"

"No, no, don't say it!"

"I'm sorry," Ethan said. He took a few more steps back.

"What are you doing? I need help!"

Flashes of Jen, her body in a similar condition, flashed in Ethan's mind. He had to get away. He turned and briskly walked off. Down the drive he went until he found a bench. He sat and put his head in his hands.

The man continued to scream at Ethan.

The hospital doors opened, and out came the nurse with a gurney. She approached the man and looked inside. She pressed her fingers on the woman's throat to check for a pulse and asked, "How long has she been in her current condition?"

"I don't know. Maybe twenty minutes."

Upon hearing this, the nurse pulled away from the woman, gave the man an empathetic look, and said, "I'm sorry, she's gone."

"No!"

"I'm truly sorry."

"What about the baby?"

"The baby is gone too."

"No, no, no, no!" the man howled in anguish and denial.

She touched his arm tenderly and said, "I am sorry for your loss. I wish there were something I could have done." She turned and hurried back inside with the gurney.

Ethan had heard the entire encounter. All his mind would imagine was Jen taking her last breath and saying, *"Ethan...I love you."*

The man sobbed. He got back in his vehicle and sped off.

"Get it together," Ethan said loudly. He ran his fingers through his hair. He tried to push the memories out, but they flooded in at a rapid pace. He sat back, pressed his eyes closed, and took in a deep breath. He exhaled and took in another. He tried to calm down, but the sight of the woman had been too much of a reminder. Frustrated and guilt ridden, he reached into his waistline and pulled out his pistol. He held it firmly and stared. A flash of Jen's lifeless eyes came forward in his thoughts. "Ugh! Stop!" He put the pistol to his temple and began to apply pressure to the trigger. With each image of Jen, more pressure was applied to the trigger, causing the hammer to begin its journey back. A thought of Chance came to mind, then the baby. He kept them front and center and pushed Jen out. He intently thought like this until his heart rate decreased, and the pressure on the trigger subsided. He lowered the pistol and set it in his lap. A sigh followed by tears came. "Fuck!" he groaned as he processed what he had almost done. He shoved the pistol back into his waistline, wiped his eyes, and relaxed further onto the bench.

This was a battle he was all too familiar with, one he'd fought many times over the year, and one he'd almost lost just then.

———

FOR SAVANNAH, the streets of Cedar City might well have been like Manhattan. The number of cars she encountered, along with maneuvering around abandoned cars and debris, put her novice driving skills to the test. Her hands and forearms ached, and her back became tight as the stress of driving began to take its toll on her body.

She scanned each building, looking for that perfect location to scavenge. She had driven past markets and stores already, but there were people there, and people she didn't know represented risk and fear. She slowly passed a street and saw a sign that read "Tony's Deli". It was half a block down on the left side of the street. She came to a stop and looked more intently to see no one was milling about. Filled with a mix of confidence and excitement, she turned the wheel hard right and drove down the street slowly.

The street was empty, not a car parked and no signs of anyone. The deli sat snug in between a Sherwin-Williams paint store and a furniture repair shop. Across the street, a large carpet and flooring retailer stretched for a quarter of the street. These stores represented the past, relics of a life where people had futures.

She pulled in front of the deli and exited. With her situational awareness on high alert, she looked left and then right, making sure she took in every detail for more than a few seconds. Confident she was alone, she approached the store. She took hold of the handle and pulled to find it locked.

She grunted her disappointment and plastered her face to the glass door. Inside, she spotted a treasure trove of candy and other snacks. She pulled the door again with a mix of frustration and hope that it would magically open. She turned to leave but stopped short of taking the steps. It was then she convinced herself she was going to get in the deli, no matter what. She had two choices: find the back entrance and see if that was open, or find something big and heavy enough to smash through the front plate-glass window. She headed down the sidewalk with her mind fixed on going with whatever presented itself first. She found an alley, turned, and stopped when sitting next to a dumpster was a broken cinder block.

"Perfect."

She picked up the cinder block with both hands and carried it back to the storefront. She didn't waste a second; she lifted it high and threw it against the window as hard as she could. The block smashed easily through, shattering the window and sending it crashing to the ground in a mix of large and small pieces.

With a fist pump, she squealed. "Yes!" She'd never broken into a store before, and with days still on the calendar until Colossus, this probably wouldn't be her last.

She carefully stepped over the windowsill and into the store, her feet crushing glass as she put her weight down. Fully inside, a pungent smell hit her; it was so strong her gag reflexes kicked in. She lifted her T-shirt to cover her mouth and nose and proceeded further. The store was quiet. She found a basket next to the register and quickly began to fill it with candy, chips, and whatever looked appealing to a twelve-year-old with a sweet tooth. She looked over the counter and now had an idea of where the smell was coming from; with the power off, the meats and cheeses were rotting.

A bang sounded from the back. She froze and listened. The bang sounded again.

"Anyone here?"

Silence.

"Hello?"

She looked to the window and contemplated fleeing but stopped short of doing so because her gut told her she was alone.

Bang.

She walked around the cash register and into the back through a swing door. To her left was a darkened hallway.

Bang. The sound came from a room on the right; the light of day cast shadows on the far wall.

"Hello!"

Silence.

She walked, one careful step after another, until she reached the edge of the doorjamb. The odor grew more intense.

Bang.

She peered around the door and recoiled upon seeing a body in a chair. It was an older man, sixties or older, and he was slumped forward so she could see the top of his head, or what was left of it. Behind him was an open window with thick heavy blinds.

Startled by the sight, she took a moment before stepping fully into the room. She carefully looked him over, her eyes taking in the sight. On the desk sat papers, notebooks, everything you'd expect to find on a desk. What wasn't usual was the semiautomatic pistol that lay there.

Bang.

Looking up, she now confirmed the source of the banging was the blinds. A breeze would come in through the partially cracked window and catch them.

Having seen enough, she went to leave, but hesitated. She looked back towards the pistol. She had felt a lot of fear on her drive, specifically in Cedar City, and wanted something to protect herself. She snatched the pistol off the desk, tossed it in with the candy and snacks, and exited the room quickly.

The odor was getting to her, and she could feel saliva

building in her mouth. She needed fresh air and fast. She hurried back the way she came and out through the window. Once outside, she lowered her T-shirt and inhaled deeply.

A smile appeared on her face. She had not only broken into a store but confronted a number of her fears. With pride, she tossed the basket of goodies into the car, hopped in, and with jubilance shouted, "Now where?" She caught sight of the pistol and took it out of the basket. She held it in her lap and stared. She'd never shot a gun before, but figured the concept was simple. Aim or point and pull the trigger. With two fingers she touched it and let her fingers trace the curves. She didn't want to use it; then again, she knew she was capable if she had to. She set it on the seat next to her and started the car. Feeling excited about what was next, she turned on the radio, and the sultry voice of Sia singing "Unstoppable" boomed from the speakers. It couldn't have been more appropriate; it was as if she had her own soundtrack. She turned up the volume as high as it could go, and sped off.

———

MELODY STARED at the vomit in the sink, then up at her reflection. The circles under her eyes were darker than before; no doubt the cancer and her fatigue were making things worse. Her stomach tightened, and saliva built up in her mouth again. She lowered her head to vomit, but nothing came this time. She gulped in a full breath and lifted her head. Her face was red and flushed. She turned on the cold water, scooped a handful, and splashed her face.

The door opened behind her. She looked up and saw the nurse she had helped earlier looking in.

"You okay?"

"I'm fine, thank you."

The nurse entered the bathroom and stood just inside the room. The door closed. "What stage?"

Melody looked at her in the reflection of the mirror. "What?"

"What stage are you?"

"Is it that obvious?"

"I've been nursing for close to ten years. I know a cancer patient when I see one."

"Stage 4."

"I figured. Call it one of my many talents," the nurse quipped. "What kind?"

"Adenosquamous carcinoma."

"Wow, that's a rare one. Aren't you lucky."

"And aren't you a smart-ass. Do you have this bedside manner with your patients?" Melody asked as she pulled paper towels from the dispenser. She patted the water from her face and chin.

"I even tell jokes." The nurse laughed.

"I could use one; hit me."

"Why do fathers take an extra pair of socks when they go golfing?"

Melody tossed the paper towels into the waste bin and replied, "I don't know, why?"

"In case they get a hole in one!"

"Oh my God, that's corny." Melody chuckled.

"Good ole dad jokes for ya."

"I'm Melody."

"Jasmine."

"How's Annette?"

"She's stable, and she'll be fine. You got her here just in time," Jasmine replied. She leaned against the wall, her hands behind her back. Her long black hair was pulled up into a bun, and her uniform was tight fitting due to the fact she'd recently gained weight. "She'll feel like new soon after the procedure."

"Thank you."

"That's what we do."

Melody headed for the door, and Jasmine opened it. The two stepped out, one behind the other.

"Why are you here?" Melody asked.

"Why am I here helping people versus off getting drunk, having crazy sex, or committing some type of purge-like thing like in that movie?"

"Yeah, why be here versus all that stuff?"

"My family is four thousand miles away. They're in Mexico City and not getting out."

"I'm sorry."

"Why are you sorry? Did you cancel all the flights and close everything down?" Jasmine asked rhetorically.

The two walked slowly, side by side, down the quiet hallway until they found themselves in front of Annette's room.

"I have thought about just leaving, but I really have nowhere to go. I'm doing good here, people come in to be helped, and even if it's just to keep them alive for the remaining days we have, why not? And if they come in for us to ease their pain, whether that be to let them leave this world in peace and dignity, we do that too."

"What do you mean leave this world?" Melody asked, curious about Jasmine's phrasing.

"We are operating like a hospice as well."

"Which means?"

Unfazed by the questions, Jasmine frankly stated it. "We administer what's needed so they can die."

"You're performing assisted suicides?"

"Yes. But we prefer to say we help them die with dignity."

Melody had judgment about it instantly, but before she got on her soapbox and began to preach, she pulled back. The world was ending soon, and did any of it matter? Was she going to lay into this woman who had just helped them by calling her a murderer? She took a silent deep breath and let it go.

"Where's your friend?"

"Who?"

"The handsome silver fox," Jasmine said, referring to Ethan with his graying hair.

"I don't know where he is, to be honest," Melody replied. She did wonder where Ethan had gone, and wanted to find him. "Thank you again for being here and helping."

Using Melody's exact phraseology, Jasmine said, "It's what I do." She gave Melody a smile and entered Annette's room.

Melody walked the route back to the front entrance. Her nausea reared its ugly head again as she entered the lobby.

She took a seat and put her head in her hands. A cold sweat broke out on her forehead. She found if she could breathe slowly and focus on each inhale, the nausea would subside enough for her to continue doing what she was doing. She practiced this, and like before, it worked. Feeling better, she lifted her head to look for Ethan and spotted him outside in the same position she had just been in, head in hands. He appeared distressed, which worried her.

She headed for the entrance but paused just before exiting to take in a deep breath as a wave of nausea swept over her once more. "Hold it together." When it subsided, she exited, her mind focused on making sure she didn't throw up all over the entryway. With each step the nausea waned until she reached him; then another surge came rushing.

Ethan looked up and saw her face was ashen. "You okay? You don't look good." He got up swiftly and took hold of her arm just as his pistol fell out of his pants and onto the ground. "Shit."

She saw it but didn't say a word, as she feared she'd vomit if she opened her mouth.

He guided her to the bench, where she fell onto it and relaxed. She took a few good breaths in and out. The nausea left as quickly as it had come on.

Feeling stupid, Ethan picked up the pistol and shoved it into his pants. "Sorry."

"You have a gun?"

"Yeah. It's just for self-protection," he replied with a nervous tone.

"I don't care. I'm glad you have one. Heck, I wish I had

one," she said as she leaned further back. "You won't believe what I just found out."

"What's that?"

"They're performing assisted suicides."

"So what?"

"So what? They're violating the Hippocratic oath."

He sat next to her. "I don't care about that or who's doing it. What I want to know is if you're okay?"

"I'm fine."

"You're not fine. What's wrong?"

She slowly turned her head, her left eye closed due to the sun, and answered, "No, really, I'm fine."

"You're lying."

She sighed and thought, *Don't tell him. He doesn't need to know.*

He kept staring at her anxiously, waiting for her answer.

"You really want to know?"

"Yes."

"I have stage four pancreatic cancer."

"Wait, what?"

"Yes, I have cancer."

"And you're going to the Ark?"

"Hold on, so if I have cancer, I'm not allowed to go?"

"I didn't mean it to sound like that. I was thinking more pre-Colossus thinking that you should be in a hospital or something."

"Yes, you did mean that, but it's fine. It's a good question to ask."

"I really didn't mean it that way," he said sincerely.

"The Ark is going to have the best doctors in the

world, at least they'd better. But believe me when I say I know how selfish it sounds. Why not give my spot to someone healthy, someone who can procreate and ensure the survival of our species."

"I'm glad you're going. And no, it's not selfish. I mean, isn't it selfish to even be healthy and going? Everyone is looking out for themselves here."

"Your turn."

"My turn for what?"

"Tell me a secret. You now know mine. What's yours?"

"I didn't know we were playing a game."

"Isn't life a game?" she quipped with a glimmer in her eye.

The way she phrased things and her overall positive attitude were attractive. He pushed any thought of desire out of his mind and thought about what to say.

"Go ahead. I'm waiting," she said playfully.

He leaned back and thought of something silly, but before he was about to say it, he stopped. He gave her a look and thought that if he was ever going to be honest with someone, now was the time to do so. "I killed my wife."

Her relaxed posture stiffened, and she returned his look with one of shock.

"Don't look at me like I'm a murderer. It was an accident."

"I don't think you're a murderer, believe me. So, what happened?"

"Car accident. I was driving."

"I'm sorry."

"Me too," he said as he nervously played with the zipper on his hoodie jacket.

"Can I ask you a favor?" she asked.

"Shoot."

"Don't tell the others. Let this be our secret."

He gave her an assuring look and said, "Deal."

"This might be a stupid question, but do Chance and Annette know about your wife? I'm sure they know, but have you shared your feelings on it, like the fact you blame yourself? I'm sure you have; I just don't want to speak out of line."

"Most of the details, yes."

"Most?"

He sat and thought about how to explain.

Seeing how uncomfortable he was, she said, "Listen, you don't have to tell me."

"I had some drinks that night."

"Oh."

"I didn't see the truck coming. She and I were laughing. We had just come from a party. She, um, she was pregnant."

"I'm so very sorry," she said, touching his arm.

"It haunts me 'til this day. I replay it all the time. If I had only looked right instead of left, or if I had maybe been going slower. If I wasn't trying to change the fucking radio station. There were so many variables, and all I needed to do was miss one or do something different, and that truck would have missed us. It would have either blown through the light before or after us, or I would have seen it and responded appropriately."

"You can't beat yourself up."

He gritted his teeth and snapped, "Yes, I can. I deserve all the blame. I deserve every ounce of shame and regret and guilt. I killed my wife and unborn child."

Familiar with people living through the stress of a traumatic event, she knew he needed to feel the warmth of touch. She reached out and took his hand.

He pulled his hand back an inch upon feeling hers, but she wouldn't relent and took his hand into hers. "Ethan, I am sorry that happened. And when I say you can't live with shame over this, I know what I'm talking about. I lost a friend because of my actions, but I've come to understand that if I were to go on with my life, I'd have to let that go."

He listened intently and wanted to understand or let go, but the concept was easier said than done. "The pistol."

"What about it?"

"I've almost eaten a bullet every day since Jen died, but something told me I needed to stay alive for Chance, and now I know why."

"Having purpose is a powerful thing."

"It is."

She squeezed his hand firmly and gave him a sweet smile.

He returned the sentiment and found he enjoyed the touch of another, especially that of a woman. He hadn't been with a woman, much less touched one, since Jen. He missed being touched; he missed affection and intimacy.

"Please don't eat a bullet," she quipped, her hand still in his.

He shot her a grin and said, "I promise."

"Good. I kinda like having you around."

They exchanged a long look before being interrupted.

"Melody!" Jasmine called from the entry.

The two looked over.

"She's out of her procedure."

Ethan and Melody again shared a look before getting up and heading back inside.

# TWENTY-SIX

## ENOCH, UTAH

SURROUNDED by empty bags of chips and candy wrappers, Savannah lay on her bed, her stomach ached, and her heart raced. The sugar rush was just starting to wear off, but the thrill of her adventure yesterday was front and center in her mind. She sat up and peered out her window to the south across the field and in the direction of Cedar City. Today she'd be venturing out, and what she'd find, the unknown of it, had her filled with excitement.

She swung her legs out of bed, her weight crinkling the bags and wrappers. The floor was ice cold as usual, even with thick socks on. Her eye caught sight of the pistol. She picked it up and sat back down with it cradled in her lap. She understood the basic concept of firing a pistol, but nothing else. She knew what the trigger was and where it was located but not the button on the grip or what looked like another button or part of the mechanism next to the slide. She pressed the button on the grip using her thumb, and the magazine unclicked. She pulled it out and saw it was mostly full of bullets. She set it down and pressed the lever; nothing happened. In movies she recalled watching people pull back on the top or slide. She did just that, causing the bullet that was in the chamber to pop out, startling her. The slide locked back in place and stayed there. She played with it, but it wouldn't move. On the side of the frame, she saw something that looked like it would affect the mechanism, and pushed down. The slide slid forward, almost catching her finger.

"Whoa."

She again pulled the slide back and locked it to the rear.

The spare bullet, which had popped out of the chamber, lay in her lap. She picked it up and held it between her two fingers and admired it. It was a 9 mm ball round. She found the shiny brass of the casing pretty. She set the pistol in her lap, picked up the magazine, and examined how she could get the bullet back in. After a few moments, she figured it out. With the magazine now loaded with the spare round, she inserted it into the magazine well located in the grip and slid it in until it clicked. She then pressed down on the slide release; like before the slide slid forward, this time chambering a round. Now all she needed to do was go test fire it. She jumped to her feet and raced outside.

The chilled January air whipped her hair and robe, but she barely noticed. Near the trash cans, which sat at the bottom of the back-door stairs, was an empty glass jar.

She picked it up and carried it across the frozen-dew grass to a post and set it up. She took a few steps back, steadied herself, and raised the pistol until she could see clearly down the sights positioned atop the slide. With her small index finger on the trigger, she pulled back until the pistol fired.

It wasn't the recoil that startled her, but the loud concussion that rattled her ears. She shook her head repeatedly and blinked heavily. Never in her life had she heard something so loud. She didn't recall people acting like that in the movies she'd seen. The pain in her ears overshadowed the fact she had hit the jar, shattering it into dozens of pieces. Pride and a feeling of empowerment spread over her.

Filled with confidence, she was ready to go back to Cedar City. She headed back for the house. In the side yard she saw Everett's body. She paused and stared, but no feelings or regret came. Had she turned into a sociopath? She questioned whether she should bury him, but again she resisted. It wasn't as if she didn't think people deserved dignity, she did, but he didn't. No, he had committed an act so heinous in her eyes. He had abandoned them and for selfish reasons. She knew her mother was an impossible person to live with, but that didn't justify why he'd left them there to suffer. While he might not have known of her predilection for violence and abuse, he still had to know something was off about her. So instead of fighting for them, he'd just left, abandoned them to years of horror.

She walked over to his body, his skin was palish blue purple in color, and the blood was frozen and appeared almost black in color. On the ground near him was the pistol he had used. She picked it up. It wasn't like the one she possessed. It was a revolver, so the shape was different than the semiautomatic. She fiddled with it until the cylinder broke free; she spun it and closed it. Thinking she might need it, she took it with her back to the house and prepared for her trip back to Cedar City.

# TWENTY-SEVEN

## CEDAR CITY, UTAH

THE CREAKING door jolted Ethan awake. He turned and saw Chance leaning out of the hospital room.

"Oh good, you're awake," Chance said, a smile on his weary face.

"Yeah, what's up, bud?"

"She's awake and doing great. Didn't know if you wanted to say hi."

Ethan nodded and looked around for Melody. "Where's Melody?"

"Not sure," Chance replied.

The sound of a closing door down the hall drew their attention to Melody, who was exiting a bathroom. In her right hand she had a balled paper towel, which she dabbed her mouth with as she approached them.

"You good?" Ethan asked, giving her a wink.

"Just my morning sickness," she quipped.

Chance raised his left brow and gave her a curious look.

"Not that kind of morning sickness," she said to Chance.

"Oh," he replied with a confused expression.

Ethan stood, his body stiff. He stretched and asked with his hand outstretched, "Shall we?"

"Yes, come say hi," Chance happily said as he opened the door fully.

Ethan allowed Melody to go first, then came in to find Annette sitting up, nursing the baby. She smiled ear to ear upon seeing them.

"Hi, you all!"

Melody went right to her side and took her hand. She squeezed and said, "You're looking great."

"I'm feeling great."

Ethan stood at the foot of the bed, a slight smile on his face.

"Hi, Dad," Annette said.

*Dad?* Ethan thought. She hadn't used that moniker before. What had changed? Was it because she had just survived a life-threatening incident? He gave her a smile and said, "Hi."

"How's our little boy?" Melody asked as she caressed the baby's leg. She loved babies and children, but little chubby babies most of all, and found it difficult to not touch them often.

"He's hungry."

"That's my son, big eater!" Chance proudly quipped.

The door opened, and in came a man. He was portly

and stood just shy of six feet, with a thick partially gray beard.

"Uncle Barry!" Annette cheered.

"How's my favorite niece?" Barry said, walking up to the bedside opposite Melody. He looked at everyone in the room and nodded. He took her vitals and gave her a big smile. "You're healthy."

"I can't thank you enough," Chance said.

"I'm happy I could help," Barry replied graciously. He gave Ethan a glance and asked, "You're the father-in-law, I suppose?"

"Ethan Kinkaid. Nice to meet you, and like my son said, thank you."

Barry took Annette's hand, gave her another smile, then looked at Ethan. "I'd do anything for family, anything."

That was something Ethan couldn't disagree with.

"I hear you're headed north," Barry said.

"Yep," Ethan answered.

Barry lowered his voice and said, "It's okay. I know."

Ethan slightly turned his head and gave Annette a look.

"Sorry, but he's my uncle."

"Listen, I'm not sure when you need to get there, but I would suggest you stop to see the rest of the family before you continue north," Barry urged.

"I'm not sure, we're in a bit of a hurry, and this stop cost us some time already. And I'm guessing she needs to stay for another overnight."

"No, she's fine to leave, just no physical activity."

"So we can leave?"

"Yes."

"Great."

"Listen, Annette said you don't have to be there until February 1. That gives you three days. Please come to Spanish Fork."

"It's true, we don't have to be there until February 1, but we can't waste any time, as I don't know what the rest of the road has in store for us. This situation is an example of that," Ethan asserted.

"Just stop by for a few hours. It's along the way; they live about ten miles off the interstate. In fact, I'm headed there today," Barry said.

"Can we, please? It would be so nice to see my parents. They could meet the baby and even you," Annette pleaded as she gave her best puppy-dog eyes.

"C'mon, Dad, it'll be a short stop, and then we'll be back on the road," Chance said, his tone signaling he really desired to visit her family.

"Spanish Fork is a little over three hours north of here, and from there you're a little over an hour to the base," Barry said.

"You can't use old travel times. There's bound to be issues, road closures, you name it," Ethan countered.

"We have three days plus. I think we can make the stop," Melody said.

All eyes were on Ethan, who stood defiantly.

"Please," Annette said. She looked at Barry and asked, "When am I able to leave?"

"Now," Barry replied.

"Then let's go; we'll be there by lunchtime," Annette said.

"You don't know that," Ethan fired back. "It's taken us days just to get here."

"He's their only grandchild. I want them to meet him," Annette said. "Please, Dad."

Now he knew why she was calling him dad. He chewed on the detour, his eyes shifting between all of them and settling back on Annette. "Fine, but just for a few hours, and then we move on."

"Yes!" Annette squealed with happiness.

Barry clapped and said, "I'll get you discharged immediately. I'll get on the road pronto and inform them of your arrival."

"But I want to surprise them," Annette said.

"Best not do that, you know how they get about unannounced visitors," Barry reminded her.

"Oh yeah, good idea."

"What does that mean?" Ethan asked.

"Her family are private people, they don't take kindly to solicitors and such, but all is well. I'll get a head start and announce the prodigal daughter is returning."

"Uncle Barry, don't tell them about..." she said and motioned to the baby at her bosom.

"I won't say a word. Now let's get you discharged, and I'll see you all very soon."

———

AVOIDING the high-traffic areas was Savannah's goal, like it had been yesterday. Even though she felt safer now, being armed, she didn't want to invite trouble. She headed back to the business park area she'd found yesterday and began her search. Street by street, she drove until she discovered what felt like the holy grail of spots, a Target distribution center. The building was massive and spanned two city blocks. She pulled the car over and carefully looked for anyone but didn't see a soul. The gate that led to the loading docks was open, and by the appearance of debris that lay strewn over the lot, she wasn't the first to come here scavenging. She pulled into the lot and parked next to a trailer at the dock. The roll door was open, allowing her to see inside. She sat for a few minutes to see if someone came out, but no one did.

With a firm grip on the pistol, she exited the car. Like a ninja, she stealthily made her way up a set of concrete stairs to the loading dock. She paused at the top to listen but didn't hear a sound. She figured if someone was inside, they'd be making noise. She couldn't explain why, but she felt a surge of exhilaration. Like she was in an action movie, she maneuvered closer and closer to the open roll door, her ears attentive for sounds.

When she reached the door, she peeked around and looked, but didn't see movement. Now confident she was alone, she entered. Skylights illuminated the massive space. Boxes and other litter were scattered along the concrete floor. The building was so vast she found it a bit overwhelming. *Where to start?* she thought.

Without a clue of where to go, she surrendered to the idea that she'd probably be there all day and headed down the first aisle. She'd treat the place like a big store she was shopping in.

Aisle by aisle she went but only found household items, furniture, and cleaning supplies. Frustration began to build. She turned the corner and entered the next aisle, and there to her left was exactly what she was looking for, snack food.

"Yes!"

She went to open the box, but it had heavy and thick corrugated cardboard and would need a knife to get through it. She grunted displeasure but wasn't about to give up. She recalled seeing a box cutter a couple of aisles back and went to get it.

She returned and began to carve the box up by removing the side. Her focus was so much on the task she failed to notice several people walk in the warehouse. It wasn't until she heard a snap that she looked up and found herself face-to-face with three young men ranging in age from eighteen to twenty.

"What are you doing?" one of the men asked. He was short, only coming in at about five feet seven inches. His hair was cropped tight on the sides with long bangs. His sweatshirt was filthy and covered in grime.

Savannah stepped back; her body tensed. She held the box cutter out in front of her instinctually. "Don't come near me."

"Whoa, girlie," the second man said. He was taller than the first, lean, and his dirty blond hair hung down to his shoulders.

The third man, equal in height to the second, stood, his arms crossed, and a devilish smile stretched across his lean face.

The men all stood eight to ten feet away from her in a semicircle.

Savannah waved the box cutter from one to the next

with hopes it would deter them from advancing, but it didn't work. The first man took a step forward and faked a lunge. Savannah swung.

"I'll cut you. I will!" she bellowed.

The men laughed.

She knew the box cutter wasn't enough to scare them, so she tossed it at them and pulled the pistol from her pocket and held it up.

The first man had advanced when the box cutter was thrown, only to stop his advance and raise his arms. "Easy."

"I'll shoot you!" she barked.

"Take it easy, girlie," the second man urged, his arms out in front of him in a defensive posture.

She pointed the pistol at him. "Back up!"

"We're not here to hurt you!" the third man said, finally breaking his silence. He brushed his long bangs from his eyes and gave her a smile.

Savannah swung the pistol towards him. "Step back!"

The first man lowered his arms and said, "You can only shoot one of us before the other two tackle you. Did you think about that?"

"And who wants to be the one I shoot?" she snapped back.

"Brian, shut up, man," the second man said to the first.

"No, fuck this little bitch," Brian crowed.

Savannah's arm trembled, so she supported it with her other. Desperately wanting some space, she took a step back. Because of his arrogance, she kept the pistol pointed at Brian. "Back up!"

"C'mon, guys, she won't do it. I've run into little shit

talkers like this before. Heck, she probably doesn't even know how to use the gun," Brian snarked.

A slight feeling of vertigo manifested in Savannah, which added to her fear. She was now afraid she was going to pass out, and if she did, it was all over. She needed to act and act decisively. With the pistol pointed directly at Brian, she pulled the trigger. The bullet roared from the muzzle and struck Brian in the upper chest, near his right collarbone.

Brian stumbled back a few steps and fell over against the boxes. He looked down at the hole in his sweatshirt, terror on his face. His terror turned to shock and a knowing he was going to die when blood appeared. "She...she shot me."

The other two men backed up quickly.

"Get out of here!" she screamed.

They turned and ran in the direction they'd come.

Savannah did the same thing; she turned around and sprinted towards the way she'd come. Her heart was beating so hard she thought it would burst from her chest. She raced through the open door, saw her car, and then saw two other men standing next to it. They immediately took chase after her. She jumped from the dock, hit the hard pavement, and tumbled. She lost her grip on the pistol, which fell to the ground and slid underneath a trailer. She got to her feet, stared at the pistol and then over her shoulder. The men were closing in.

"Get her. She shot Brian!" the second man hollered as he exited the warehouse, with the third man by his side.

Savannah jumped to her feet and raced for the

entrance to the parking lot. She heard the thumps of the men's feet close behind.

"You're not going to get away, bitch!" one of the men hollered.

Never in her entire life had she run so hard or felt such fear. While living with Susie had been torment, she knew what to expect. The pain these men meant to exact on her would far outweigh anything Susie had done to her.

She reached the open gate and took a right onto the street. Ahead of her was the main road. If she could get to that, maybe someone could help her. She didn't bother to look over her shoulder, she knew they were there, and any movement would slow her momentum. Her arms thrust and her legs stretched, but she knew they were closing fast, as their footfalls grew louder, and she could now hear their breath.

Ahead, not half a block, was the main road; she was almost there.

An arm reached for her; the fingertips touched the back of her jacket. The man who had attempted to grab her fell and spilled to the ground.

She was close enough to the main road to see a vehicle coming. "Help!" she screamed, her arms raised in the air, and waved. Only feet now to the main road. She ran onto the road, not a concern for getting hit, and stood in the path of the vehicle, her arms up. "Help!"

The vehicle screeched to a full stop inches from her.

The men stopped feet from her when they saw a man exit the driver's seat, a pistol in his grasp. "Back off, now!"

"They're trying to hurt me!" Savannah screamed at the men.

The men backed away, and once they were distant enough, they turned and ran off.

"Are you alright?" the man from the vehicle asked.

She looked at the men racing away, then back to him, and replied, "I am."

The passenger-side door opened, and a woman stepped out. "Where are you going?"

Savannah gave them both an up and down and answered, "I was getting supplies when they surrounded me."

"Do you need us to take you home?" the woman asked.

Savannah shifted her gaze from the woman to the man, who had now put the pistol away, and replied, "I live in Enoch, a few miles north of here."

The man looked at the woman and snarked, "I'm guessing we're taking her home."

"Yes."

"See, this is what I was talking about," the man said as he got back behind the wheel.

Savannah approached the woman and said, "My name is Savannah."

"Hi, Savannah, I'm Melody."

# TWENTY-EIGHT

## ENOCH, UTAH

TELLING everyone I told you so was on the tip of Ethan's tongue. He'd literally called it at the hospital when Annette had asked if they could stop in Spanish Fork. He knew they'd run into a deviation, detour, or distraction that would cost them more time. This distraction, though, was a little girl named Savannah, and if he opposed, he'd live the rest of his life in regret. While he hated losing precious time, he couldn't say no to a child.

His mind was also troubled by the fact he wasn't going to be able to go and just how he'd explain that to Chance. He hadn't even bothered to reach out to Eric, what was the point? It was like him to wait until the last minute to have uncomfortable conversations, plus the one benefit of dying shortly after said conversation was he wouldn't be around to dwell on it.

Melody could see and feel the stress in Ethan in

between her conversations with Savannah. She knew the importance of getting to Hill Air Force Base on time, but also had discovered during her original cancer treatment the importance of human connection. Couple that with her love of children and the need to protect them, she was not about to leave Savannah.

"I'm sure your parents are going to breathe a sigh of relief when they see you," Melody said to Savannah, who had only muttered a few words along the drive from Cedar City to Enoch.

"Yep," Savannah replied.

Ethan made the turn onto Minersville Highway, looked into the rearview mirror at Savannah, and asked, "Now where?"

"Just up ahead on the right."

"Like a mile?"

"See that white house?" Savannah replied, her index finger raised in the direction of her house.

"Got it."

Ethan reached the drive and turned in. He put the vehicle in park and said, "Here you go, kid."

"Thank you," Savannah said and rushed to exit the vehicle.

"Maybe I should walk you to the door," Melody said as she opened her door.

"No, I'm fine," Savannah muttered. She jumped clear of the vehicle without saying goodbye or thanks.

"Are you sure?" Melody called out.

Savannah ignored her and raced towards the house.

Ethan leaned his weight against the steering wheel and lifted his gaze ahead. At first his mind was confused;

then he saw it, the body lying in the side yard. "Um, Mel."

Upset, Melody got back in the vehicle. "I'm not so sure about her. Did you see her face?"

"Ah, Mel."

"I think something is up with that girl," Melody said.

Annette, Chance and the baby were in the back, asleep, ignorant of even being at Savannah's house.

"Mel!" Ethan snapped, his finger pointed in the direction of Everett's body.

"What?" Melody replied curtly. She shot Ethan a look, saw he was pointing at something, and looked to see the body too. "Is that...a body?"

"Yeah."

"What's going on here?"

"I think you were right, something is up with her," Ethan said.

Not waiting a second, Melody opened the door and exited without closing it behind her.

"Mel, no, don't," Ethan called after her. His raised tone woke Annette and Chance.

Chance raised his head and asked, "What's all the fuss about?"

"Get behind the wheel, and if you see anything out of the ordinary, get the hell out of here," Ethan ordered. He exited the vehicle, pistol at the ready, and advanced towards the front of the house, where Melody was now, her hand up and ready to knock.

"Savannah, open up!"

"Get away from the door. You have no idea what's going on here!" Ethan barked, his tone showing his deep concern, and understanding the threat they could possibly be under.

"Savannah, open the door!"

"Go away!" Savannah hollered back behind the closed door.

"Savannah, we see the body at the side of your house. Who is that?" Melody asked. Her focus was on Savannah with no regard for her own safety.

Ethan's eyes went to each window to see if anyone was there spying on them, but saw no one. He reached the foot of the stairs and halted his advance. His grip on the pistol was firm, and his heart thumped hard. As he surveyed the house and the yard, he picked up on the decay and neglect and made a spot judgment that Savannah's household reflected the human relations of those who occupied it.

"Savannah, if you don't open this door, I'll kick it in!" Melody exclaimed. She stood a foot from the door, her hands firmly planted on her hips. "I will."

The dead bolt slapped open, and the door opened. Savannah stood just on the other side. "What do you want?"

"Whose body is that?"

"My dad," Savannah coldly replied.

"Are you in any danger?"

"Not anymore."

"Can I come in?"

"No."

"Are you alone?"

Savannah didn't answer.

Her silence told Melody what was going on; she was alone and in need.

During their exchange, Ethan made his way to the side yard and discovered the graves. "Hey, Mel, there's two fresh graves too!"

Melody sighed. "What's going on, Savannah?"

"That's my brother and mother."

"I know you're alone unless you have another sibling in there."

Again, Savannah remained quiet.

"What happened?"

"Can you go now?" Savannah asked.

"No, I'm not leaving until you tell me what happened, and you let me help you," Melody insisted.

Sensing Melody's determination, Savannah decided to be honest. "My brother was killed trying to run away from my abusive mother. Shortly after, I killed my mother and then my father, who abandoned us for years, shows up, and then kills himself."

The information was gut wrenching. Melody lowered her head and gently shook it in disbelief.

Ethan reappeared, his pistol lowered. "Well?"

"It's a story, that's for sure," Melody replied.

Curious, Chance exited the vehicle, but stayed close.

"Can you please go? Leave me alone," Savannah urged.

"We're not leaving until I know you're not in any danger," Melody answered.

Savannah grunted and walked away, leaving the door ajar.

"What's going on?" Ethan asked. He cleared the stairs

and walked up to Melody, who hadn't moved from her position.

"She said the body is her dad and that he killed himself. And the graves are her brother, who got killed somehow running away from the mother, whom she killed."

"This is a true crime documentary in the making here."

Melody turned and faced Ethan. "We need to help her."

He could see by the look on her face what that meant. "Help her how?"

"She needs us."

"You don't know that. She seems quite capable, she killed her mother, and she could have quite possibly killed her entire family."

"So you think she's a homicidal maniac?"

"Yeah, she could be. Killers come in small packages too."

"Don't be ridiculous," she smirked.

"Savannah, come out here and talk to us," Ethan cried out.

No reply.

"I'm going in," Melody said as she turned and pushed the cracked door fully open. She disappeared inside.

"Ugh," Ethan grunted and raced in after her. The second he stepped across the threshold, a musty odor hit him. His eyes adjusted and allowed him to see that the decay and neglect predictably continued inside the house.

"Savannah?" Melody called out.

"Up here!" Savannah replied from the attic.

Melody reached the foot of the darkened stairs and looked up. "Come down, please."

"No."

"Please come down so we can talk."

"This is foolish. We don't know her or if anyone else is in here," Ethan said, his head swiveling from side to side.

"Please, sweetie. We're not here to hurt you; we want to help," Melody urged.

Savannah appeared from the shadows and stood at the top of the stairs. "Why do you want to help me?"

Melody thought that was a good question and imagined for a girl her age who might have suffered abuse, trust wasn't something that came easily.

"Tell me why I should trust you?"

And there it was, just as Melody thought. "We're good people; you've met us all. We didn't harm you; we saved you and took you home."

"But why not just go on, leave me? Why are you trying to help me?"

"Because that's what good people do," Melody replied. "And because I grew up in an abusive home too." She waved her arms around at various objects in the house and continued, "I grew up just like this."

"So what?" Savannah snapped back.

Ethan couldn't control his thoughts. "She wants us to go, so we should go."

Melody ignored him. "I know this life. I know trust is something you don't have much of. I have trust issues too."

"And?" Savannah snarked.

"Let us...let me help you."

"How can you help me? We're all going to die soon anyway," Savannah said.

Ethan's ears perked when he saw Melody's mouth open; he knew what she was going to say before she said it. "No, don't."

"We're not going to die, and you don't have to if you come with us."

"Melody!" Ethan stressed.

Melody lifted her hand and motioned for Ethan to be quiet while keeping her attention on Savannah. "Come with us. We're going to safety."

"That's a lie."

"No, it's not."

"Mel, what are you doing?" Ethan urged.

Melody ignored Ethan, again, and continued, "Have you heard of the Ark?"

"No," Savannah answered.

"It's a safe place the government built. We will survive the asteroid there."

"You're going somewhere safe?"

"Yes, and we want you to come with us."

Ethan came up alongside Melody, leaned in close, and said, "We don't have enough spots."

"Yes, we do."

"No, we don't."

"Wait, what are you telling me?" Melody asked, curious now why he was being so urgent.

Seeing what appeared to be a disagreement between Ethan and Melody, Savannah asked, "What are you two saying?"

The two ignored Savannah.

"I'm telling you we don't have enough spots," Ethan flatly said.

"You have four, and I have two. There's an extra spot."

"No, I have two."

"But you said."

"I only said we had spots."

"So you lied."

"Yes...no, I...I had enough spots originally, then along came Annette, now the baby."

Melody pulled back and cocked her head angrily. "That's why you wanted me to come. I had your extra spot."

He paused.

"Yeah, that's it. Just admit it."

"Yes, I thought maybe you'd let us have your extra spot, but it's not for me, it's for the baby." Ethan touched her arm with hopes to calm her.

She pulled her arm back hard and snapped, "No, you lied."

"Please, it was never for me, I'm staying."

"We're taking her, I don't care what you say, and if they don't allow us all to go, she can take my spot."

"Melody, please."

"I'm dying anyway." She turned away from him. "Savannah, we were just discussing the details. Would you like to come with us?"

"Is there really a place we can go to survive?" Savannah asked. "A safe place?"

"Yes."

"And you'll take me?"

"Yes."

"Mel," Ethan interrupted but was cut short.

"You shut it," Melody snapped at Ethan. She gave her attention back to Savannah. "Come with us if you want to live."

A mix of thoughts and feelings swept through Savannah. While she had trust issues, she believed Melody, and if there was a time in her life she was to know commitment and love, this couldn't have been a better time.

Melody lifted her arm with an open hand. "Savannah, let's get you to safety."

Surrendering to the moment, Savannah descended the stairs.

# TWENTY-NINE

## FILLMORE, UTAH

THE DRIVE to Fillmore was excruciating for Ethan. Melody wouldn't look at or talk to him, and the tension was palpable. Chance had decided to drive, leaving him to his thoughts, and like always they eventually went to Jen. As he drifted back to that dreadful night, the heaviness of the past day weighed on him, and fatigue began to take hold.

In the middle seats, Savannah and Melody chatted, keeping their voices low so as not to wake Annette and the baby in the back. Savannah shared few details of her life, but what she did share was her love for her brother, EJ. Melody didn't ask, nor did Savannah offer what specifically had happened to her family. It really didn't matter to Melody. What she saw in Savannah was a version of herself, a child who had lived a hard life with an abusive mother and an absent father; the only thing missing was the younger sibling. Melody's thoughts meandered to her condition and what she had told Ethan. In the moment she'd meant what she said: she would give up her seat for Savannah and give the other for the baby. She was dying, and even if they had the best doctors in this bunker, her odds weren't good. This was her fate, her destiny, her purpose, she now believed. She had always asked why she was born, and maybe it was just for this very moment, to save a little girl. She let the fear of death, something she had dealt with often over the past years, pass through her. She didn't know what happened after death or if she really believed in God, but knowing that her legacy would be Savannah and a baby, she was content.

Chance slowed when he spotted a Flying J station ahead, they needed fuel, and he needed to use the bathroom. He exited, made a left at the stop sign, and crossed over the highway.

The vehicle jolted when it hit a pothole.

Jarred awake from his slight slumber, Ethan lifted his head. "Where are we?"

"Need gas and a pit stop," Chance answered.

Ethan rubbed his eyes. His body felt tight, and his skin had the sensation as if it were dried and stretched over his bones. He hadn't had a good sleep in a long while, and the accumulative stress of everything was now wearing his emotions thin. He looked over his shoulder at Melody, who cut her eyes at him.

In the western sky, the sun was about to dip below the horizon. What was supposed to take three hours to get to Spanish Fork would probably become closer to eight or more, just as Ethan had predicted.

Cars and trucks dotted the gas pumps, with people coming and going, giving the appearance of pre-Colossus days. All appeared normal.

Ethan sat up and looked for anything out of the ordinary.

"Looks fine," Chance said as he made the turn into the pump area.

"Head on a swivel," Ethan reminded him.

"I know, I know."

Chance pulled up to a vacant pump and turned off the engine.

"Go do your business, and I'll fill it up," Ethan said. "Does anyone else need to go?"

Melody and Savannah both said yes, and Annette, now awake, replied no.

"Escort them inside, and take this," Ethan said. He handed Chance the pistol. "Can never be too safe, crazy days."

Chance took the pistol without complaint.

Ethan exited the vehicle, took a long stretch, and walked around to the pump. He lifted the nozzle, hit the button, and heard the pump kick on. Not one for prayer, he pressed his eyes closed for a moment and thanked God the station had power and fuel. He inserted the nozzle into the tank, looked up, and was face-to-face with Melody as she exited. "Hi."

She didn't say a word.

"Mel, we need to talk."

Savannah came around to meet Melody. She gave Ethan a sweet smile.

"Hi there," Ethan said with a big smile.

"Hi," Savannah replied.

"Get any sleep?" he asked Savannah.

She shook her head.

"You should try," he said.

"I don't sleep much."

He chuckled and replied, "Same here."

She looked into his eyes. "You seem sad."

"I do?"

The comment made Melody look at Ethan, but she could only hold her gaze for a few seconds.

"Yeah, your eyes, they're sad. They remind me of my little brother."

"I heard you talking about him. He sounded like he was a smart boy."

"He was and fun too."

Melody put her arm around Savannah and said, "Let's go use the bathroom."

"Guys, let's go!" Chance chirped. "I'm going to burst."

Melody and Savannah joined Chance, and the trio retreated into the store.

A shiver from the cold spread over Ethan. He looked north to the mountains, where the sun's final rays lit the snowcaps and painted them a yellow-orange. They were closer with each mile, but he still couldn't shake a feeling of impending doom. He never allowed himself to dwell on such thoughts for too long, using a technique his therapist had taught him. After Jen had died, he fell into a deep and paralyzing depression. It was his therapist who gave him tools to at least manage life, and for that he was grateful.

A tap on the window broke him from his thoughts. He

looked and saw Annette waving. He opened the door. "Hey."

"I think I should go in too. Can you watch him?"

"Ah, yeah, of course. But don't you think you should wait for Chance?"

She got out and with care handed him the baby, who was swaddled tightly. "I'll be fine."

Ethan watched, nervous that he should go with her, but his concerns vanished when Chance appeared from the store and took her in. Left with his grandson, he looked down at the chubby face. "Hey there."

The baby swallowed, his little lips moving with the motion.

An intense sensation of love flowed over Ethan. He drew the baby closer and began to sway. "You're a handsome boy; you definitely got my looks." A smile graced Ethan's face. "I'm going to protect you, little one, I promise you. You're going to live; you're going to survive this." Back and forth he moved. A song came to mind, a song he hadn't thought of since Chance was a baby. He hummed it at first, then started to softly sing. *"Puff, the magic dragon, lived by the sea. And frolicked in the autumn mist, in a land called Honah Lee..."*

# THIRTY

## SPANISH FORK, UTAH

THE WIND GUSTED and spread a layer of fresh white powdery snow across the road, which was all that was visible with the headlights. No signs of Barry's tire tracks were visible, leaving them to believe he must have arrived much earlier. A large wrought-iron gate with a prominent sign posting *PRIVATE DRIVE* stood in between them and the long gravel road, which stretched into the darkness.

"This is it!" Annette chirped with excitement. She knew she was drawing close and had spent the last ten minutes to brushing her hair, braiding it, and applying a modest amount of makeup. Her jovial mood was infectious, with even Ethan feeling good and looking forward to a home cooked meal, a drink, and a much-needed break from the road.

For Ethan, finally making it to Spanish Fork gave him

a sense of calm. They were close, just hours now from Hill Air Force Base, with two-plus days to spare.

"I'll get the gate," Chance announced. He opened the door to get out, and the sight of headlights appeared in the distance.

"A welcoming party?" Ethan asked.

"Yes, that's probably my dad or one of my brothers," Annette replied.

"I'll stay put, then," Chance said.

A large white Ford Excursion rolled to a stop twenty feet from the gate and sat. No one exited.

"Should I get out?" Chance asked.

"No, you're fine," Annette replied.

Ethan leaned towards Chance and whispered, "What are they waiting for?"

"Not sure."

"Have you met her family?"

"Nope."

"This could be interesting, then." Ethan chuckled.

The driver and front passenger doors opened, and out stepped two large men, each standing easily over six feet tall with broad shoulders. They wore thick coats and donned cowboy hats. The man from the passenger side walked towards the gate; he was younger than the driver. He had a thick dark beard, and even from Ethan's vantage point he could see the man's piercing blue eyes.

"That's my brother Ezra," Annette announced.

"And who's the driver?" Ethan asked.

"That's Daddy."

Ethan put his focus on him. Like Ezra, Annette's

father's face was covered in a thick full beard, which hung just underneath his chin, and he too had piercing eyes.

Ezra unlocked the gate and swung it open with one push. He stood in the center of the road and stared at Ethan for a moment before turning back to the Excursion.

"He's a bit scary," Chance said under his breath.

"Yeah, both of them are," Ethan fired back.

The men got into the Excursion, turned it around, and headed down the road.

Ethan followed.

They drove for what felt like thirty minutes. To either side of them was darkness. Not a sign of life, no lights, just pitch black.

"Did you grow up out here?" Ethan asked.

"Yes. Born and raised."

"Must have been a long trip to school," Melody added.

"No, I was homeschooled."

"Remind me, how many brothers and sisters do you have?" Ethan asked.

"I have two brothers, Ezra is the oldest of all of us, and I'm the youngest."

"Aw, the baby of the family," Melody replied.

"Three of us, there were four, but he died young. There's Ezra, Judah, then me in that order."

"How old is Ezra?"

"Oh, he's twenty-seven."

"Wow, your mom was popping out the babies one after the other," Melody quipped.

Annette laughed. "She's a fertile one, that's what daddy always says."

"What type of crops or livestock do you have out here?" Ethan asked.

"Oh, we have done various things over the years. We have about a thousand head of cattle, and we also have greenhouses where we grow our own food. And then we also have bees, the women harvest the honey, and we sell it at the market in town."

"A thousand head, that's not a joke!" Chance exclaimed.

Filled with curiosity, Ethan asked, "Does all your family still live here?"

"Yes, they do. It's one big happy family."

"But you left?"

Annette grew quiet for a moment. "I wanted something more, so I went to college."

"And how did they feel about that? Your parents?" Ethan asked.

"They weren't happy, but they came around eventually."

"And they know you're married and know about the baby?"

"Yes and no."

"Dad," Chance said quietly.

Picking up the cue, Ethan shifted the conversation. "I'm sure it was quite a childhood living out here."

"It was magical."

Savannah leaned in towards Melody and whispered, "I can't wait to see what it looks like."

Melody reached and took Savannah's hand. She squeezed and whispered back, "This is fun, isn't it?"

Savannah nodded. "Besides Cedar City, I've never left home before."

"Then you have many adventures ahead of you."

The bright red of the Excursion's brake lights shined. Its headlights illuminated another large gate with barbed-wire fencing stretching from it to either side. Ezra exited and opened the gate. The Excursion drove in, leaving him on the outside.

Ethan followed and kept his eyes forward, though he could feel Ezra's hard stare as he passed him.

The Excursion stopped, and moments later Ezra appeared and got back in.

"Are we close?" Ethan asked.

"Just ahead, I promise. I'm sorry this has been a long drive, but I also promise they'll have hot tea or coffee and even cocoa, Savannah," Annette said happily as she rocked back and forth with the baby swaddled in her arms.

The snow continued to whip in front of them, but it was now heavier, forcing Ethan to use the windshield wipers.

Lights appeared in the distance.

"There's home!" Annette crowed.

"Thank God," Ethan snarked quietly.

"Dad, c'mon," Chance admonished.

"Sorry, but my ass hurts, and I need to pee."

The Excursion pulled up to a large two-story home. If Ethan were to guess, it had to be at least six to seven thousand square feet. To the right of them was a four-car, two-story garage, and to the left was a series of outbuildings.

Standing underneath the covered entryway was a

woman; she wore a thick coat and had a thick wrap over her head, which partially covered her face.

"That's Momma!" Annette squealed with excitement. "Stop, please."

Ethan did as he was told.

"Open the back, please!"

Chance jumped out and did as she requested.

Annette got out, handed the baby to Chance, and moved as quickly as she could towards her mother, who came towards her. The two met and embraced firmly and warmly.

"Hi, Momma!"

"My baby is home, finally! I couldn't believe my ears when Barry said you were coming. It's a miracle, a true miracle of God."

Chance approached, the baby held close to his chest.

Annette released her embrace, looked at Chance with a smile, then to her mother, and said, "Momma, this is Chance, my husband, and may I introduce your grandson."

Annette's mother smiled broadly, and a few tears streamed down her face. "May I?"

Chance handed over the baby with care.

She took the baby and pulled him close. "Oh my, he's beautiful, Annette, just perfect. God's perfect creation."

"Isn't he?"

"What's his name?"

"We haven't officially named him yet, but since we're here, I think it's time, so soon, I promise."

Ethan and the others exited and walked up.

With a warm smile, Annette's mother said, "Welcome

to our home, and may I now say it's your home too, as we're all family, I understand."

"Oh no, I'm not related. My name is Melody, and this is Savannah," Melody replied, her arm draped over Savannah's shoulder.

"Hello."

"Hi, I'm Savannah. Nice to meet you." She had her hand out.

"What a polite little thing, and you're Ethan, Chance's father, I presume?"

"Yes, nice to meet you," Ethan said.

"I'm Beth, and did you happen to meet Ezra and my husband, Olson?"

"Not officially," Ethan replied.

Olson and Ezra suddenly appeared behind Ethan and startled him. He looked at Olson. "Hi."

"Hello," Olson replied, his expression emotionless.

Ezra walked past and went inside without saying a word.

"Let us get inside and get warm," Beth said. With the baby still in her arms, she opened the large knotty alder front door and welcomed them in.

# THIRTY-ONE

## SPANISH FORK, UTAH

STEAM ROSE from the coffee mug. With his hands wrapped around it for warmth, Ethan took the moment to look around the house from his perch in the dining room, which sat adjacent to the great room. If he could describe the size of everything in one word, from the house to each room he'd been in so far, that word would be massive.

Just outside the foyer, which itself was large enough to accommodate them all with space to spare, was the great room. The ceiling, which towered above them at a height of twenty-eight feet, had thick large beams, which spanned the width and connected with an even larger central beam. In the center of the room was a seating area with two large couches and two chairs, which faced each other. On the far wall a roaring fireplace stood and was tall enough for a child to stand up in. The hearth was made of a large slab of granite, and above it, a mantel of old oak, stained dark, stretched across the eight-foot expanse. The chimney was constructed from river rock and stretched all the way to the ceiling.

Throughout the great room, sitting on end tables and shelves among the many tchotchkes were personal memorabilia, from framed pictures of family generations back to Olson's baby shoes encased in bronze. It was obvious to Ethan, Annette's family came from money, something he wasn't expecting. To him he imagined everyone living in small ranch-style homes and who were just rednecks.

"Want some more?" Beth asked, holding a pot of freshly brewed coffee.

Ethan looked to her and replied, "I'm good, thank you." He could see Annette in Beth, with her long blonde hair pulled back into a bun, fair complexion, large doe eyes, and thin lips. He guessed she had to be in her early fifties but didn't look a day over forty.

She sat down opposite Ethan, folded her hands, and leaned in. "Tell me, Ethan, what do you make of our kids being married?"

"Can I be honest?"

"I would hope so, we're family now," she replied with a pleasant smile.

"I didn't know they were married until just a few days ago. In fact, I didn't even know of Annette until then."

She widened her eyes and cocked her head. "That gives us some relief. We found out a few weeks back, about the marriage that is, not the baby."

"Relief? I don't understand."

"We thought it was just us she was afraid of telling. It

appears your son was the same. I guess we both have had some issues with our children."

"You could say that," Ethan answered with calm. He felt at ease with Beth; she had a way about her, a pleasant demeanor that soothed him.

"Issues? It wasn't us; it was her and you. You spoiled that girl," Olson growled in his raspy voice from around the corner just outside the room. He stomped in, his big heavy feet making equally heavy footfalls. He went to sit down, but before he did, Beth snapped, "Hat!"

Olson took off his hat and set it on the chair next to him. He clasped his hands together in front of him on the table as if he were praying, and leaned in. "Annette told us you and your son haven't spoken in years."

Shocked by the forward question, Ethan replied, "We had some stuff we've been working through, but I can tell you it's not because I didn't try."

"So it's your son's fault?"

"Um, I wouldn't put all the blame on him, but we had our troubles early on."

"You're not really a family man, that's what I heard," Olson asserted.

"Olson Francis, don't be rude to our guest," Beth admonished as her usual silky voice hardened.

Ethan's shock turned to irritation. "You don't know me."

"I've heard enough to know," Olson shot back, his piercing eyes locked on Ethan.

"Olson, stop it!" Beth snapped.

Olson fixed his gaze on Beth. The two locked stares

until he relented. He stood abruptly, grabbed his hat, and stomped out of the room.

"I'm sorry, he's been grumpy since he found out about Annette and this Colossus mess; he's been on edge."

"I can appreciate his surprise with Annette," Ethan replied with sincerity. It's not easy being a parent, much less dealing with issues of estrangement with a child.

"He's also upset about...you know."

"Colossus?"

"No, the other thing."

"What?"

"That you're going to the Ark."

Upon hearing this, Ethan wanted to not just leave the room, but get out of there and back on the road.

"Why's he upset about that?"

"He just feels it's not right. He has these notions of who should be able to go or not. It's not for you to worry about. The rest of us here are content in the notion. We have all come to terms with it, and if this is God's plan, then so be it. His will is my way."

With a desire to connect with Beth, he said, "I was ready to give it all up before I heard about Colossus, but that rock gave me purpose, and now I'm sitting here with you."

"I'm sorry."

"About what?"

"Annette told us about your wife and the baby. I'm truly sorry, I know loss, so I can understand how you feel."

"Annette has shared a lot."

"We are family now; there's nothing to hide," she said,

her pleasant smile back gracing her face. "Let me go get a fresh pot. I'll be right back."

Beth departed and left Ethan to ponder the altercation with Olson. He found it unpleasant but could understand. Facing death is something we all know is coming one day for us, but we as humans put off that fact until something thrusts itself into our lives to remind us. It can be the death of someone close or an illness. Most people will do anything to prevent death, the self-preservation instinct is strong, but pain can override that. Emotional pain specifically is the wedge that can dislodge a person from wanting to live, and he had been riding that razor's edge up until recently. With his mind contemplating much, he took in the room more. His eyes traveled from an ornate sconce on the wall with its small leather lampshade to the rustic mirror. There he paused when he caught sight of his reflection. He looked rough. Days of thick stubble on his face. The lines and wrinkles around and underneath his darkened eyes were made worse by the dry Utah air, and he was sure he didn't smell great.

Beth entered the room with the same elegance she had left. In her right hand was a fresh pot of coffee.

"You brewed that fast," Ethan commented.

"Two coffee makers. When you have all this family who love this dark elixir, you need more than one." Holding up the pot, she asked, "Can I freshen your cup?"

"Sure." He held out his cup, and she filled it. "Um, where's Chance?"

"The kids are in their room with the baby."

"And where is that?"

"I forgot, you haven't been taken to your room. I'm sure you're ready to get cleaned up."

"After this cup."

"Ethan, I apologize for my husband."

"It's fine."

"No, it's rude, and he's just not been the same. He's a good man, not perfect, but none of us are. I pray many times a day he will just let go of this idea he can survive this thing. He's been looking at topo maps, trying to find caves and whatnot. He's holed himself up in his office, not spending what time we have left together; it's just so frustrating."

"I'm sorry."

Tears filled her eyes.

Feeling a bit uncomfortable, Ethan took a large gulp and said, "I think I'll excuse myself. How do I get to their room?"

Beth wiped her eyes before they teared down her face. "I apologize. Ugh, that man, he just gets me going sometimes. But yes, you should go get cleaned up for dinner. Rebecca, my sweet angel of a daughter-in-law, is cooking us up something wonderful."

Melody appeared from around the corner. Her hair was wet and combed back. She was in a fresh set of clothes, and the smell of lavender wafted off her. "I smell coffee." She saw Ethan, gave him a half smile, then looked at Beth. "I can't tell you how amazing that shower felt. Oh my God, it was just what I needed." She fell happily into a chair opposite Ethan.

"I'm so happy to hear it." Beth smiled. "Want a cup?"

"Yes, I do," Melody answered with glee. "If you have half and half, I'll be in heaven."

"We don't have that, but we do have cream straight from the cow, not a day old," Beth said. She held up a small cup and smiled.

"Even better." Melody sat and watched as Beth poured her a cup of coffee.

"Your house is gorgeous, and it's so big. I think I almost got lost finding my way back down here. I might need a map going back."

"Thank you," Beth replied as she poured a splash of heavy cream in her cup and offered her a spoon to stir.

Melody cradled the hot steamy cup close; her face hovered over the steam. "Ahh."

"Where's Savannah?" Beth asked.

"In her room, she's relaxing on the bed. I had to laugh; the second she saw it, she started to jump up and down on it."

Beth laughed.

"I'm sorry, maybe she shouldn't have done that."

"Oh, no, dear, it's fine. Happy children is what we love around here. And it's an old mattress that won't mean much in a week's time anyway."

Beth's comment hit them with the realization that everything around them would soon be gone, wiped clean.

"Melody, tell me how you two met?"

Melody and Ethan looked at each other and waited for one to begin explaining.

Melody cleared her voice and answered, "It started with a flat tire."

"Hold that thought," Beth said. She jumped up and raced out of the room; when she returned, she had a bottle of Bailey's Irish Cream. "This story sounds like it might go better with this."

With a broad smile, Melody yelped, "Beth, you're my kinda gal."

Beth opened the bottle and poured a heavy-handed amount in Melody's cup and hers, she went to pour some in Ethan's, but he waved his hand. "None for me."

"Oh, c'mon," Beth snarked.

"We're only here for a few hours; then we need to get back on the road," he said.

"Oh, hon, you're not getting back on the road tonight, there's a heavy snow coming in, and more than likely it will continue until the morning. You'll have to wait until Ezra and Judah plow the drive before you can get out."

Ethan laughed as he shook his head.

"What?" Beth asked.

"Oh, he's about to tell me, *'I told you so,'*" Melody answered. She took a sip and smiled. "This is perfect."

"Told you so, about what?" Beth asked.

"It's nothing, inside joke."

Ethan stared at Melody, he couldn't keep his eyes off her, and he couldn't explain why. He hadn't had anything to drink yet, so he couldn't explain it away with alcohol. She looked vibrant, happy, and beautiful. Her skin glowed, and her blue eyes twinkled. He noticed for the first time a slight dimple in her left cheek when she smiled. The sweater she wore hung loose, but tight enough to show she wasn't wearing a bra.

Melody noticed his stare and cut him a look.

Embarrassed, he looked away.

Her hand still hovered with the bottle of Bailey's. Beth waited for his final verdict.

Knowing what his fate was until the morning at least, Ethan surrendered to the moment. He slid his coffee cup towards Beth.

With a devilish smile, Beth poured the Bailey's. "Now where were we? Oh yeah, a flat tire."

————

ETHAN'S HEAD swooned as he exited the shower. Enveloped by steam, he walked to the mirror and wiped it to see his reflection. He rubbed his hand across his face. "Time to look civilized."

As he shaved, he recalled the time he had just spent with Beth and Melody. It was the first time in a long while since he could say he enjoyed himself. He had even lost count of the number of drinks he'd had. The Irish coffees had turned into cocktails, but before it became straight whiskey, Beth made him go get cleaned up.

He was finding it difficult to get Melody out of his thoughts. He hadn't seen her the way he saw her tonight, and because of that, he felt guilty as if he had cheated on Jen. He pushed his impure thoughts of Melody out of his mind and lathered up to shave.

A loud knock at the door was followed by Chance saying, "Dad, dinner is ready."

"I'll be right there; say ten minutes."

Ethan finished shaving, slid into a fresh pair of jeans and a sweater. He slipped into the slippers he'd found at the foot of his bed and exited the room. In the wide hallway he was welcomed by the savory aroma of the meal Rebecca had made. His mouth watered, and his stomach growled at the prospect of the meal.

One by one everyone appeared in the dining room. They took the seats Beth chose and waited for what would be a great reveal.

Ethan was the last to arrive. He saw all the smiling faces and looked for an open seat.

"You're right next to Melody," Beth informed him.

He walked past Savannah, who was next to the head of the table on the left, and then Melody. To her right was his seat. He sat and nervously looked at her. "Hi."

"You look...clean."

"I feel great."

"You smell good," she said.

"Oh, thanks. Just the soap. And you... you smell nice too."

The two acted like teenagers who had just encountered a crush they had chemistry with.

"Who's hungry?" Beth asked.

Ethan tore his gaze away from Melody and looked around the table. Next to him were Chance and Annette, with the baby in a bassinette in between her and Beth, who was at one head of the table. Across from him, going from right to left, was Judah, an empty seat most likely for Rebecca, Ezra, Barry, and seated at the other head was Olson.

Rebecca entered the room holding a platter, and on it was a large rump roast. She set it near the head of the table where Olson was and headed back to the kitchen.

After a few more trips, the table was full of bowls and plates. From mashed potatoes, a vegetable medley, freshly baked dinner rolls, butter, and gravy, Rebecca had provided a feast for the entire family and guests. Filled with pride, she went to her seat next to Ezra.

Olson clasped his hands together and lowered his head. "Let us pray."

Everyone lowered their heads and closed their eyes.

Ethan opened his eyes and peeked at Melody, to find her peeking back. He gave her a wink, which elicited a smile from her.

"Dear Lord, thank you for all the bounty you have given us. But today I'm thankful to you because you brought our girl home. She graces our table with our grandson, a gift, thank you. And Lord, thank you for the family who sits at this table, a family who appreciates what family means. And Lord, thank you for the food we have here and the hands that made it. I send this to you through your son, Jesus, amen."

In unison everyone said, "Amen."

Chatter broke out around the table as food and plates were passed back and forth.

Olson picked up a knife and honing rod. He swiped the blade along the rod a few times, then began to carve the roast. He set each slice on an adjacent plate, neatly displaying them. "Ethan, are you a vegan like most of your fellow Californians?"

Beth cleared her throat and shot Olson a look, but Olson ignored her.

"I'm a meat eater, Olson; give me several slices if you

don't mind," Ethan answered. The two exchanged a look that could only be described as animosity.

Beth interrupted the uncomfortable exchange and asked, "Who wants wine?"

Olson snarled, "I think we've had enough for today."

"Blah," she shot back. She got up and left the room, only to return with two bottles of Prisoner, a red blend of wine. She handed the bottles to Ezra, then stepped over to Olson, kissed him on the cheek, and said, "Cheer up, you ole grump. Our baby girl is here with our beautiful grandson."

"But for how long?" Olson growled under his breath.

Ethan took note of the comment but brushed it off. As a father, he could understand Olson's anger, even disappointment.

Back and forth friendly conversation went, with even Olson laughing about a story Annette recalled from her past. Dinner turned to dessert without further rude comments from Olson.

Rebecca excused herself from the table, took a few plates in, and returned with a large cake covered in chocolate frosting. "Who wants my world-famous chocolate-chocolate cake?"

"Right here," Ezra replied as he patted his belly. The gruff Ezra had disappeared halfway through dinner and hadn't returned, no doubt compliments of the wine and its sedative effects.

Olson too seemed more relaxed, while Beth was the same.

Rebecca set the cake down and began to cut it into

thick slices. She set them on small plates while Beth handed them out.

The table grew quiet as everyone ate.

Savannah hadn't said much since she sat for dinner. She was immersed in the family environment and rich food. She was in heaven, and if Colossus slammed into them that night, she'd die happy and full.

The baby cooed loudly and drew Annette's attention to him. She wiped her face and picked him up. "How's my little prince?" She held him tight. "Everyone, we have an announcement."

"I love announcements." Beth clapped.

"They're just surprises we're told we're supposed to like," Olson complained.

"Daddy, don't be like that." Annette sighed.

"Go ahead," Olson grumbled.

"Me and Chance have been going back and forth, and we have finally decided on a name for our beautiful baby boy."

"I'm so excited," Beth said, her hands clasped in front of her, with her eyes wide.

"Ethan Olson Kinkaid," Annette announced.

Chance took her hand, a big smile on his face. "We wanted to honor our son with the names of two men –"

Olson slammed his fist onto the table. The china, glasses and silverware clanged. "Bullshit!" He glared at Annette, then Ethan.

"Olson, how dare you!" Beth crowed.

"How dare I? She leaves us, runs off to college, then gets knocked up by some –"

"Daddy!" Annette howled in protest.

"This is your latest insult!" he fired back. "I should throw you and this riffraff out into the snow right this very second."

"So you'd toss your only grandchild out?"

"You're not worthy. Poor Rebecca here, she's a good woman, a decent and moral woman. She loses her child, but you, you dishonor your family by running off and getting pregnant before even getting married."

Annette began to cry.

"That is enough. Get out of here now before you say something so horrible you'll never be able to take it back," Beth warned.

"He's already done that, I think," Melody chirped.

Olson cut his eyes at her, then put them back on Beth. "We're all going to die in a week. I think it's fine to express how I feel. I may never get a chance again," Olson exclaimed.

Ezra rose, took Rebecca by the hand, and escorted her out of the room once he saw she too was crying.

"Annette, you disgraced and dishonored your family when you abandoned us. You then dishonored God when you lay with this boy. He's the spawn of a man –"

"Easy, buddy," Ethan warned.

"What are you going to do?" Olson asked.

Ethan rose, his fist clenched. He'd had enough disrespect. He knew he was outnumbered and most likely outmatched one-on-one with Olson, but there was always a time one must stand up for the dignity of oneself and family, and this was that moment.

Beth slammed both her hands onto the table; her wineglass tipped over, the white tablecloth soaking up the deep red purple wine. She shot up from her seat, her face red with anger. "Get out of here, Olson! I'm sick and tired of this talk! It's precisely this behavior why our little girl left home."

Olson's eyes bulged with fury. He opened his mouth to counter her comment but was stopped cold when she shook her head. He knew what that meant, she was done, and if he continued, it would only get worse for him. He gave her and Ethan one last look, turned and stormed out, knocking his chair to the floor on the way out.

Annette, with Ethan Junior in her arms, and Chance rose and left, as did Judah, who had remained silent all night.

"I think I'll go get ready for bed," Barry said. He wiped his mouth with the napkin. "I apologize for my brother," he said to Ethan before standing and leaving the room.

"I'm so sorry for my husband. This news of Colossus has made him upset."

"Can I go to my room?" Savannah asked.

Seeing Savannah was upset, Melody asked, "You okay?"

"I just want to go to my room."

"Want me to come with you?"

Savannah shook her head and marched off.

Beth gave Melody and Ethan a look and said, with tears now forming in her eyes, "I'm so very sorry." She turned and left, leaving only Melody and Ethan.

"Wow!" Melody exclaimed as she relaxed from the tense exchange.

"He's a bit high-strung. Should you go check on Savannah?"

"No, I think she needs some space."

Melody grabbed the bottle of wine, stood up, gave Ethan a wink, and said, "I need another drink. Wanna join me?"

"Maybe I should check on Chance and Annette."

"They're fine, but if you must, go ahead."

Ethan only needed a moment to ponder. "Fill her up."

———

SAVANNAH CLOSED the door behind her and pressed the lock. She needed to be alone. The fantasy of a happy family was destroyed in the matter of minutes during Olson's unhinged rant. What was it about people? She thought. Here was a family that had so much, they had wealth, a beautiful home, and if you looked at the numerous framed photographs which adorned many tables and walls, you'd think they were the perfect family. What she experienced steeled her beliefs that most families had dysfunction and weren't what they showed the world.

She lay on the bed and stared at the ceiling. Her thoughts drifted back to growing up in Enoch and Susie. All she had ever wanted was to be happy and safe; and happiness came in second living with Susie. Life under her roof was filled with terror. You never knew when you'd be attacked either physically or verbally. It was a brutal life.

She was hoping life with Melody and the rest would be happy and safe, but after what she just saw she wondered when she'd finally get to see their real faces.

When would she experience their dysfunction? Or when would she come face to face with a situation which made her feel unsafe. Was there a place she could find safety, true safety, and peace? She pressed her eyes closed but opened them quickly when images of Susie came front and center.

She grunted her displeasure and sat up. Maybe she should go find Melody, or even Annette; whom she also felt safe around. She swung her legs out of bed but just before placing her weight down and getting up she stopped. She didn't know what she'd encounter by going back downstairs and if she saw another episode of anger, she'd probably lose it.

Surrendering to her solitude, she looked around the room. It was a large space, easily twice the size of her bedroom from home. The bed itself was the most comfortable thing she'd ever laid in with its down comforter and smooth to the skin sheets. On either side of the full-sized bed were nightstands, their rugged wood construction fit the house perfectly and the pinecone-shaped lamps added to the woodsy mountain motif.

A chest of drawers made from the same material as the nightstands sat under a large window; it was too dark to know its view, but atop it sat books. Curious she went to examine the titles. She hadn't been much of a reader, but she found herself a bit bored and wasn't tired enough to sleep.

"Moby Dick?" she muttered loudly. She pulled the book and looked at the cover. It was a hardbound cover and there wasn't an illustration to give her any insight into what it was about. She turned it over and on the back didn't find anything. She opened it, read a paragraph but lost interest. She set it down and picked up the next, on the cover was a colorful drawing of a girl peering into bushes. Above the image was the title, *The Secret Garden*. The image alone captivated her with the title speaking to her love for mysteries and the unexplained. With the book in hand she fell into the bed, opened the cover and began to read.

# THIRTY-TWO

SPANISH FORK, UTAH

THE ROARING FIRE cast warmth and dazzled as the flames danced and crackled. Its light was the only source in the room, a relatively small den at the end of the main hallway. Melody and Ethan had found the den when they searched for a space to relax away from the others. The room was round with tall narrow windows that encircled it with a view unknown to them due to the darkness of the night. In the center wall sat a fireplace, which they'd found lit, as if awaiting their arrival. A couch covered in thick throws and pillows faced the fireplace, with two rustic end tables on either end. On the floor in between the couch and the fireplace lay a thick shaggy rug, which beckoned Melody's romantic side and harkened back to a trip she and Jared had taken to the mountains of Colorado.

Like all memories and thoughts, one produced several

more, which spawned even more. Those fond memories soon turned into scenes of Jared's lifeless eyes staring at the ceiling. Her dark thoughts quickly manifested into her recoiling her legs and going quiet.

Ethan had been telling her a story from his days in college when he saw she had become withdrawn. "You okay?"

His question jarred her back. She took a gulp of wine and answered, "Yeah, sorry, just had a bad memory."

"Care to share?"

She took another drink, emptied the glass, and replied, "Nah." However, in her thoughts she wanted to. She desperately wanted to unburden herself of the grisly act; some might even consider it a crime. But if she told him, what would that do to their relationship? What would that do to Savannah?

"I hate to bring it up, but I am truly sorry for lying to you. I should have told you we only had two spots; that wasn't right," Ethan said. He too finished his wine and set the empty glass on the floor next to him.

"It is what it is."

"But they might let us all go, let's hold out hope."

"Ethan, I'm dying, literally, whether that's in a week – is it a week? I lost track of the days now – or sometime in the not-too-distant future. Even if they say we can all go, I'd rather give my spot to another child."

"Nope, not happening, we're not picking up more strays," he quipped with a wink

"Savannah isn't a stray?"

"I'm just joking."

"Better be, now pour us some more wine."

"No more."

"Let's go find some more."

Ethan stared at her face intently. The glow of the fire hit her just right, increasing her allure for him. This was a feeling, an emotion, he hadn't felt for some time, yet here it was. From his chest down, he felt drawn towards her. Consciously he didn't want to have this sentiment towards another woman, but his desire was building, and he was finding it difficult to control his thoughts and himself.

Seeing how his gaze had changed, she continued, "Hello, more wine."

He wanted more wine, but knew if he did, he would do something he'd regret. He needed a distraction; he pushed his thoughts to Jen and that night. "Did I tell you the last words she said to me?"

"No."

"I love you...those were her last words to me. She was looking right at me and said, 'Ethan, I love you.'" He lowered his head; emotions ranging from sadness to anger began to rise in him. "She loved me like no one ever has. She was the only woman I have ever known who I can say was my soul mate. We had a connection that was intense. But in the time it took to blink, it all happened. I looked down to adjust the radio station to find a song. I took my eyes off the road. If I hadn't, I would have seen the truck coming through the intersection, I could have swerved, I could have braked. I wanted a stupid fucking song, and boom, this fucking truck slams into us, into her side of the car. We flipped and rolled. I was out for a moment, not sure how long. I woke in a pile of glass and blood. I was out of my seatbelt and lying on the ceiling of the car. I looked up, and she was dangling upside down. Blood, there was so much blood. I hadn't seen it then, but a piece of the door had pierced her side; she was bleeding out. I took her hand, and she woke; she looked at me, her big beautiful green eyes. She looked into my soul, and I told her she'd be fine, but she knew, I swear it to this day she knew she was going to die. The paramedics and police got there and were trying to pull me out. I wouldn't go. I kicked and screamed and held on to her hand."

Tears fell from his eyes. "You see, I was telling her she'd be fine, but I knew too, I also knew she was going to die and that it was my fault. The very moment I came to, I knew it had been my fault." He paused to wipe his face. "I can't get it out of my thoughts, it's seared into my being now, that moment, and I replay it every single fucking day. This is why I don't deserve to live, why I don't get to go. My penance is to stay and let you all go. I couldn't save her. But maybe I can save you, Melody; maybe they have gathered the best and brightest doctors in the world. God, I hope they did; otherwise, what's the point?" He wiped more tears and laughed about his last comment. He looked into her eyes and said, "I want you to live."

She leaned in and kissed him.

He accepted the kiss for a moment before pulling back.

"I'm sorry," she said.

"No, I'm sorry." He took her hand. "I...um...I think you're beautiful, and I do want to kiss you, but I just can't."

She squeezed his hand. "I understand."

"I'm really sorry."

She leaned back into one of the thick pillows, turned

her head, and looked at the crackling fire, which needed to be stoked. Her thoughts spun from the embarrassment of the kiss to why she was even there. Her journey from discovering Jared's whereabouts and infidelity to sitting across from Ethan in Utah and her brief future in the Ark, to those spots being for children, was built upon death. Someone had to die for her to be where she was.

"Maybe we should go to bed, call it a night," Ethan said, although a part of him wanted to stay and kiss her back.

"I killed them," Melody blurted out, her eyes still fixed on the flames.

"What?"

She looked at him and with a sober tone repeated herself, "I killed them."

"Killed who?"

"I got the passes from my fiancé."

"Melody, what are you talking about?"

"I'm telling you that I'll stay back. I don't deserve to go to the Ark."

Confused, Ethan leaned close to her and again asked, "Mel, who did you kill?"

"He worked for the government. I found him cheating on me."

"Your fiancé?"

"The argument turned to a fight, and they both died."

Ethan didn't know what to say; he simply stared at her.

"I stabbed him in the neck, and his girlfriend, I hit her in the head with a rolling pin."

"It was self-defense, I assume."

"And if it wasn't?"

"That would make you a murderer in most people's eyes," Ethan replied with an uneasy candor. He adjusted his position on the couch, partially because he was feeling a bit uncomfortable with her possibly being a killer.

She stared hard at him.

"It was self-defense, right?" he asked again.

"Yes, it was, but I still feel horrible about it. Jared's girlfriend attacked me. She had a knife. I hit her in the head. Then Jared came at me; he started to strangle me. I felt like I was going to die, I tried to get him to let me go, but he wouldn't. All I remember is I found the same knife his girlfriend had just tried to stab me with, and I stabbed him in the neck."

"Sounds like self-defense," Ethan said.

"I didn't know anything about his passes to the Ark until afterwards."

"Why are you telling me this?"

"Because I don't deserve to go. Those passes aren't mine, they belonged to Jared, and I took them. Now they'll be put to good use for Savannah and the baby."

"We might still be able to make it, we must have hope."

"Ethan, I won't be going to the Ark. I'm set on it, if you give me a pass, I'll just give it away."

"Stop that talk."

She took his hand, rubbed her thumb along his knuckles, and said, "You can choose to stay with me at the end, but if you get a pass, use it. But I'm staying. I just ask that you don't say anything to Savannah until we get there. She's been through a lot in her life, and seeing me die later won't help her. Can you promise me?"

"I won't say a word, but I'm still hopeful."

"Are you not listening to me? I'm not going, you can give me a hundred spots and I'll hand them out to every child I find."

"But –"

She put her index finger to his lips. "Sssh. There will be no more discussion on this matter. We can either get another bottle, or we can go to bed. Um, not together, I mean separate." She began to blush. "So, what will it be?"

Seeing she wasn't going to be persuaded tonight and not one to press anything after too many drinks, he relented. "Fair enough."

"And?"

"We should call it a night. Not because of everything, just that I can already feel the hangover, and I don't want to be so smashed I can't function tomorrow." He wanted to stay and talk more, but knew it was getting late, and if he did drink more, he might do something he'd regret.

"Good point," she said and rose slowly from the couch.

He followed, and the two found themselves facing each other.

"Thank you," she said.

"For what?"

"You didn't judge me, you listened. You know how many people don't do that? So many people don't hear when you talk; all they're doing is waiting their turn to talk."

"How can I judge? You found yourself in a precarious situation, and something tragic came of it. I'm just sorry you had to deal with that."

She wrapped her arms around him and squeezed. She

liked the feel of his body, his chest was broad and firm, and his height was perfect. She rested her head against his chest and stayed there for a moment.

He returned the warm embrace. His hands spread wide so his fingers could feel her more. He missed the touch of a woman, and her smell sent waves of passion through him.

The two let go of each other at the same time.

"I'll walk you to your room," he said.

She nodded, and the two headed to their bedrooms with no other words exchanged except goodnight.

# THIRTY-THREE

## SPANISH FORK, UTAH

*Ethan gingerly rolled off Jen and lay next to her. He looked up at the ceiling fan as its blades spun, providing much-needed cool air to their hot skin.*

*She touched her belly and the sweat they had created together.*

*Needing to touch her again, his fingertips found their way to her slender neck. Taking his time, he slowly caressed his way down, passing over her perfect breasts until he arrived at her stomach, where he found her hand still resting. Interlocking their fingers, he turned on his side and said, "I love you."*

*She faced him, her green eyes gleaming with a loving response that needed no words.*

*"I do, I really do," he said softly just before kissing her sweetly on her shoulder. With his lips, he took in the saltiness of her skin, and with it came the accompanying sweet,*

*floral aromatic smell she always possessed. He just loved how she smelled. It was something he would long to experience and something he'd miss just after being gone a few hours. He lifted his gaze and looked into her eyes. "That face, oh, how I love that face."*

*"What was it you used to tell me when we first started dating?"*

*He needed no time to come up with the answer.*

*"Do you remember?" she purred.*

*"Oh, I remember."*

*"Then tell it to me again, like you used to," she seductively whispered.*

*He leaned in, his mouth close to her ear. "I'm here to guard your heart and fuck your brains out."*

*She let out a soft moan as goosebumps covered her once smooth skin. Unable to control herself from having him once more, she looked deeply into his piercing green eyes and said, "You've guarded my heart, now..."*

---

ETHAN OPENED his eyes and stared at the ceiling. His head throbbed, and his mouth was parched. He rolled over and groaned about the dream he'd just had. It was one he'd often experience and one he enjoyed more than the one about that tragic night, but it still left him melancholy.

A knock on the door pulled him fully away from his thoughts, and he was grateful.

"Yeah?" he called out.

"Open up," Chance replied.

"What is it?"

"Dad, open up."

"One sec." He sat up slowly, the pounding in his head dictating the pace. He made his way to the door, unlocked it, and opened it to find Chance standing there with a look of palpable agitation etched on his face.

"Do you know what time it is?"

"Nope."

Chance leaned in and sniffed. "Are you drunk?"

"I guess I could still be," he quipped.

"I can smell it on you."

"Did you come here to give me grief?"

"No, just to tell you that you missed breakfast, and now it's almost lunchtime."

Ethan ran his hand over his face and groaned. "Shit."

"Well, there's no reason to be too upset. The drive has two feet of snow, which means the highway does too."

"Damn it."

"Ezra isn't sure when they'll get the drive plowed, but promises they'll get it done by midday."

"What time is it exactly?"

"Just turned eleven."

"Fuck."

"Did you and Melody?"

"No. But why do you ask?"

"Because she looked as bad as you do."

"You've seen her?"

"Yeah, down at breakfast."

"Let me get cleaned up. I'll be right down. And, Chance..."

"Yeah."

"You and Annette doing okay? Last night was quite the show."

"She's okay. She said it was a reminder and validated why she left."

"Okay. I'll be right down," Ethan said and closed the door. He regretted the excessive drinking he'd partaken in. He searched his memory for a replay of the evening and recalled he and Melody had kissed and that she'd confessed to killing her fiancé and his girlfriend. He wondered if she remembered, and if she did, was she too regretting the night?

In the bathroom, the small window over the toilet gave him a glimpse of the day, and it appeared as Chance had described. Feet of snow lay under the gray sky, with flurries still coming down. From his vantage point, he could see the driveway hadn't been plowed. The regret of drinking quickly turned to a greater regret of stopping. He'd never thought about a snowstorm, much less considered weather when he set out on his drive. This was where being a native from Southern California came to bite him in the ass; when you live in a place where the weather isn't a factor, you lose sight of the fact it is in most other places.

———

A HOT SHOWER was exactly what he needed to alleviate some of the hangover. It's always amazing just how something so simple can feel so good and underappreciated until you haven't had it in a while. And not knowing when he'd get another one made it more enjoyable.

His gait had lost some pep, but nothing that a hot cup of coffee, breakfast and fresh air couldn't fix.

Ethan descended the staircase; his left hand glided over the railing as he took each step. To his left he saw the others were huddled in the center seating area of the great room. At first, he didn't notice no one was talking and that each one wore an odd expression. Even Melody, who was not the quietest of people, sat, her back erect and hands on her lap. He shot her a look to say hello, but her facial response screamed something was wrong. He opened his mouth to ask Melody a question when Olson barked out a command.

"Sit down and keep your mouth shut!"

Ethan craned his head towards Olson and again went to speak but stopped when he saw the muzzle of the pistol. Instinctually, he put his hands up to say don't shoot.

"Just sit down next to your girlfriend and keep quiet," Olson roared.

Ethan did as he was told. Across from him sat Barry, Chance, Annette and Ethan Junior. In the chair to his right was Beth and to his left Rebecca. On the couch with him were Melody and Savannah. He looked but didn't see Judah or Ezra. "Olson, I'm not sure what's going on here."

"Shut your mouth!" Olson snapped.

"Dad, why are you doing this?" Annette said, her eyes filled with tears.

"Hold on, what is he doing?" Ethan asked.

"Shut up!" Olson ordered Ethan, the pistol leveled at him.

Ignoring her father, Annette answered, "He's taking our passes and going to the Ark."

"You can't do that!" Ethan barked.

"I can and I am!" Olson growled.

Ethan looked across at Beth, who he now saw wore a red handprint on her face. She sheepishly looked up at him for a second before putting her gaze back on the floor. The defiance he'd seen her display the day before was gone.

"Hand over the passes to the Ark," Olson ordered Ethan.

Most people normally would be filled with fear if they had a gun pointed at them, but Ethan wasn't. He was angry and wouldn't allow his family's survival to be determined this way. "No."

"I don't have any issue hurting you to get them," Olson threatened.

"Do what you want," Ethan snapped back.

"I'll shoot you."

"And if you do, you won't be able to get the passes."

"Dad, please stop this. Please, I beg you. This isn't you. This isn't the father I know."

The front door opened, and in stepped Ezra. His big brown eyes scanned everyone as he approached Olson. Rebecca looked at him; tears covered her face. He gave her a quick smile as he stepped up to Olson. He leaned in and whispered.

Olson grimaced. "And Judah?"

Ezra whispered his reply.

"Fine. Take care of it."

Ezra faced everyone and said, "Rebecca, Mom, come with me, oh and you too, Uncle Barry."

Rebecca didn't hesitate. She stood and walked around the couch towards Ezra. Beth didn't move; she sat, tears flowing.

"Mom, come on."

"I'm not going. I won't be a party to this."

"Then you don't have to," Olson fired back, his nostrils flared in anger. He turned to Ethan. "Where are the passes?"

It was then Ethan realized Olson had no clue about how the passes were sent or what they were. "I said no."

Barry stood hesitantly, gave a look to the others, and said, "I'm sorry about this."

"Did you have something to do with this?" Annette asked.

"No, no, I'm just sorry this is happening," Barry said, fear cracking his voice.

Ezra escorted Rebecca and Barry out of the room.

"Now I'll ask one more time," Olson warned.

"Do you think you can just use my passes? Are you a fool? They have my name and image. My brother is expecting me on the other end. He works for the president's chief of staff. They'll arrest you at the checkpoint the second you try to use them."

"That's not true."

"Yes it is. Who told you they were just blank passes?"

"That's not what I heard. Now hand them over," Olson growled. He took a step closer to Ethan, who sat confidently in his seat.

"Ethan's right. You can't just use any pass. They're

linked to a name and social security number," Melody retorted.

Upon hearing what Melody had to say, Olson visibly grew agitated. His body tensed, and the veins in his neck and temples pulsated. He waved the pistol between Ethan and Melody in a threatening manner.

Ethan saw the tension building in Olson and worried he'd accidentally pull the trigger. He was tempted to lunge towards him but hesitated, as the pistol was pointed directly at him, assuring he'd be gunned down. As he pondered his next step, motion from his right caught his attention. Before he could even react, Chance launched himself at Olson, his arms wrapped around his waist, and with the force of his forward motion, he took Olson to the floor.

Upon the forceful impact, Olson, lost control of the pistol. Chance straddled him, clenched his fists, and began to pummel Olson's face.

Ethan leapt into action, as did Melody.

The commotion was loud enough to draw Ezra back into the room, a pistol in his hand. He saw Ethan make for Olson's firearm, it was something he couldn't allow to happen, but at the same time, he wasn't prepared to kill him either. He raised his pistol and pulled the trigger. The deafening crack stopped everyone; they froze as if playing the old children's game freeze tag. Ezra approached; his pistol now leveled at Ethan. "Don't do it."

Inches were what separated Ethan from the pistol, his arm and fingers were extended, all he need do was stretch and he'd have it in his hand, but at what price? Not wanting to die, he retracted his arm and raised it to show he was surrendering.

Chance stopped his brutal assault of Olson and slid off his father-in-law, who lay unconscious.

Beth ran to Olson; she knelt and took his hand. While she wasn't happy with him, she still loved him, and seeing him get beaten brought out her caring heart.

Annette stayed with Ethan Junior; her tears had become uncontrollable as she wailed.

With the pistol hovering out in front of him, Ezra confidently closed in on Ethan. He pressed the muzzle against the back of his head and said, "Face down on the floor."

"Don't you hurt him!" Beth cried out. "There's been enough pain and suffering."

"He was going to get that gun and do God knows what," Ezra said.

"Look at me, son; there's been enough of this. Put down that gun; we're family here."

Ezra saw Chance, then looked at Olson, his face swollen and bleeding. "Look at what he did to Dad. He deserves to get shot." Ezra swung the pistol in Chance's direction.

"Stop it!" Annette shrilled.

Barry and Rebecca came into the room. Like before, Rebecca was still crying. She was a sweet and innocent woman who reviled violence in any form. "Husband, please, it's over; this isn't who we are."

"But –" Ezra said before being interrupted by the front door opening.

All eyes turned to see it was Judah who entered the

foyer, removed his cowboy hat and, as he went to hang it on the rack, saw everyone. He continued placing his hat, turned and asked, "What's going on, Ez?"

"They attacked Dad. He's unconscious."

Judah's face turned from curiosity to anger in the span of a second. He marched towards the group. "Who did it?"

"He did!" Ezra barked, his index finger pointed at Chance.

"Don't you dare hurt that boy!" Beth hollered. She jumped to her feet and put herself in front of Chance just as Judah walked up, his fist clenched.

"Step out of the way, Mom."

"No, we're not having any more of this. Enough is enough! We're family here! This is not what we do! This is not who we are!" she roared; her voice bellowed through the great room.

Judah, his build like Ezra's and Olson's, towered over Beth. He looked deep into her eyes and said, "Mom, step out of the way."

"No. Son, if you want to get him, you'll have to hurt me first."

If a pin were dropped, it would echo through the room. All eyes were fixed on the standoff.

Beth touched Judah's chest, just above his heart. "Son, I love you. Please don't."

Judah stood, his breath heavy.

"This isn't who we are. These are our family now, and they're good people. If God chose for us to survive what's coming, he would have made it happen, but not like this, not like this."

Judah's expression quickly changed. Beth's touch and

soothing words melted the anger, exposing the pain and sadness underneath. "We can't die." He paused and lowered his head. "I don't want to die."

"Me either, believe me. I love life, but our time is at an end, and this is not how we go on; this is it. Let us share these final moments as a loving family, together having fun and laughter."

Judah cried. He lowered himself down and rested his head on her shoulder.

Like any adoring mother, she caressed his neck and held him. "My sweet boy. I love you so."

Olson grunted and shook his battered head. "Beth."

She looked back. "Yes, my dear."

"I'm sorry, I just don't want this to be the end."

"I understand, Olson, but like I told Judah, this isn't who we are. Let's just accept this and be happy that our beautiful baby girl and her son, our family, will survive. Your bloodline will continue. We don't end. We go on."

Olson lifted his weary arm and beckoned.

Judah and Beth went to him.

Defeated, Ezra lowered his pistol and tossed it on the couch.

Beth looked to him and held out her hand. "Come."

Ezra and Rebecca joined them on the floor next to Olson.

Ever a forgiving person, Annette too went to her father's side. When her face appeared to him, he mumbled something unintelligible through his tears and drew her close with a hug.

"Forgive me," Olson said.

"Of course, Daddy. I love you."

"I love you too."

Looking on and happy the altercation that had happened so quickly was over just as fast, Ethan walked to Chance and embraced him firmly. "I'm proud of you."

Chance shook. His entire body was still in a state of shock. He wasn't known to be a violent man, but he had proved himself today.

Melody sat with a silent Savannah, who had sat motionless and quiet like a field mouse. "Are you okay, sweetie?"

"The world has a lot of messed-up people in it," Savannah said.

"It does."

"Can we leave now?"

Melody looked to Ethan, who nodded.

It was time to go, time to make the final leg of the road trip and see what the future held for them.

# THIRTY-FOUR

## SPANISH FORK, UTAH

ETHAN WATCHED with careful eyes as Judah and Ezra removed and plowed the snow from the drive. What he hoped would only take an hour had now stolen almost three and left Ethan with the promise of driving at night up what would be a snow-covered Interstate 15 into the city limits of Salt Lake City.

Olson had offered to send Judah ahead with the plow to carve a route, but Ethan declined. Even if he had agreed, how much could Judah have realistically done? He didn't quite trust Olson and for good reason and just wanted to get away from them. His SUV was four-wheel drive, and he'd just have to take it slow through the twenty-four-plus inches of snow that awaited them on the interstate.

"Are you as anxious as I am to get out of here?" Melody asked, stepping up next to Ethan.

Resting against a column of the portico, Ethan craned his head towards her and laughed. "Anxious isn't the word I'd use."

"Hey, I want to talk about last night."

"What about it?"

"I had a bit to drink…"

"We both did."

"Yeah, but I shared some stuff that I wish I hadn't now, and I was hoping you could just forget about it."

"Forget about what?" he quipped.

"Ha ha."

"Think nothing of it. Life is complicated, and in the wise words of whoever coined it, shit happens. You're a good woman, Mel, I trust you, so pay no mind to whatever you're concerned about."

"Thanks."

"Think nothing of it."

"And I'm sorry about the other thing."

"Oh…the kiss?"

"Yeah. I got a bit carried away."

He faced her and said, "Mel, it's all okay. Please don't apologize. You must know that I…I really like you, but it's complicated for me. I want to, but just can't; if we had more time…"

She touched his arm and said, "No need to go on."

"Okay."

"And we don't have more time."

"Five days until that big ole rock smashes into us."

"It's crazy to even get my head around the fact that this all will be gone, poof, just like that. What took eons for humans to build will be wiped out in a matter of hours. So weird to really think about."

"I know."

"And this Ark, how many are going? How long will they have to live down there? There's so many questions, and none that I know of have been answered. All everyone, me included, heard was we could survive, and we're ready to go without asking a word."

"Who knows. When I talked with my brother, he didn't provide much detail. He wouldn't even tell me where it was. I had to leave that up to the news, and with so much fake news, I don't know what's real anymore."

"I'm serious about not going, by the way, no matter what."

"I know you are."

"Good, I'm glad we finally got that cleared up," she quipped with a wink.

"Where will you go?"

"This is going to sound crazy, but I've never been to the ocean."

"Any ocean?"

"Not a one."

"Well, due west from the base, you'll run right into the Pacific. Maybe I'll take you, but I still have hope my brother can pull one last Hail Mary pass."

"This talk, you've really accepted that I'm staying and you're going?"

"Yep, I don't like it, but it's your choice," he said, his arms folded across his chest.

"Good. And no word of this to Savannah."

"Not a peep. And nothing to the others about only having two passes."

"Not a word, I swear. Any place in particular I should go, like a beach I should see?"

"You won't have time to make it to SoCal, so like I said, head west. There's Big Sur, and oh, I know, a beach called Ten Mile Dunes. I went there years ago, before Jen; it's beautiful."

"Noted."

The sun broke through the late afternoon cloud cover and cast its warmth on them.

"Ah, that feels good," she purred, her eyes closed and face lifted towards the sun.

"I never asked, so don't get weird, but how old are you?" he asked.

"Thirty-two."

He chuckled.

"What?" she asked.

"I'm forty-seven."

"I figured you were an old man; the graying hair and deep crow's feet around the eyes gave it away," she jabbed.

"You like your men old, then."

"Not exactly."

"Then what type of man does Melody...you know something, I don't know your last name."

"Sinclair."

"Kinkaid," he said, pointing at himself.

"I know."

He laughed.

"Go ahead. What were you going to say?"

"What type of man does Melody Sinclair like? Wait, let me guess, big muscles?"

"I don't mind muscles, but it's not necessary. I will say this, though, if a guy is too in shape and his social media is nothing but him with his shirt off, that's always a red flag."

"Red flag for what?"

"Narcissism. And believe me, girls fall for them all the time. I have girlfriends who have left guys, stating they're narcissists, and boom, next thing they're DMing guys on Instagram, and their pages are nothing but shirt-off pics from the gym. I'm like, girlfriend, you're going from one self-centered narcissist to another. I swear people never learn."

"So you don't like narcissists or guys who have social media accounts filled with posts of themselves half naked...check."

"Okay, so what do I like...hmm, let me see. I like them to have hair."

"Check."

"Just not on their backs."

"Check."

"To be honest, there's not a look, so to speak, I just like kind; and before you say something about the bad-boy thing, which is true, by the way, for many women, I like a little mystery, smarts, quick-witted and not a pushover. But when we're together, I want him to be kind. And let me be clear, kind doesn't mean a nice guy," she said, putting air quotes at the end.

"Kind isn't nice?"

"The nice-guy thing is really targeted towards guys who let women walk all over them. You know, the simps."

"Simps?"

"You don't know what a simp is? Ha, you are a boomer."

"Hold on, first thing, I'm not a boomer, I'm a Gen Exer, and I'll say it loud and proud. We're the best generation besides the greatest generation, who fought World War II."

"Oh my God." She laughed, her hand holding her face.

"Laugh all you want. But go ahead, educate me on what a simp is."

"It's that type of guy who allows a woman to walk all over them. A woman can treat them like shit, and they'll keep coming back for more. They'll shower her with gifts and words of affirmation with hopes it'll win her over. They're really just a bunch of weak-kneed men who lack confidence."

"I think I understand. We call those guys pussy-whipped," he quipped.

"Same thing."

"Then why not say that?"

"Us Millennials prefer to use more up-to-date vernacular, not outdated phrases." She lightly jabbed him with her elbow.

"So you like men with hair, even if it's gray, no ape men, and if they're kind, that's the winning trait."

"Kindness is key. I don't mind my guy taking charge or opening the door for me. I'm old-fashioned that way. If we have a one-car garage, he allows me to park in it and not on the street. But I don't mind if he's strong-willed and can take a stand on principles and beliefs he has; just be kind to me. People confuse the notion."

"Check, check, check, and check."

"What are you checking?"

"That I hit all those marks."

She laughed. "Look at you, all cocky. Just because I kissed you last night doesn't mean you made all the checks; maybe you're just the only available guy around."

"Wow!"

She laughed more.

He smiled broadly and looked at her dimples and the way her eyes glimmered. His stomach ached. A strong urge welled up in him to pull her close and kiss those lips.

She caught sight of his stare and stopped laughing, but her smile remained.

The two looked into each other's eyes for about thirty seconds or more. No words needed to be exchanged as they shared this special connection.

The front door opened and pulled them back to reality.

She looked away and brushed her hair behind her ear.

He put his gaze on the drive and cleared his thoughts, but his stomach still ached, and the physical desire still remained.

Beth stepped out holding a tray with two steaming cups of coffee. "I thought you needed something to stay warm and alert."

"Oh, thank you," Melody said, taking a cup.

Ethan took one as well and asked, "This is just coffee and cream?"

"Yes, but I can get some Bailey's."

"No, I'm good."

"Same here," Melody said.

"I want to apologize again."

"Please, no, let's just move on. It happened, and no one was...killed. I was going to say hurt, but that wouldn't be accurate," Ethan said.

Beth rubbed his arm. "You're a kind man."

Ethan and Melody looked at each other. Ethan winked and smiled.

"Yes, he is a kind man," Melody said sweetly.

The door opened and out stepped Savannah, her backpack slung and the book, *The Secret Garden*, in her hand.

"Hi, Savvy," Melody said with a smile.

"Hi."

"What's that?" Melody asked pointing at the book.

"Oh, it's a book."

"I can see that, which one?"

Savannah held it up for her to see.

"That's such a good book," Melody fawned.

"It is and I'm happy Savannah is taking it with her," Beth said warmly as she rubbed Savannah's arm.

"That's nice of you," Melody said.

"I offered her more, but she only took a few others, like what are we going to do with them," Beth said.

Everyone nodded.

"When are we leaving?" Savannah asked.

"Soon, very soon," Ethan answered.

# THIRTY-FIVE

## SEVEN MILES SOUTH OF DRAPER, UTAH

THE INTERSTATE WAS A MESS. Abandoned cars and snow made the drive arduous. It was almost three in the morning, and for Ethan, it felt like he'd been awake for days. Having stayed up late drinking the night before was wearing on him. He caught himself nodding a few times but decided to keep pushing to at least the city limits of Salt Lake.

During the drive, he played out how the farewells would go. If he didn't get another pass, just how he'd explain it to Chance and if he did, how he'd say goodbye to Melody. Even in his imagination, he felt the pang of sorrow. Yes, he'd only met her days before, but there was something about her that he could safely now say he'd fallen for. He questioned his fondness for Melody as real or just a man who hadn't been with another woman in a year and the height of emotions leading up to Colossus' arrival. He knew the psychology could literally be she was an avatar for desire, and it might not even be about her, but about someone longing for him. This recalled a quote from the philosopher Friedrich Nietzsche, *"Ultimately it is the desire, not the desirer, that we love."*

These feelings for her always ran headfirst into his memories of Jen, which would then fill him with regret. He was perfectly in his right to find love, even by the societal standards of the Victorian era, but for him, he just felt awful.

Like the tide his thoughts went. He'd see Melody's face in his mind, her dimples when she smiled, her lips, and those blue eyes. He'd hold that vision only for it to be washed away as Jen's face would come. He hated this conflict but reminded himself that soon there wouldn't be any.

The weight of fatigue again gripped him. He nodded in sleep for a few seconds, caught himself, and jerked back to life. He pinched his leg hard and shook his head. It didn't help that he had turned on the heat to keep everyone warm. While they slept comfortably, the heat made it feel cozy and fueled his desire to sleep.

He nodded again, this time longer, closer to ten seconds. When he came to, the vehicle was headed at a road sign. He jerked the vehicle hard to the left. The motion was enough to wake Melody, Savannah, and Chance.

"You okay, Dad?" Chance asked just after a big yawn and stretch.

"No, I'm not."

"Pull over, and I'll drive," Chance offered.

"Good idea."

"What's that?" Melody asked, her finger pointed out the window towards a dim light waving back and forth.

Chance and Ethan looked closer. They saw the light, but it was too dim to be headlights.

"I think that's someone in the road, waving a flashlight," Melody said.

Annette had woken and said, "Melody is right. That's someone in the road."

Upon them saying it, Ethan too saw the person. He wasn't driving fast, so he slowed to a stop, keeping a good distance between them and the person they now could see was a woman.

"She must need help; let me go see," Chance said, his hand on the door handle.

"No," Ethan said firmly.

"Why?"

"Let's assess this."

"It's just a woman; she's harmless. Ran out of gas or something," Melody said.

"Mel is right," Chance said and opened the door.

"No, damn it. Let's just wait a moment," Ethan barked.

"Are we doing this again?" Melody fired back.

Savannah watched the two go back and forth a few more times before she added, "Ethan is right."

Melody looked at her with a curious expression, her brow raised.

"Thank you, Savannah," Ethan said.

Chance closed the door and waited for a consensus.

The woman hadn't moved since they stopped. She stood in her spot, flashlight pointed towards the ground, with the headlights of a minivan illuminating her and the surroundings.

Ethan turned around to face everyone. "Listen, guys, we're close, like an hour or more because of the snow, but nevertheless very close to the base. I just don't feel this is legit, or at the minimum, we can't take any chances."

"He's right," Savannah said again.

"We know how you feel about this," Melody snidely replied, not giving her a look.

Savannah winced at the comment.

"I understand how you feel, but we should help people when we can," Melody continued.

"I agree," Annette added.

Ethan turned his head slowly to Chance. He already knew his thoughts on this.

"I'm with them. Look at her; it's a woman, all by herself."

"You don't know that," Ethan argued.

"There's three votes yes and two no," Melody said; she now reached for the door handle.

"No, this isn't a democracy," Ethan spat.

Melody mumbled something under her breath. She donned her knit cap, threw on her jacket and gloves, and exited the vehicle.

Ethan grunted his disapproval as he watched her post-hole through the almost two feet of snow until she was feet from the woman.

"Maybe I should go," Chance offered.

"No, I'll go. Slide over here, and be ready to react."

"You sure?"

"Yeah," Ethan replied. He got out, press checked his pistol to confirm a round was chambered, and slid it into his jacket pocket. He could hear Melody and the woman talking, but it wasn't clear enough to make out what they were discussing.

Melody and the woman walked to the minivan.

Ethan had his hand on the pistol still in his pocket; the grip felt good in his palm.

The side door of the minivan opened. Two men emerged; pistols pointed at Melody. She jumped back but not before the woman pulled a pistol she had in her pocket and put it to Melody's temple. The men came alongside Melody and the woman and stood, pistols raised towards Ethan.

Ethan froze. It happened so quickly that his response was muted.

"Where are you going?" the woman asked Ethan.

"We're going to Idaho."

The woman pressed the pistol hard against Melody's temple and said to her, "Is he lying?"

"No."

"Let me see your phone," the woman snapped.

"It's in our car," Melody said.

"Tell everyone in your car to get out. I want them to put all their phones in this bag," the woman ordered, holding up a plastic grocery-store sack.

The man next to her grabbed the bag and walked towards Ethan. "If anyone shoots me, we will kill her."

Ethan was tempted to fight, but like Gila Bend, he wasn't confident enough in his skills to know if he'd win this fight. He hollered at the man, "My son, his wife and grandson are in the vehicle, oh, and a young girl. But what do you want with our phones?"

The man stopped feet from Ethan. "Don't play us like fools. You're headed towards that base, and we know all about the passes being sent either by e-mail or text."

"What passes?"

"Just give us your phones and tell us how to access them. If we don't find any passes, you can move along."

"I don't know what you're talking about."

The man lifted the pistol and aimed it at Ethan's face. "Tell them to get out and bring me their phones."

Ethan gritted his teeth. His anger swelled. All he wanted to do was pull his pistol and put a bullet in each of their faces. He was sick and tired of people.

"Tell them. All we want are your passes, nothing else."

"Get out with your phones and bring them here!" Ethan hollered.

Chance exited, his arms over his head. In his hand were his and Annette's phones. He tossed them in the bag and stepped back.

"Keep your hands up." The man looked in the bag. "There's only two phones. I want everyone out of the car now!"

"That's my phone and my wife's. Savannah doesn't have a phone," Chance replied.

The man swung the pistol towards Chance's face.

Ethan's grip on his pistol tightened. "I told you who was in the vehicle."

"I want everyone out of the car...now!" the man screamed.

"Fuck you!" Chance barked defiantly.

"What did you say, boy!" the man growled. With anger in his eyes, he marched up to Chance and put the pistol in his face. "I should shoot that smug face."

"Leave him be. We don't have passes, and our phones will prove it. Now please just check so we can get out of here and towards Idaho. We have family waiting," Ethan said.

"I need everyone out of the car so I can go through it."

Ethan hated being controlled, but he didn't have the leverage. "Annette and Savannah, get out, please!"

A moment passed.

"Hurry up!" the man hollered.

"My wife is carrying an infant; give her a minute," Chance seethed. He wasn't deterred by the pistol in his face not to sneer and comment, but it was enough to stop him from doing anything. His encounter at Annette's family had steeled him.

The driver's side rear door opened, and out came Savannah, looking sheepish, followed by Annette with Ethan Junior swaddled tightly in her arms.

"Over here," the man commanded. "You, step over there with them," he barked at Chance.

Chance glared before doing as the man said.

"You too," the man said to Ethan. "But I need your phone too."

Ethan unzipped his coat and went to reach in but was stopped.

"Hold on!" the man said. He stepped over and with his pudgy fingers reached inside and came out with Ethan's phone. He tossed it in the bag.

Ethan's mind was spinning with ways they'd not just

survive this but do so with their phones and the passes they so desperately needed.

"I've got three phones here," the man hollered back. He looked at Savannah and asked, "What about you? Got a phone?"

Savannah shook her head.

"You ain't lyin' to me, are you?"

"No, sir."

"She says her phone is in the car," the woman hollered back. "In the seat back pocket."

The man headed towards the SUV.

If there was a moment to act, this could be it. Ethan motioned with his head to Chance towards the man. "You get him, and I'll get them," he said under his breath.

"Okay," Chance replied.

Headlights appeared from the south.

"Lance, car comin'. Hurry up!" the woman called out.

"One sec," Lance answered, his upper body fully in the SUV, digging around.

"Go," Ethan said.

Chance ran towards the SUV.

Ethan ripped the pistol from his coat and raised it towards the other man.

Seeing Ethan and Chance acting, Melody did too. She elbowed the woman in the ribs and with a clenched fist swung back and struck her in the face.

The second man looked at Melody, then back to Ethan, who he saw had a pistol trained on him. He went to lift his pistol to engage, but it was too late. Ethan fired off two rounds, one missed, but the second struck him in the chest. The man lowered the pistol, looked at the hole in his coat, and cried out, "He shot me!" A trickle of blood came from the entry wound and down his navy-blue coat. He dropped to his knees and toppled over in the snow.

Chance reached Lance, who turned just as he arrived. Chance tackled him to the ground. The two began to grapple.

Melody's assault on the woman produced the results she wanted. She had the woman back on her heels. Like Chance, Melody ran at her and pushed her to the ground. When she hit her, the pistol dislodged from her grip and flew into the deep snow.

Melody reached and came up with it, but before she could pull the trigger, the woman straddled her.

Ethan took aim and fired. He missed; the round struck the minivan. He fired again; this time he struck her left side, just below her armpit. The woman grunted and fell over into the pristine white snow, turning it red. She coughed, blood exiting her mouth.

Melody scooted away, eyes fixed on the woman as she went through her death throes.

The woman kicked and flexed her arms, then gasped. Her eyes stayed open, staring into the dark sky above.

Like the time with Jared and Tabitha, Melody stared at the woman's eyes stuck in a death stare.

The commotion between Lance and Chance got Ethan's attention; he turned and heard the crack of a pistol. He stopped when he felt the sting in his side. He grabbed at it, looked, and saw a hole in his coat on the left side. He looked at his hand and saw blood. "Damn it."

Another crack of the pistol sounded.

Chance rolled off Lance. He lay in the snow, his breath

rapid. The snow underneath Lance turned crimson, and like his friend, he lay there with his eyes open, lifeless.

As if she'd transported herself there in a second, Melody was next to Ethan. "Are you okay?"

"Ahh, I think I've been shot."

Hearing Ethan, Chance lifted himself out of the snow and called out, "Dad!"

Ethan unzipped his coat to find the lower part of his shirt was soaked in blood, and it was seeping into his jeans.

Not wasting a second, Melody's training kicked in. She lifted his shirt and saw the wound easily. She wiped the blood with a dry part of his shirt and quickly discovered it was superficial.

"Well?" Ethan asked.

Chance was now there, his face showing the strain of concern.

Annette and Savannah reappeared from the safety of the far side of the SUV. Upon seeing Ethan, their relief turned to distress.

"Let's get you to the vehicle. I need to clean this up and get a better look," Melody said. She wrapped her arm around him and walked him towards the SUV.

Chance and the others followed.

Inside the back, interior lights on and a flashlight in hand, Melody examined him more closely. "You're lucky, my friend. The bullet only grazed you." She lifted her head and looked to Chance. "Get me the first aid kit."

"Okay," Chance answered. He turned and watched as a truck slowly drove by. In the front passenger seat was a woman, who stared at him, then at the body of Lance on the ground. The truck sped up; its tires spun out briefly. "Yeah, yeah, keep going," Chance snarked.

Chance returned and handed the kit to Melody, who went right to work. All eyes were on Melody as she meticulously treated the wound.

Ethan was a good patient. He occasionally grimaced as she applied alcohol to clean the wound and only grunted once when she stitched it.

When she was done, Melody leaned back and smiled with pride. "All done. You're a new man."

Ethan gave her a smile. "Thank you."

"I told you it was a good idea to bring her along," Annette chimed in.

"You were right," Ethan replied.

"I haven't been right lately, hence why I wanted to remind you of this one time I was correct."

"Who's ready to get out of here?" Chance asked.

Everyone voiced their desire to leave and headed for their seats. Before Melody could move, Ethan took her hand. He tenderly squeezed it. "Thank you."

"It's what I do."

"I know, but I'm truly grateful for you." He slipped his fingers into hers, and the two shared a look of genuine fondness.

Chance cleared his throat from the driver's seat.

Embarrassed, Melody pulled her hand back.

"Are you staying back there?" Chance asked.

"Ahh..."

"You can. I want to lie down," Savannah said and disappeared as she stretched out on the bench seat. She turned on a small flashlight and opened her book.

With her decision made for her, Melody grabbed the strap to the rear gate and closed it. She resumed her seat next to Ethan but sat upright and kept her hands in her lap.

Annette, with Ethan Junior in her arms, took the front passenger seat.

"Next stop, Hill Air Force Base," Chance said. He put the SUV into gear and drove down the freeway. As they passed the minivan, he looked at the bodies of the man and woman. He shook his head. "Fools."

In the back, Ethan was happy Melody stayed with him. After having what could have been a brush with death, he felt even more drawn to her. Unable to control himself, he reached over and took her hand.

She didn't resist. She allowed his fingers to slip in between hers. His touch and the sweet attention he gave her made her feel warm inside.

"Forty-eight miles!" Chance called out when he saw the sign.

Hearing this filled Melody with dread. Soon she'd possibly be alone. Knowing her time with Ethan could be limited, she decided not to care what anyone thought. She stretched out next to him, rested her head on the pillow where his was, and gently laid her arm over his chest.

"Hi," he said, his eyes locked on hers.

"Hi."

"Have I thanked you yet for saving my life?"

She laughed. "I didn't save your life. It's just a flesh wound, all you need to worry about is infection."

He leaned in and kissed her. "Believe me when I say that you did save me."

# THIRTY-SIX

## HILL AIR FORCE BASE, UTAH

THE LINE of cars getting off the exit for the base was backed up for miles. Car horns and yelling could be heard all around. In the distance, the lights from the base glowed and illuminated the sky as if it were a small city.

"We haven't moved in hours. I think we need to walk in," Chance said, his frustration showing.

"I think you're right," Ethan said. "Let's get our stuff and prepare to hike the rest of the way."

Everyone poured out of the SUV.

"Only bring what you need; everything else stays," Ethan said loudly to overcome the noise outside.

Next bag was Melody's, he gave he a look and she nodded. She was going to play the game up until she had to tell Savannah. He leaned in close and whispered in her ear. "I've been trying to reach my brother, there's still hope." Ethan had been trying often, but no reply via text or voice had seemed to make it through.

"My answer is still the same," she replied calmly.

He looked deeply into her eyes and could see a defiance and confidence.

She looked over his shoulder at the immense crowd that was on the highway, then saw the hordes walking across the overpass. Seas of people were making their way towards the base, which was a mile and a half away.

"This isn't going to be easy," she said.

"I always like a challenge," he replied with a cocky tone.

————

SIDE BY SIDE, they slowly trudged through the packed-down snow up the exit ramp, weaving in and around people hauling luggage, pets, and an assortment of items the base security would certainly tell them they couldn't take.

Ethan wondered how many had passes versus the numbers who were just coming with hopes of getting on a transport. It was unclear, but what was evident was a large number of people were determined not to die. They hadn't come to grips with their own demise, and it was understandable. Not two weeks before, they had learned of Colossus; that wasn't much time to get your affairs in order or even process death.

They reached the street at the end of the ramp and merged with the hordes coming from the west side. People were spread across the width of the street and sidewalks and parking lots. As they drew closer, the pace of the advance slowed and slowed. People were everywhere; some were finding ways to scale buildings, looking for shortcuts.

In the air, loudspeakers from the base boomed an announcement.

*"Only entry for those with valid Ark passes. If you do not have a pass, you will be turned back. Do not come if you do not have a pass."*

It was chaos, and they were still a mile from the base entrance. They were at a full stop in the street and hadn't moved in twenty minutes.

"This is crazy!" Chance exclaimed.

"We'll make it. God is with us," Annette countered.

"I think we could use some prayers right about now!" Ethan said.

As they inched closer, the mass of people compacted tighter like the crowd at a concert near the stage. Melody grew concerned they'd accidentally get split up. "Take my hand," she said to Savannah, who obliged without hesitation.

"We need a plan here," Chance said.

People bumped into him, and the space grew tighter and tighter.

The pain from Ethan's wound was a distant memory, only to be rekindled when someone nudged him. He too was getting concerned about the size and the lack of movement. To his left he spotted several people cutting holes in a chain-link fence. They crawled through and disappeared. He wasn't sure where it led, but what was certain was staying where they were wasn't getting them anywhere. "Follow me!" He took Melody's hand and pulled.

She and Savannah followed, with Chance, Annette and the baby coming right behind.

He pushed his way past people until they reached the fence.

"Ethan!" a voice boomed from the crowd.

He looked but didn't see anyone. Thinking he misheard, he ordered everyone through the hole in the fence.

One by one, everyone did as he asked until he was the only person on the other side.

"Ethan! Ethan!" the voice again boomed.

He looked around and saw a woman wearing a beanie cap waving at him. He didn't know who it was, but they knew him.

"Ethan, over here!" the woman cried out, her arm waving frantically.

"Dad, let's go!", Chance barked.

"One second," Ethan replied. He wanted to see who it was.

The woman pushed her way through the crowd until she was face to face with him. Just behind her was a boy. She embraced him tightly. "I can't believe it's you."

Shocked, Ethan stood still unsure who it was.

The woman pulled back and looked at him. "Don't you recognize me? It's me, it's Jamie."

"Jamie? What are you doing here?" he asked now knowing who it was. Jamie was Jen's older sister and the boy in tow was Jakey, her nine year old son. Jamie was divorced and had been for a few years, no significant others so to speak except an occasional boyfriend. Jamie was attractive and in her mid-forties, but found it hard to find another long term relationship after her divorce. It wasn't that she didn't try she said, just that the men, or lack of serious men, was the issue. Now here she was, with Jakey.

"I could ask you the same thing," she said, a big smile on her face. She grabbed him again and squeezed. "It's so good to see you."

"Yeah, likewise."

"Are you going to the Ark?" she asked bluntly.

"Yeah and you?"

Tears formed in her eyes. "Can we come with you?"

"Ah, I'm sorry, but..."

"Please," she begged taking his hand.

"Dad, we need to go!" Chance barked.

Not wanting to get into a back and forth and still holding out some hope, he said to Jamie, "I can't promise anything, but come with us."

It was as if someone breathed new life into her as her hazel eyes widened and a large smile graced her slender face. "Thank you."

Ethan stepped out of the way and let Jamie and Jakey pass through the fence. He followed right behind.

"Now where?" Chance asked.

"We know the base is that way; let's just keep moving in that general direction. We're going to make it, I promise," Ethan answered confidently.

They were in what appeared to be a business park,

with lines of identical-looking steel buildings all laid out evenly on both sides with a paved road separating them. To their right, beaming over the roofs of the buildings, the bright lights of the base and the booming announcements gave them the direction they needed to go.

The lights from the base provided enough ambient light for them to navigate the streets. They went right, then left, then right, each block getting them closer and closer.

They made a right turn and could see the end of the street ahead. It was a fence, and the base entrance was just on the other side of it.

"We're close," Melody cheered. She came up alongside Ethan and asked, "Who's that?"

"My sister-in-law, Jamie and her son, Jakey."

"Do they have passes?" Melody asked.

"Nope, but there's still hope." He faced forward and exclaimed, "Let's hurry; every second we waste, we'll be that much further behind."

A series of bright direct lights hit them. Like a spotlight on a stage performer, they were lit up and the center of someone's attention.

"Halt!" a voice boomed over a bullhorn.

They froze.

"You cannot advance; turn around. You're on federal property and are trespassing!"

"We have passes!" Ethan hollered.

"Turn back around and go to the street and follow the signs to the proper entry!"

"We have passes. Please!" Ethan cried out.

"Turn back around, now!"

"My brother is the president's assistant chief of staff. His name is Eric Kinkaid; please contact him. We have passes to the Ark!"

"Dad, get your phone out and call Uncle Eric. We might have service here!" Chance said.

"Good idea." Ethan got his phone out. His hands were shaking, making it difficult to scroll to Eric's number. He found it and hit call. The phone rang and rang, then clicked over to voicemail. "Eric, it's Ethan, I'm at the base, but I can't get in. It's a shit show here. If you get this, please tell them who we are and to let us in."

"Turn around and leave, or we will remove you by force."

Ethan pocketed the phone and got an idea. "We're not moving."

"Turn around!"

"No!"

"What are you doing?" Chance asked.

"I'm assuming this works."

Shadowy figures began to advance from behind the lights. Ethan could make out they were armed, but would they really hurt them? Would they injure women and children? He was betting they wouldn't.

"I'm Ethan Kinkaid. I have passes to the Ark; we all do. My brother is the assistant chief of staff for the president of the United States!"

The men advanced.

"Will they hurt us?" Savannah asked as she hid behind Melody.

"They won't hurt us," Melody replied.

Ethan took Melody's free hand and squeezed. "We're going to be fine."

Three Air Force Security Forces personnel moved up to within ten feet, their rifles at the ready and pointed at them. "Turn around!"

"My name is Ethan Kinkaid. My brother is the assistant chief of staff for the president of the United States!"

"Turn around!"

"Call your superior, please! There's no way to gain entrance. There's too many people."

The man in the center stepped forward, his rifle pointed at Ethan. "Turn around now, sir!"

Ethan's phone rang. He pulled it out and saw it was Eric. He answered and put the phone on speaker. "Eric, we need help!"

"Put your phone down and turn around," the man, a staff sergeant, commanded.

*"Ethan, what the hell is going on!"*

"Hey, bro, I need your help to get inside the base."

*"Put whoever is there on the phone now!"*

The staff sergeant shot Ethan a look, which showed he was now nervous that Ethan wasn't lying.

*"Whoever is there, this is Eric Kinkaid. I'm the assistant chief of staff to President Reynolds. These people all have access per presidential order."*

"Did you hear him, huh?" Ethan asked.

The staff sergeant advanced a few feet and leveled his rifle at Ethan's chest. "Turn around, sir."

"Please listen to him," Ethan begged.

*"Listen, this is the assistant chief of staff to President Reynolds."*

The staff sergeant leaned in this time and listened. "How do I know you are who you say you are?"

*"Who is this?"*

The staff sergeant didn't reply.

*"Who is this?"*

"This is Staff Sergeant Collins."

*"Staff Sergeant Collins, these people all have access. Please let them in."*

"But how do I know you are who you say you are?"

*"One second. Stay right there."*

The phone went silent, as did everyone there.

Ethan and Collins kept exchanging looks, with Ethan doing his best to stay calm. They were close now; all they needed to do was just be patient.

Collins' radio crackled to life in his ear. He pressed to talk and said, "Yes, sir. Yes, yes. Sorry, sir. I'll let them in right away. Yes, sir, I'll send them to the receiving checkpoint."

Like a blowtorch to snow, Ethan's anxiety melted away.

"Sorry, sir, you're all clear to enter. Let me escort you in."

*"Ethan, you there?"*

"I'm here." He took the phone off speaker and put it to his ear.

*"Get your ass in there. The last wheels up is soon."*

"I need some extra passes, I really do, if I don't, I'm not coming."

*"I'll see what I can do. But, there's no time to waste. We*

*were wrong about Colossus' arrival. It'll make impact in a day and a half."*

"What?"

*"Yes, there's n–"*

The phone went dead.

"Eric, hello, Eric?" Ethan looked at his phone. It read Call Dropped. "Shit!"

"What did he say?" Melody asked.

Not wanting her to worry, he replied, "He said our timing was perfect."

# THIRTY-SEVEN

## HILL AIR FORCE BASE, UTAH

THE BASE WAS JUST as chaotic inside as outside. With Colossus arriving earlier than they thought, panic set in, not just for everyday folks but for the government personnel trying to plan the evacuations and final preparations.

As promised, Collins escorted them inside the base, but instead of taking them to a secure location, he took them to the front of the boisterous line at the entrance. A flank of Air Force Security Forces personnel lined the road and the fence line. Just on the other side were those unlucky souls who didn't have passes.

It was there Ethan came face-to-face with those without passes and desperate to live. Their fingers clinging to the chain-link fence, tears on their faces, eyes swollen and filled with terror. What struck him most was the children; there were so many.

A young senior airman with a tablet stood in front of Ethan. "QR codes?"

Pulled away from the weeping people at the fence, Ethan found his phone and scrolled to the text from Eric. He found the QR code and held it up. The name tag on the senior airman's coat read Sorvino. Taking note, Ethan said, "Sorvino, any relation to the actor?"

Sorvino ignored him and said, "Please hold up the phone so I can see it clearly."

"Sorry, I'm a bit jittery." Ethan repositioned the phone and heard an audible beep. His heart fluttered upon hearing it as he waited for Sorvino's response.

Sorvino looked at Ethan, then to the others behind him. "I'm showing three. Who's going?"

Ethan let out a sigh, Eric had come through on another pass and quickly. He gave Melody a look. She had heard Sorvino mention three. Her heart ached. She would now be all alone in the final days.

"Three? That's not right!" Annette chirped.

"That's all I have here, three," Sorvino confirmed.

"I have passes too," Melody said. She pulled Jared's phone from her coat pocket. As soon as she saw the screen, a pic of her and Jared, she paused. It was so hard to believe he was dead, and here she was in Utah. So much had happened and in such a short amount of time.

"Ma'am?"

"Sorry." She presented it to Sorvino, who scanned it. Right after the beep, he looked at her and said, "Jared..."

"Um, yeah, he –"

"Ma'am, I don't care. Who's in your party?"

She stood and looked at him blankly; this was her moment. She could go. This was it.

Savannah looked at her, but she froze.

Moving on, Sorvino turned back to Ethan. "And you, who are the three?"

Like Melody he froze.

Jamie came up alongside him. "You don't have enough for everyone?"

He shook his head.

"I need someone to give me an answer. I've got five passes and eight people," Sorvino pressed.

Ethan and Melody shared a look. He could see the struggle in her eyes.

"Eight people?" Annette asked. "You can't be counting the baby, no, he's just going on my lap."

"Ma'am, the head count is for the bunker, not the transport."

"But he's a baby," Annette fired back.

"It's about resources, ma'am, and a baby will grow."

"But –"

"Ma'am, I'm sorry, you have five passes and eight people."

"This is stupid. It's a baby!" Annette snapped. Her nostrils flared. She was showing an anger not typical for her.

"I'm sorry, ma'am."

"No, we need to speak to your manager," Annette blared.

Sorvino cocked his head and said, "My superior officer will tell you the same thing. We don't budge on that."

"Why?"

He lowered the tablet and with deep sincerity said, "Ma'am, this child will grow to be an adult in the bunker and may spend the rest of their life there. This isn't a temporary thing."

His comments silenced everyone. No one knew what the projections were going into this, and hearing him say they'd live there until they died was heavy.

"Now, who's going?"

Jamie tugged on Ethan's sleeve.

He gave her a look and knew what she was going to ask.

She pushed Jakey towards him and said, "Please take him, please."

"Dad, no! We need you to go!" Chance exclaimed.

"But he's a boy, he should go!" Jamie shot back.

"I don't even know who you are, but my dad is going, not your kid!"

"This kid is your cousin."

"Step-cousin," Chance retorted. "And you show up last minute thinking you're going!"

Back and forth Chance and Jamie argued.

"Enough! It's my son, daughter-in-law and the boy, you're taking the boy."

With Ethan declaring who was going with his passes, Melody spoke up. "She's going and the other pass is for the baby."

Savannah gripped her arm tightly. "No."

Melody knelt to look Savannah in the eyes. "I have to stay." She's paused and continued, "There's something I haven't told you."

"There can't be anything you can say that would make sense."

"I'm dying. I have cancer, it's bad."

Warm tears streamed down Savannah's flush rosy cheeks. "Is that why you're always getting sick?"

Melody nodded.

"You can't die; you can't go, please." Savannah wrapped her arms around Melody's neck and put her face against hers.

The warm tears felt good against Melody's chilled skin. "I'm sorry. You have no idea. I want to come, but this is the right thing to do."

"Dad, what are you doing?" Chance barked, raw emotions straining his face.

Ethan wanted to talk but couldn't as the commotion all around was becoming distracting and chaotic.

"Is this final?" Sorvino asked. "We don't have much time, last transport leaves in an hour."

Those at the fence and gate howled, their frantic voices becoming so loud it was almost impossible to hear.

"Dad!" Chance hollered.

Ethan could hear him but was lost in thought.

"Dad!"

Ethan broke free of his thoughts and turned to Jamie. "He's going, okay, Jakey is going."

She threw her arms around Ethan's neck and kissed his cheek. "Thank you, thank you so much." She then turned to Jakey and began to explain what was happening.

"Dad!" Chance screamed. He took Ethan's shoulder and turned him around. "What in the hell are you doing?"

As if under the influence of something divine, Ethan said, "I'm not going."

"Why?"

"I'm not going, sorry son."

"Stop being stupid. Now c'mon, we need to go."

"No, I'm staying with Melody."

"But we have our spots." Chance hollered emotionally.

"My decision is final." He pulled Chance aside. "I need you to know that wasn't my original plan. I had two passes and only just now got a third pass."

"I don't understand," Chance cried.

"I never had the passes. I had intended this was just going to be me and you. I never knew about Annette or my beautiful grandson. No, son, this is the right thing to do."

"No, I won't accept that, contact Uncle Eric."

"I did, he just now got us a third pass and now Jakey, your cousin is going."

"This is bullshit!"

"Son, I've spent the past year wanting to kill myself; in fact, I was so close after finding out about this asteroid; then your uncle called. I've lived my life. I had my time at bat. I want someone else to take my spot, someone who has a chance at living a full life, to have a future."

"This is stupid."

"Please take your beautiful family, go, raise Ethan to be a man like you."

"Dad, no!"

Ethan grabbed Chance by the collar and pulled him in. He embraced Chance firmly, his arms wrapped tightly. "I love you."

"Dad, this isn't right."

Ethan pulled back from the embrace. "This is my life, and I'm giving it to someone who hasn't had the years I have."

Like Chance, Annette was exasperated by what was happening.

"Why? Why are you doing this?"

"Because it's my time; it's been my time for a while. Please take care of Chance and my grandson."

"Dad, you can't," Annette pleaded.

Ethan hugged her and kissed Baby Ethan on the forehead. "Goodbye."

"We need to move it along!" Sorvino announced.

Ethan gave Chance another hug and whispered, "Have a good life!"

Chance knew his father well enough to know his answer was final. He took Annette's hand and said, "Savannah, Jakey, let's go."

Jamie kissed Jakey one last time, and nudged him to go with Chance.

"Mommy, no."

"Go!" Jamie stood, tears flowed heavily. Without saying another word, she turned and disappeared into the crowd behind her.

"Mommy, no!" Jakey shrieked.

Savannah took Jakey's hand. "Hi, I'm Savannah, I'll look after you."

"But my mommy!"

"Move it people!" Sorvino barked.

With Chance leading the way, the group marched off towards a large transport near the end of a runway.

Ethan watched as they walked away, taking a mental snapshot of the moment.

Chance looked over his shoulder; like Ethan, he imprinted the sight of his father standing there. He stopped for a moment, turned and waved.

Ethan returned the wave.

Taking one last image of Ethan, Chance turned back in the direction he'd been heading and walked on.

Melody came up alongside him, slipped her hand into his, and put her head on his shoulder. "You're full of surprises."

"Yeah, I've heard that before."

She squeezed his hand and said, "You're pretty darn amazing."

"If watching my life walk away, literally and figuratively, is being amazing, I guess I am. By the way, where's Jamie?"

"She walked off that way."

Ethan looked around for her, but she was gone. Like fate, she had appeared just in time to deliver salvation for Jakey. It was poignant as Jakey and Jen's blood in him.

"Now what?" she asked.

He faced her, looked deeply into her eyes, and said, "We go to the beach."

# THIRTY-EIGHT

## INGLENOOK FEN - TEN MILE DUNES, CALIFORNIA

CARS WHIZZED by Melody hunched over along the side of the road. She expelled the potato chips and iced tea she and Ethan had snacked on just an hour before.

Graciously and with care, Ethan held her hair back and rubbed her back tenderly.

In between convulsions, she joked, "I never saw you as a hair holder."

"I have many unknown talents," he quipped.

She lurched again.

"I can't imagine the salt and vinegar are good coming back up," he joked.

She wanted to laugh but couldn't.

Ethan looked around; it was nice not seeing the snow any longer for several reasons, one being it made their drive much easier. The briny sea air engulfed them each time a chilled easterly breeze washed over them. They were close to the ocean, and soon Melody would be able to check this experience off her bucket list.

She went to wipe her mouth with her hand, but Ethan was there with a wet wipe.

"The benefits of having a baby as a passenger," he said.

Happily, she took it and cleaned her face, lips and hands. The smell of the wipe brought her back to when she worked in the well-baby nursery as a nurse. "Thank you," she said, facing him.

He reached up and tucked a loose strand of her hair back behind her right ear. "You good?"

"Much better, and no, salt and vinegar taste horrible coming back up."

Like a man prepared for any occasion, he handed her a bottle of water and a piece of gum. "Wash your mouth out, and the gum is self-explanatory."

"You're the best. Like seriously better than any girl-friend I had to hold my hair while getting sick."

"Now I'm being compared to girlfriends?"

"You know what I mean."

"No, I don't think I do."

A large truck roared past; the vortex caused by it whipped their hair and clothes.

"Headed to the beach," Ethan said.

She gave him a quizzical look.

"It's a game I play. I make up where people are going. I've been doing it since this mess began."

A car raced by.

"Headed to see his mother," she said.

"His mother?"

"Yeah, didn't you see the look on his face?"

"No."

"That guy looked like he was rushing home to mommy."

Another car whooshed by.

"Beach," they both said at the same time.

"Jinx." She laughed.

He opened the passenger door. "My lady."

"Why, thank you." She climbed in and sat, her hands in her lap. She gave him a sweet smile.

He ran around and got in. Before he put the vehicle into gear, he said, "I'm really happy –"

"Me too." She took his hand into hers. "Thank you."

The way she took his hand told him she thought he was going to say something romantic. However, the reality was he was happy they were close to arriving at their destination. He thought about following up to be precise but stopped short upon seeing the joy her eyes.

She glowed, and the happiness that was radiating from her was contagious. In fact, the two had been filled with a jovial attitude since leaving Hill Air Force Base. They knew what their decisions portended, but having made it, they both felt a weight lifted off them. These were their last hours, and they meant to enjoy them to the max.

He pulled off the side and back on the road.

She couldn't stop looking at him. No one had ever done something so thoughtful or sweet. He literally gave his life so she wouldn't be alone in these last hours. "Can I say something? And don't think it's morbid," she asked.

"Noted, don't think whatever you're about to say is morbid," he replied, giving her a wink.

"Everything that we're doing now, or will do coming

up, will be the last time. Me throwing up, I'm praying that's the last time I ever do that. And driving on this road, I'll never see that tree again or that sign."

"Not morbid."

She looked ahead as the road stretched out west. The sun was now nearing the horizon. "This will be our last sunset."

He squeezed her hand and said, "This is our last day." He chuckled awkwardly for a moment. "Sorry, just sounds so weird to say it."

"It's not weird."

The two grew quiet for a minute.

"Let's just have fun. Can we do that? I mean, we can be..." She lowered her head and blushed.

"What?"

"We can be romantic if you want, but let's not get too serious or depressing."

"My middle name is fun."

She pulled his hand to her lips and kissed the top of it.

He inhaled heavily as thoughts of Jen came rushing in.

"Something wrong?" she asked.

"No, I'm good. Just depressing thoughts that I'm pushing away. I'm here to have fun on our last day."

She relaxed into the seat, his hand still in hers.

He stopped at an intersection and pointed to his left. "See that?"

She leaned forward and looked. "Oh my God, the ocean."

"We're very close now, just up here."

Childlike joy came over her. Her posture became erect and alert. Her focus entirely fixed on the left side of the SUV, she vowed not to let the ocean view out of her sight.

Groups of people walked in the same direction they were driving, and soon they found themselves behind a line of abandoned cars, both lanes and even the shoulder impassable. He stopped, put the vehicle in park, and said, "I guess we walk from here."

She didn't care. With glee, she opened the door and jumped out. She patted the hood and said, "Goodbye, Mr. Suburban."

Ethan stepped out and stretched. By a rough count, he saw at least thirty people ahead of them, some individuals, others in groups of four and five. He went to close the door but stopped when he felt the weight of the pistol in his waistband. He pulled it out and looked at it. Memories of the past year came back, mostly sad. Times where he almost used his old friend to end it all. "This is the end of the road for you." He tossed the pistol on the seat and closed the door.

Melody witnessed this but didn't say a word. She came around the front of the vehicle, took his hand, and gave him a smile.

Not needing directions, they followed the others. Many were holding hands, some laughing, some crying, all knowing their time would soon come to an end.

They came to a bridge, and there to the west she saw them, the dunes. The white sand rolled with patches of grass just like Ethan had described it. The only thing that separated her and the ocean was a single-track dirt trail.

"We're really close now," he said, a broad smile gracing his stubbled face.

"I can't wait."

"I'm happy I get to do this with you."

"It's always been on my list, and I can now mark it off. Unfortunately, the rest of my life will go unchecked," she quipped with a slight laugh.

"Yep."

When they reached the sand of the dunes, she pulled off her shoes and tossed them aside. She dug her toes into the cool sand and outstretched her arms.

He watched her with joy in his heart. Here was a person fully enjoying themselves and letting go.

She turned around, wearing a flirtatious smile, the westerly breeze blowing loose hair across her face. "Wanna race?"

The old Ethan would have said no, but that Ethan was gone. "Sure."

Before he could even remove his second shoe, she took off running, her laughter catching the attention of those around them.

"I see how it is!" He yanked his second shoe off, removed his socks, and sprinted after her.

Spinning around to face him, her smile wide, she waved and beckoned him to her, teasing and taunting.

Just as he closed the gap, she pivoted and took off with greater speed. Up and over the last set of dunes she went, stopping in awe when she saw it. There before her was the wide and beautiful Pacific Ocean.

He caught up and, like her, took in the moment. Stretching in both directions were hundreds of people, all sitting and enjoying the view. Fires, blankets, chairs and even a keg were in view. People had come to enjoy this moment, and why not? It would be their last.

"I want to jump in," she said, ripping off her shirt.

"It's going to be freezing," he warned.

Not paying him any attention, she took her pants, panties, and bra off. Naked and without a care, she raced towards the roaring waves.

He applauded her courage.

She hit the ocean at a sprint, the frigid ocean temperature not stopping her pace. She high kicked for a few feet, then dove in. She disappeared for a moment, then sprang up, arms high, and screamed happily.

Ethan smiled. Seeing her so happy inspired him.

"Come on!" she screamed to him just as a wave knocked her down.

"What the hell, why not!" He tore off his clothes and raced down the beach and into the water.

People cheered from the beach.

"We have an audience," he joked.

"Audience? I don't see anyone but you."

Ethan nodded with a smile.

The two splashed and laughed. He joked about the chilly temperatures while she offered a comment about the salt water in her eyes. The two embraced briefly, their eyes locked. He pulled her close. She wrapped her legs around his and surrendered her weight to him.

"Thank you," she said softly, her eyes not leaving his.

"For what?"

"Taking me to the beach and being with me."

"I can say the same to you." He wanted to kiss her but

found it difficult not to think of Jen just now. In some way he felt like he was cheating on her.

Growing impatient, she placed her lips on his.

He didn't resist.

The two kissed and got lost in each other.

# THIRTY-NINE

## ANTARCTICA AIRSPACE

THE PLANE DROPPED and shifted violently.

The sour smell of vomit mixed with the overpowering odor of sweat and breath.

Packed in tight, shoulder to shoulder and knee to knee, with no concern for safety, the last plane from Hill Air Force Base descended into Antarctica airspace.

Many on board exchanged glances; their gazes locked in an acceptance of how fortunate they each were to be there. Fear was still present, but a confidence could also be seen. Each looked at the other, taking in the people who would soon be some of the few remaining humans on the planet. These people would be their neighbors, their companions, and some even friends or lovers. This flight represented the last people from the United States who would survive Colossus' impact.

Annette had tried to sleep, but the cold air inside the

turbulent fuselage prevented it, not so much because she had a difficult time sleeping, but because Ethan kept waking. She scanned the weary and nervous faces of her companions, taking in each person. When she'd make eye contact, she gave them a smile and nod. Chance, on the other hand, had no problem sleeping and had even slept through the in-air refueling. She took his hand in hers and squeezed. Her other hand tenderly rubbed Ethan's tiny foot through the swaddling.

The plane lurched and dropped.

Chance sprang up, wide-eyed, and looked around. "Where are we?"

"We're landing soon. They just announced it," she answered.

He leaned over and looked at Ethan's face. "He's so handsome."

"Like his dada," she said, her eyes lovingly looking at Ethan.

Chance grew silent.

"Is it your dad?"

"How did you know?"

"I can see the sorrow on your face."

"I'm sad for sure. It had been years since we'd seen each other. He swoops in to save us, and now he's gone, like, gone forever. In a matter of hours, he's gonna be dead. There's no going back."

"He did something very honorable," she said, taking his hand.

"Yeah, but."

"Look at him," Annette said, nudging him to look at

Jakey, who was asleep, his small body nestled into Savannah's.

"I get it, I do, but he should be here," Chance retorted.

"I know you're upset. Your father felt that boy deserved life more..."

"Annette, please..." He shifted in his seat and gave her a look, his eyes telling hers that he was sorry. "I had ideas of us all living together, three generations of Kinkaid."

She put his hand on her lap. "I love you, Chance, I do, and our family is more than us now; we have Savannah and Jakey. You're not just a father to Ethan, but to those two. Your father saw that you were capable, and you are. I know you're going to miss him, and I wish it had worked out differently too. I'm just choosing to see this as positively as I can. We're going to live; your father did that; I'll be eternally grateful to him."

There it was, that word grateful. Chance's thoughts went back to the day at the dam. Ethan had stressed the importance of being grateful. He let that memory sink in and understood. He'd had an expectation, and it hadn't worked out, but he disliked when things didn't go his way. He needed to let go of that emotion as well as having a defined expectation of an outcome. His life ahead would be uncertain going forward; he needed to move past that way of thinking if he was going to be the leader of this big family he now had.

A loudspeaker came to life, but with so much chatter, Chance couldn't hear. "Everyone, be quiet; they're announcing something!" Chance hollered.

People around them quieted.

*"We're making our final descent into the Ark airbase. We ask that everyone remain seated, as we're expecting some heavy turbulence."*

"Finally," Chance said.

A sigh of relief could be heard throughout the plane. They'd been in the air for close to sixteen hours, and the weariness of the long flight could be seen on everyone.

The plane shuddered and dropped.

Several people cried out in fear.

"That was a big –"

Again, the plane jerked. It was down, then up and over to the right. The violent motion elicited many fearful responses.

"They weren't joking about turbulence," Chance said.

Annette leaned in close, her arm wrapped around his. "I hate flying."

"We'll be fine. These pilots are some of the best in the world." Chance looked at Savannah and saw her consoling Jakey, who was now awake and crying. Another big drop in altitude made Chance's stomach flutter. "That was a doozy."

"You sure about these pilots?" Annette asked.

"How about we say a prayer," Chance said. He closed his eyes and recited a short prayer.

Upon saying amen, he could feel her tight grip ease up as well as the plane settle down.

She lifted her head, kissed him on the cheek, and said, "The power of prayer."

*"We've been cleared to land. We'll be on the ground in ten minutes. Again, we need everyone to remain seated."*

"God is good," Chance said and kissed Annette on her forehead.

"What do you think your dad is doing right now?"

"Not sure."

"I have an idea."

"What does that mean?"

"I just mean that he's still a man and Melody is a woman and the two are probably together. I'm sure whatever it is, it's a touching moment and not touching like physical, or maybe it is."

# FORTY

## INGLENOOK FEN – TEN MILE DUNES, CALIFORNIA

THE WOOD POPPED and crackled as the flames slowly devoured it. Its warmth provided heat for six people, including Ethan and Melody, who, after a twenty-minute splash in the sixty-plus-degree water, needed it.

The beach had turned into a scene from any major holiday. Tents, canopies, blankets, and even a volleyball net dotted the sand. The air was filled with conversation, laughter, and music.

The strangers Ethan and Melody were sharing the fire with were a jovial group. The older man, Cliff, strummed a guitar while his girlfriend, Cindy, detailed hilarious stories of her childhood.

A voice called out from across the beach, "Forty-five minutes until impact!"

The group and many around grew quiet upon hearing the announcement.

Melody drew closer to Ethan, her arm wrapped around his.

They all shared a look and waited for one to talk first.

Marie, a striking woman with long black hair streaked with gray, cleared her throat and said, "My dad, I'm grateful for how he raised me. He showed me what a man was and how he should love. He set the example for me, set that bar high, so when I came across this guy, I knew he was the one." She took the hand of the man next to her, looked into his eyes, then leaned in for a kiss.

Her declaration and the knowledge they had little time left shifted the mood.

One by one, each shared something they were grateful for. When it came to Ethan, he paused. He could feel their eyes on him. When he reflected, he found so many things to have gratitude for. His life had been blessed, yet he could also find the numerous times in his memory he'd taken those things and people for granted. "We've all heard the talk about what's important in life, about what we'll want when we're facing our end. And it's true, it's all true." He stared deeply into the fire, then shifted his gaze to the other faces; the shadows of the flames danced over them. "I'm grateful that I had Jen for as long as I had her. She was a light in my world. People say they have a home; she was my home. People talk about soul mates, and I know she was mine. I'll admit I have some fear about what's about to happen, but I'm also happy because I'm getting ready to go back home."

Tears covered the faces of all there, including Ethan.

"And I'm also grateful for Melody here. She came into my life just when me and my son and daughter-in-law needed her. It was like divine intervention, and I say that as a nonbeliever, or maybe I'm not anymore."

"There aren't atheists in foxholes," Cliff blurted out.

Ethan nodded and continued, "I still remember turning around to walk out of that store and there..." He faced her. "And there you were. My son and his wife are religious, not me, but if there are angels, you are one. You saved my grandson, my daughter-in-law, Savannah, and me. I'm grateful that I get to spend these last moments with you."

Touched by his words, Melody slipped her hand into his. She stood and pulled him to his feet.

"Leaving us?" Cliff asked.

"Just going for a walk," Melody answered. "Goodbye to all of you. You're all truly beautiful people." She had the blanket the group had offered in her hands and asked, "Can we take this?"

"Of course. And you keep yours too," Cliff said to Ethan.

"What about you? What are you grateful for?" Cindy asked Melody.

"So many things, but right now, this guy right here."

"Thank you and goodbye," Ethan said to the group. They turned, and he leaned into Melody. "Where are we going?"

"Anywhere, I just want to be with you these last minutes, just us."

"Is this the romantic thing you –"

Interrupting him by putting a finger to his lips, she said, "I'm not looking for anything specific. I just want your company, and maybe you could spare a warm embrace."

"I can do that."

The two walked down to the water's edge, hand in hand.

# FORTY-ONE

## ARK AIRBASE, ANTARCTICA

UNEASE SPREAD THROUGHOUT THE PLANE. They'd been on the ground for what seemed like an eternity. If Chance were to guess, which he had to since he'd lost his watch, they'd been sitting for over thirty minutes.

The unease among the passengers turned to concern, with some teetering on the edge of panic.

One such man, who had crossed over to panic, stood and began to scream, "Open the doors! Let us out of here!"

Another man followed suit. "Is this it? Are we meant to die on this filthy plane? Huh? Talk to us; what's going on?"

"What's going on?" Annette asked, her voice calm but showing some disquiet.

"I'm sure it's nothing; we were one of the last planes. I imagine it's chaotic out there. We'll off-load soon."

Looking into Chance's eyes, Annette said, "I love you."

"I love you too."

The two men who had complained turned into six, then a dozen. They chanted, "Open up, open up!" Soon the dozen had become forty. People were standing, with some banging on the sides of the plane.

"I'm scared," Jakey cried.

"It'll be fine," Chance said to him, giving him a wink of encouragement.

"Why are these people mad?" Jakey asked Savannah.

"They're just scared."

"Like me."

"Not like you, you don't act like a child," Savannah quipped.

A man a few feet away who had been chanting overheard Savannah. "You calling me a child?"

Not shocked by an adult threatening her, Savannah replied with calmness, "Yes, I am."

The man moved towards her.

Chance sprang to his feet and got in between the two. Chance gave the man a look. He could see the anger, as well as the fear. "Just go back and sit down."

"Tell your daughter to zip it!" the man growled.

"I've seen bullies like you, adults who like to hurt children," Savannah spat.

"Shut your mouth, kid!"

"Go sit back down," Chance ordered.

"Fuck you!" the man screamed as he went to shove Chance.

Chance grabbed his arm and held it. He squarely looked the man in the eyes and snapped, "When I let go, you'll go sit back down, or you'll be going into the bunker with a broken arm."

The man snatched his arm back and leaned away from Chance. "I'm going to die anyways!" the man wailed.

"You're not going to die. Calm down. You're frightening the children and others."

His eyes bulging with anger, the man moved towards Chance.

An alarm sounded throughout, followed by the loud-speaker coming to life.

*"We've been cleared to approach the hangar. Sorry, but there's a lot going on."*

The plane lurched forward.

Cheers erupted, and people embraced.

The man stopped his advance, went back to his spot on the floor, and sat down. His anger turned to calm as his wife consoled him.

Seeing the situation was over, Chance turned towards Savannah. "Sorry about that."

"Like I told him, I'm used to bullies."

"You were brave," Jakey happily said to Savannah.

"He's just a scared man, nothing more," Savannah said confidently.

Annette reached up and took Chance's hand in hers. "Were you really going to fight that guy?"

He sat down, grinned, and replied, "Yeah, I was."

She returned his smile and rested her head on his shoulder. "My man."

# FORTY-TWO

## INGLENOOK FEN – TEN MILE DUNES, CALIFORNIA

"COLOSSUS ARRIVES IN TWENTY-FOUR MINUTES!" a voice cried out.

"Twenty-four minutes. It's crazy to think that's all there is. This is all going to be over soon. You, me, everyone here, all the animals, the trees, the fish – everything is going to be dead in a little over twenty-four minutes," Melody calmly said. Her head rested on Ethan's arm, and her body faced his, with her left arm draped over him.

"Let's just not worry about that and just lie here."

"Good plan."

"I feel stupid, but I never asked what you used to do for a living."

"Does it matter?"

"It does to me."

"I was a technical writer."

"This sounds stupid, but technically speaking, what is a technical writer?" she mused.

"Ever read instructions or manuals for, say, your television or anything you've ever purchased?"

"Yeah, and I hate it."

"I write that type of stuff. I used to prepare instruction manuals, how-to guides, journal articles, and other supporting documents to communicate complex and technical information more easily."

She pretended to snore.

He laughed and said, "I couldn't agree more, but it was a nice paycheck."

"I'm sorry, I shouldn't make fun."

"Please do; it is or was boring as hell. I always had a desire to write a novel, but never did."

"Now, if you said you were a novelist, then I'd have to jump your bones; that's sexy."

"Both are writers," he countered with a smirk.

"Correct, but one is boring, and one is interesting and sexy." She winked.

"Whatever."

"Oh, look," she said, her index finger pointing towards the darkened sky. "Shooting stars."

"Oh yeah. Wow, lots of them."

People around also saw the shooting stars and began to comment loudly with oohs and ahhs.

"It's beautiful," Melody softly said. She nestled closer to him.

He cocked his head and stared into her eyes. "You're beautiful."

She laughed. "Yeah, dark circles under my eyes and gaunt cheeks are so pretty."

"You are, truly." He pulled her closer, and the two continued to watch the pre-show display of Colossus.

# FORTY-THREE

## ARK AIRBASE, ANTARCTICA

THE CRAGGY SNOW-COVERED mountains to the southwest towered over the valley. With no moon and the sun having set, the only thing the pilots had were the red and green lights of the taxiway to guide them to the massive hangar. The temperature outside was just at freezing, balmy for a late summer southern hemisphere Antarctic day.

Inside the plane, cheers of happiness continued. The epic long flight, the severe turbulence, and then the extended pause on the tarmac had caused many to wonder if they were going to die on their way to being saved.

The stench was becoming unbearable, but soon the nose of the C-5 Galaxy would open and allow in fresh air and allow them to get off.

Savannah was happy, but mainly she'd be able to get

337

her right hand back from Jakey. He had held on too tightly for most of the flight.

"When is the asteroid coming?" Jakey asked.

"Soon, but not before we get to a safe place," Savannah answered. She had wondered what the timeline looked like but felt sure they'd make it down in time.

Jakey began to cry.

"What is it?"

"I miss my mom."

"I know, I'm sorry."

"Where's your mom?" he asked, wiping tears from his face with his sleeve.

"Um, she's dead."

"Oh."

The loudspeaker crackled to life.

*"Ramp opening; be prepared to move quickly."*

"We should stand," Savannah said.

Jakey stood without complaint.

A loud beep sounded, followed by a rush of cool air, which swept through the fuselage. Gone was the foul smell, replaced by dry frigid air.

"Kids," Chance called out from a few feet away, "wait for us. Don't separate."

Like cattle moving in a cramped pen towards a small gate, they all shuffled along.

It took fifteen minutes, but Chance and the others made it to the top of the ramp just as a loudspeaker boomed in the hangar.

*"Colossus impact in ten minutes. Move to elevators. All personnel, move to elevators immediately!"*

The announcement caused panic, with some behind Chance shoving and pushing. Those in front of him sprinted for the elevator doors at the far end of the hangar.

Two Air Force Security Forces personnel hollered, "No time to get your personal belongings; move to the elevators...NOW!"

*"Everyone proceed to the elevators!"* the loudspeaker blared. *"We are closing the blast doors in three minutes...ten minutes to impact!"*

"C'mon, let's go," Chance said, his arm firmly draped over Annette's shoulder as they hurried along with Savannah and Jakey in tow.

They entered an elevator. It was the largest one Chance had ever seen in his life. It spanned thirty feet by twenty feet. People piled in, stacking up like dried corn stalks.

*"We are closing the blast doors in one minute...eight minutes to impact!"*

# FORTY-FOUR

INGLENOOK FEN – TEN MILE DUNES, CALIFORNIA

THE SOUNDS of crying and weeping grew as the time for impact was again announced.

The meteor shower became more intense as small, advance chunks and fragments of Colossus entered the atmosphere. What some had found beautiful at first now portended their fate and reminded them the mother of these would soon be arriving with a vengeance.

Lying wrapped in each other's arms, Ethan and Melody stared at the meteors coursing across the sky, providing a light show that was fantastic and equally terrifying. Thoughts of Jen would come to Ethan, but he put them aside. He believed he'd soon be with her, but until then, he would seek comfort and provide the same to Melody.

"Is it weird to say that I love you?" Melody asked.

"I suppose to say you love someone so soon isn't conventional, but under these circumstances, I think it's the heightened state of emotions we're both going through. I'll admit this, and this isn't typical Ethan when I say this, but I feel strongly for you."

"Feel love?"

He skipped past her question. He cared for her and as a person loved her, but Jen was the love of his life; he couldn't utter those special words to anyone else, even Melody. "Mel, I can't explain any of it, but for some reason we were meant for this moment together. You and me, here on this beach at the end of it all."

"It is so strange to think that from the second we were born, we were destined to be here together."

"Yeah, it is strange to think of it that way," he replied and paused. "What would you have done if I hadn't stayed?"

"Probably driven somewhere like a park, then sat and waited for it all to end."

"From the moment you said you were going to stay, I kept imagining you at the end. It made me sad to think of that, of you all alone."

"Well, I'm not," she said softly and squeezed him. "Any regrets about not going?"

"None."

"Me neither. I mean, there's some regrets of things from my past, but I'm ready. I've had to prepare for death twice, both cancer diagnoses, so I'm experienced at thinking of my own demise."

"I'm sorry you're in so much pain."

"Not for long...say, how about we stop talking and just hold each other," she said with a dimpled smile.

"Deal."

# FORTY-FIVE

## ARK, ANTARCTICA

THE RUMBLE of the massive steel door closing filled the space.

Huddled together, Chance had one arm over Annette and another over Savannah, who in turn had both of her arms protectively holding Jakey.

All were silent in the elevator save for the cries of fear coming from adults and children alike.

A loud metallic boom sounded. The bright fluorescent light turned green, followed by a significant shuddering of the entire elevator as it began its descent, slowly at first; then its speed noticeably increased.

"I'm scared," Jakey whimpered.

"We're safe now," Savannah assured him. She looked up at Chance, who responded with a simple nod.

The loudspeaker came to life, startling many.

*"Impact in three minutes."*

A tangible shift in mood and energy could be felt as unintelligible chatter erupted throughout.

"Are we going to make it in time?" Jakey asked, his hand finding Savannah's. He gripped her fiercely.

"We're going to be fine."

"Promise me," he begged.

"I promise." Uncomfortable having to say those words, her thoughts went back to EJ and how she'd made the same declaration before. She'd failed at holding up that promise but steeled herself to not fail again.

The elevator slowed.

"Are we almost there?" Jakey asked, his voice cracking with fear.

"I think so," Savannah replied with confidence.

*"Exit the elevator and move towards the blast door."*

A voice commanded from the loudspeaker.

The green light turned bright white again, and the elevator doors opened.

Ahead of them was a large room. Yellow arrows painted on the tall gray walls and floor pointed in the direction they needed to go.

Everyone hastily poured from the elevator and into the room, only to be stopped by a large steel blast door. Safely in the room, the elevator door closed and another steel blast door closed, sealing them in the room.

*"Impact in ninety seconds."*

# FORTY-SIX

INGLENOOK FEN – TEN MILE DUNES, CALIFORNIA

A SERENE CALM had settled over the beach. The music was gone, and all that could be heard were waves crashing along with crying and hushed chatter. The chilled breeze which had been blowing most of the day, continued into the evening.

Ethan and Melody were now sitting, their eyes on the darkened ocean. They knew the impact would occur to the southwest, across the ocean.

"I'm scared," Melody confessed, her right arm wrapped in his left and her hands clasped tightly to his.

"Me too."

"What will it be like? Will we see it, you think?"

"I imagine we'll see something." He then heard her start to cry. "I'd ask if you're okay, but that's a stupid question."

"I'm just having silly thoughts about my life, you know,

little, heck, big regrets. Why did I date Jared for so long? I felt he wasn't the one, but I was so insecure. I was even engaged to him. Hell, we even went to Vegas to get married, and he wouldn't do it. I knew then, I just knew. God, I was so unhappy but lied to myself that I wasn't. What I was really doing was being comfortable. He gave me just enough to feel okay now and then. It just pains me to think I could have been with someone else who truly loved me. I wasted years with him. Or why didn't I pursue my career in nursing earlier versus wasting all those years doing dead-end jobs? Or why –"

He leaned down and kissed her lips.

Stunned by his kiss, she asked, "What was that for?"

"All those things you did, those choices you made put you here with me, and for one, I'm happy. Me personally, I never spent much time in regret until Jen. I used to proclaim how it was such a waste of energy and thought. This isn't to say we shouldn't reflect and learn from our past, but it's gone, the choice was made, and the consequence came. You and I are here together because of consequences of many choices."

"Or it's fate."

"I suppose it can be that too."

"But you know what I mean about wishing you'd done this or that?"

"Yeah, I do, but all I want to do these last few minutes is just be...with you. I don't want to think about anything else now. I can't do anything about it. There's not even a future to strive for where those mistakes are used for wisdom; this is it. I want to enjoy you and this time, nothing more."

She pulled him close and put her head on his chest. "I'm so happy you're here."

"Me too."

"Impact!" a man cried out from the far side of the beach.

Ethan and Melody looked into the darkness for any sign of Colossus' arrival.

"This is it," Melody said, holding Ethan tightly.

He returned her embrace.

The horizon began to glow. It started in one small spot in the southwest, then grew until the entire sky was aglow.

She squeezed tighter to him.

He kissed her forehead.

Minutes passed.

Wails and cries grew in volume as the brightness increased in the western sky.

A rumble sounded, and the ground began to shake violently.

The two held tight to each other; there were no words to express as they watched the sky turn a searing red.

The rumble was deafening and overpowered the cries of terror.

The temperature rose by tens of degrees in seconds, and the shaking became so violent they found it hard to sit up.

In a surreal moment, Melody watched the water's edge recede rapidly.

Ethan knew it was coming and fast. He pressed his eyes closed and waited.

Melody pressed herself even tighter against Ethan, her head tucked into his chest. She closed her eyes and wept.

Ethan brought an image of Jen to mind and focused on it. The heat was becoming intense, but he kept his thoughts on Jen. He could see her standing tall, her arms outstretched, and beckoning for him to come.

Wrapped in the other's embrace, they sat until the nine thousand mile per hour ejecta cloud made contact leaving nothing in its wake.

# FORTY-SEVEN

## ARK, ANTARCTICA

"TEN, *nine, eight, seven, six, five, four, three, two, one.*"

Prayers and crying were all that could be heard.

Chance, his eyes pressed closed, held Annette and Savannah tight, with Jakey holding onto Savannah, his arms wrapped firmly around her waist.

"When is it going to happen?" Jakey asked.

Savannah remained quiet. She didn't have an answer. She didn't know if they'd even feel anything. In her imagination she'd seen the ground moving and cracking open. Molten rock along with winds and walls of fire coming towards her. Maybe this was happening above, but below, all seemed peaceful, almost too much so.

Thirty minutes went by.

"Is it over?" a voice asked in the back.

"Did it hit us?" another asked.

"We survived. It's over; we survived!" a woman near the front sang out.

People hugged and congratulated themselves.

A low rumble sounded, then another. As each second passed, the rumble grew louder.

Several people started to wail while others loudly prayed as the joy of the moments before turned to terror.

The floor shifted, and the walls shuddered.

The shaking intensified along with the rumbling until it reached a crescendo of violence.

"Mommy, I'm scared. I don't want to die," a girl cried out.

Unable to stand, they dropped to their knees.

"Will the doors hold?" a man asked loudly, fear vibrating in his voice.

"It will, it has to," another man replied, his response sounding more like a reassurance than an honest answer.

"Is it getting warmer? I think it's getting warm. Are we going to be burned alive?" a woman wept.

Unable to tolerate people vocalizing their fears or doubts, Annette shouted, "Can everyone please be quiet!"

Silence fell over the room.

The rumbling became a deafening roar; the lights went out, shrouding them in total darkness.

Chance tightened his grip on the others; he could feel them physically shaking. With fervency, he prayed for it to stop.

As if God answered his prayer, the roar subsided.

The lights turned on, and everyone slowly lifted their heads.

"Is that it?" a man said from the back of the room.

Chatter erupted.

"Do you think that's it?" Annette asked.

"I have no idea; this is my first asteroid impact," he quipped.

The crackle of the loudspeaker jolted them all. They craned their heads in its direction and waited eagerly.

*"Colossus impacted 313 miles northeast of the Hawaiian Islands. Time of impact was 0444 Zulu. Bunker is secure."*

# FORTY-EIGHT

## ARK, ANTARCTICA

SO, *it's over, the world is gone, and Dad is dead. Now what?* Chance thought. He looked at Annette, Savannah, and Jakey. This was all he had, they were the future, but what did that future hold? Who knew? He was in the unknown now.

He got to his feet and helped the others up.

"You okay?" he asked Savannah and Jakey, who both nodded.

Another set of blast doors opened behind them. Intensely bright fluorescent light spilled into their room. A long wide hallway stretched out before them. At the end of it was a massive open space filled with potted trees and plants, tables, chairs and even artwork adorned the walls.

A woman, dressed in black slacks and a white cotton collared shirt, confidently walked into the room. She held herself in a distinguished and authoritative manner. Her black hair was pulled back in a tight bun and her skin glowed as if she had just come in from sunbathing. She stopped just feet from the group and said, "Hello, my name is Corrine Carr. You're our last guests to arrive. May I be the first to welcome you to your new home."

Several others came in and stood behind her in a line. They wore similar clothing and each gave off the same air of confidence Corrine did.

Corrine lifted a tablet and began to call out names.

One group after another acknowledged their names, stepped forward and were escorted away.

"Ethan Kinkaid," Corrine called.

Chance raised his hand. "Here."

"I have three in your party."

"Yes."

"Come forward; Mary here will take you to your quarters." Corrine pointed to a young woman in her mid-twenties, her hair pulled back tightly in a ponytail.

"We're traveling with them." Chance pointed to Savannah and Jakey.

"And whose pass –"

"Does it matter now?" Chance retorted.

"Only to get them to their assigned quarters," Corrine answered.

"We're family. They come with me. We're not getting split up."

Corrine opened her mouth to reply, but upon looking at them, she nodded and said, "Mary will find you quarters that will suffice...your family."

Chance, with the others following, walked towards Mary, who stood with a warm smile on her youthful face.

As they passed Corrine, Savannah stopped and stared into the vast vivid space at the end of the hall. She saw children playing. They wore clean clothes, with joyful smiles stretched across their faces.

"Is this yours?" Corrine asked as she bent down and picked up a book.

"Huh?" Savannah looked confused. When she saw the book, she recognized it. "Yes, that's mine."

"Great book. Are you enjoying it?"

Savannah nodded.

Corrine handed it to her and asked, "You like reading?"

Savannah nodded.

"Well then, you'll be happy to know we have an extensive library with every book ever published."

"That's nice."

"Movies, do you like to watch movies?"

Savannah nodded and said, "I do but I've only watched a few."

"What's your name?"

"I'm Savannah."

"Well Savannah, we have every movie ever made for your viewing pleasure. The Ark was designed and outfitted for everyone's comfort."

The laughter of the children echoed down the hall, distracting Savannah for a brief moment. She looked at them happily playing and felt a tug of joy. But as fast as the joy came, it was swept away with a skepticism borne from a life of hardship.

"But is it safe?" Savannah asked.

"Safe?"

"Am I going to be safe here?"

Seeing her unease, Corrine held out her hand and said with a confident smile, "Yes, you're safe now. I promise."

Savannah looked at her hand, then to the others waiting for her at the end of the hall.

"Come, let me give you a personal tour of your new home," Corrine said.

Savannah took her hand.

Hand in hand, the two walked down the hall and into the comforting warmth of the brilliant light.

THE END

# ABOUT THE AUTHOR

G. Michael Hopf is a *USA Today* bestselling author of over forty books, including the international bestselling post-apocalyptic series, *THE NEW WORLD*. He is a prominent name in the post-apocalyptic, western and paranormal genres. To date he has sold well over one million copies of his books worldwide with many being translated into German, French and Spanish.

He is the Co-Founder and Managing Partner of Beyond The Fray Publishing and is a proud veteran of the United States Marine Corps.

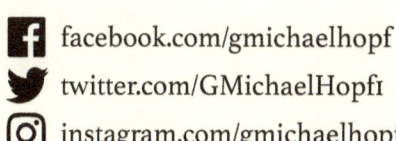

facebook.com/gmichaelhopf

twitter.com/GMichaelHopf1

instagram.com/gmichaelhopf

# ALSO BY G. MICHAEL HOPF

## THE NEW WORLD SERIES

THE END

THE LONG ROAD

SANCTUARY

THE LINE OF DEPARTURE

BLOOD, SWEAT & TEARS

THE RAZOR'S EDGE

THOSE WHO REMAIN

## NEMESIS TRILOGY

NEMESIS: INCEPTION

NEMESIS: DEAD CENTER

NEMESIS: REVENGE (COMING SUMMER 2023)

## THE NEW WORLD SERIES EXPANSION

EXIT

LOCKDOWN (with L. Douglas Hogan)

## THE WANDERER TRILOGY

VENGEANCE ROAD

BLOOD GOLD

TORN ALLEGIANCE

## THE BOUNTY HUNTER SERIES

LAST RIDE

THE LOST ONES

PRAIRIE JUSTICE

## THE DEATH TRILOGY (with John W. Vance)

QUARANTINE

ERADICATE

EXTINCTION

## STANDALONE APOCALYPTIC BOOKS

HOPE (with A. American)

SEVEN DAYS

DAY OF RECKONING

MOTHER (MISSIONS FROM THE EXTINCTION CYCLE 2)

DRIVER 8

CRIES OF A DYING WORLD

## STANDALONE WESTERN BOOKS

JUDGMENT DAY

THE LAWMAN

THE RETRIBUTION OF LEVI BASS

RIGHTEOUS KILL

## HORROR

THE DOLL (with Savannah Hopf)

DETOUR (Apocalyptic Horror)

## SCIENCE FICTION

BINARY (USA Today Bestselling novella)


## PARANORMAL NONFICTION

BEYOND THE FRAY: BIGFOOT (with Shannon LeGro)

BEYOND THE FRAY: PARAMALGAMATION (with Shannon LeGro)


## CHILDREN'S ILLUSTRATED BOOKS

DOGGIEVILLE

HUDSON WHAT'S YOUR TAIL NUMBER (with Andrew Drykerman)